BATMAN COVER TO COVER

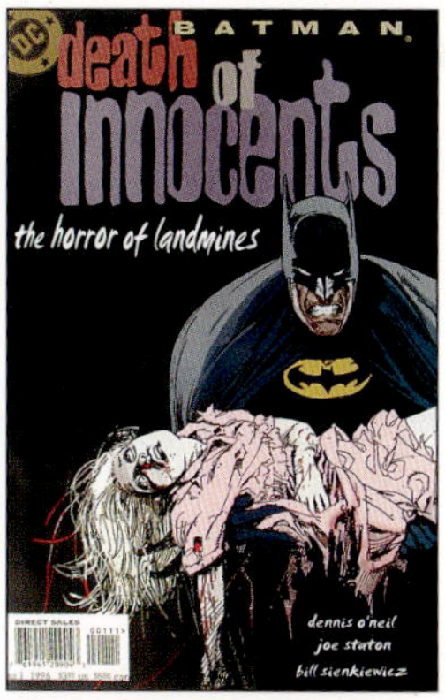

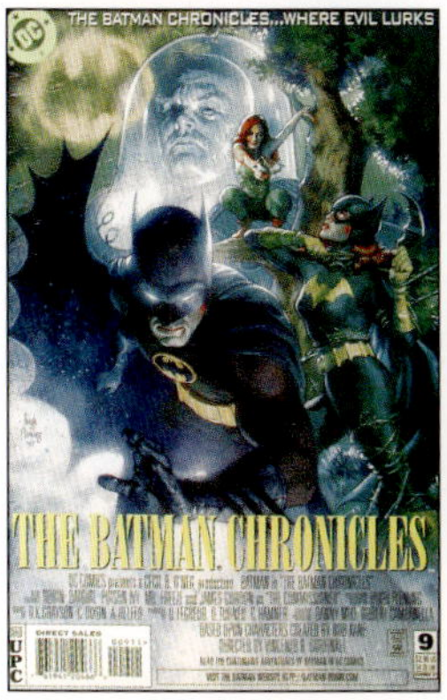

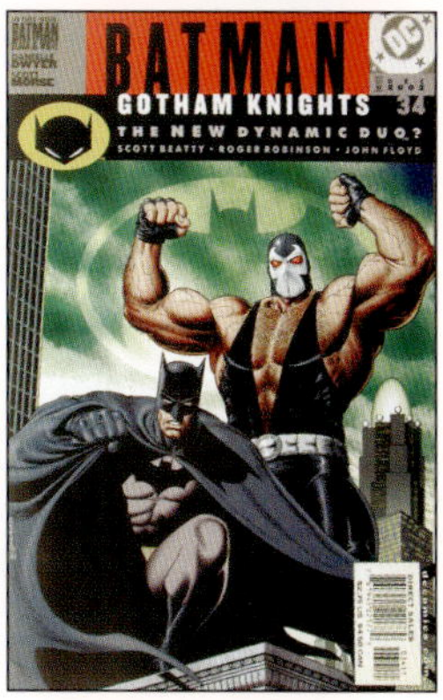

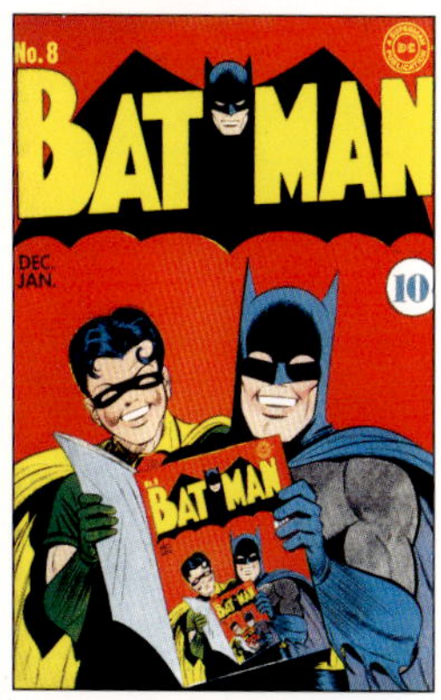

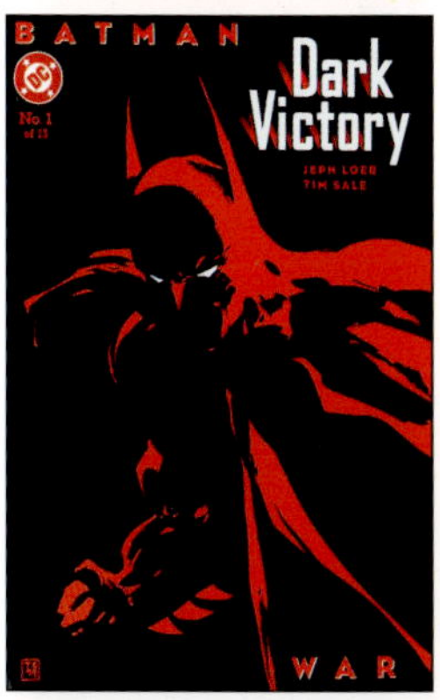

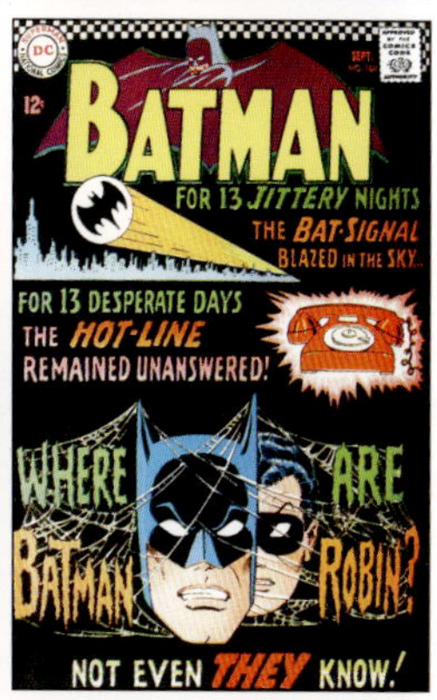

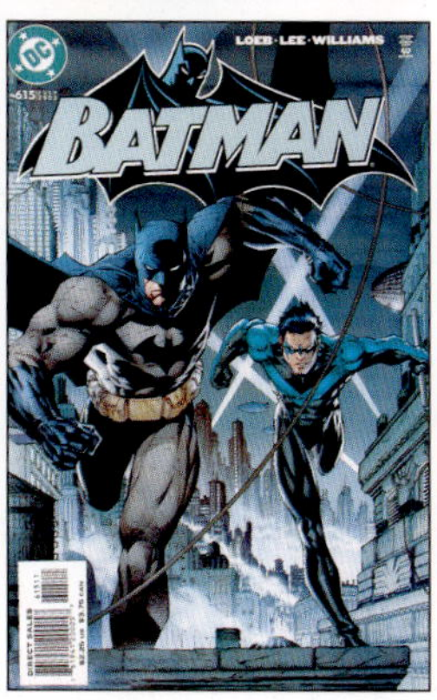

The Greatest Comic Book Covers
of the Dark Knight

BATMAN CO

ER TO COVER

BATMAN: COVER TO COVER

Published by DC Comics.

DC Comics
1700 Broadway
New York, NY 10019

A Warner Bros. Entertainment Company
Printed in Hong Kong.
First Printing.
ISBN: 1-4012-0659-X

Special thanks to Spencer Beck, John Wells, Mark Waid, Mike Wilbur of Diamond International, Allen Ross, Kevin Sorensen, and Steve Korté.

Batman created by Bob Kane

Cover pencil art by Jim Lee

The cover is the most important visual aspect of a comic book. If among the countless other titles on the shelf the image doesn't entice you to pick it up, then the story goes unread. The cover can make an impact through the use of the character, its story elements, the design/composition, its color and even the placement of the logo.

Since 1939, Batman (his friends, family and foes) has appeared on over 2000 comic book covers. The Dark Knight, as you will see on the following pages, has brought out the very best in artists for over 60 years. Choosing "the Greatest" of these covers is a daunting challenge.

To narrow down the choices, it was decided that each cover had to actually feature Batman and not just members of his extended family. As the covers were reviewed, scrutinized and debated, they started falling into several categories, which

were then applied to organize the book. Countless hours were spent looking in the company's Print Library and many other sources, to find those that gave a thrill, a chill or stood out from the rest.

To provide another perspective, the challenge was opened to people who wrote or drew some of these adventures, or in some cases, helped bring these characters to life. Their choices often, but not always, dovetailed with those already selected. It was telling that four of the contributors all chose the same cover.

Turn the page and see for yourself the engaging, exciting and entertaining images that have delighted readers for decades. It is always hard to define the "Greatest" with so many powerful covers to choose from, and the book could easily have been twice as long. Let the debate begin.

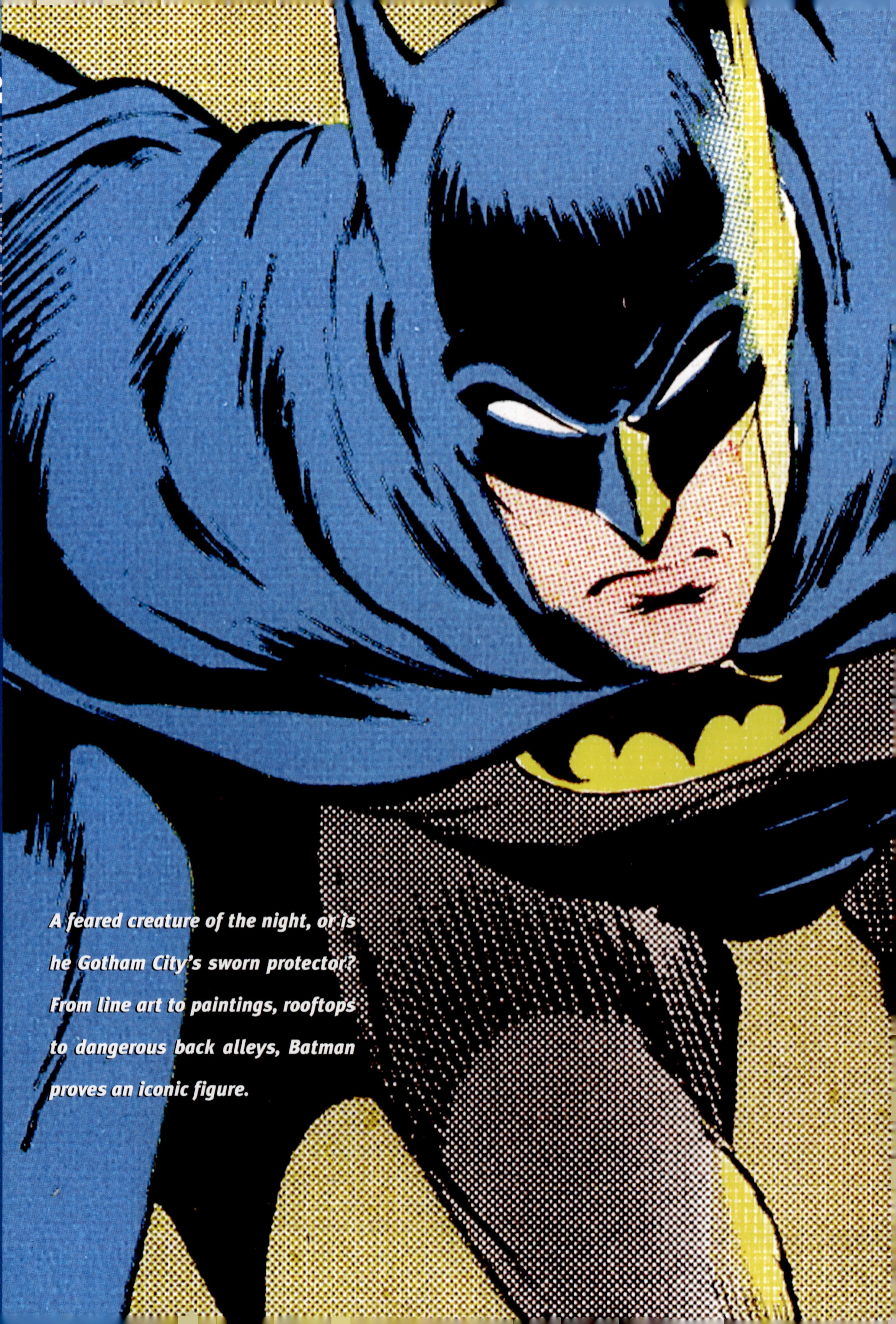

A feared creature of the night, or is he Gotham City's sworn protector? From line art to paintings, rooftops to dangerous back alleys, Batman proves an iconic figure.

Batman: No Man's Land #1

1999

Art by Alex Ross

Batman #608

2002

Art by Jim Lee & Scott Williams

With writer Jeph Loeb, Jim and Scott produced a best-selling year-long epic that began with this issue.

Batman: Gotham Knights #57

2004

Art by Jae Lee

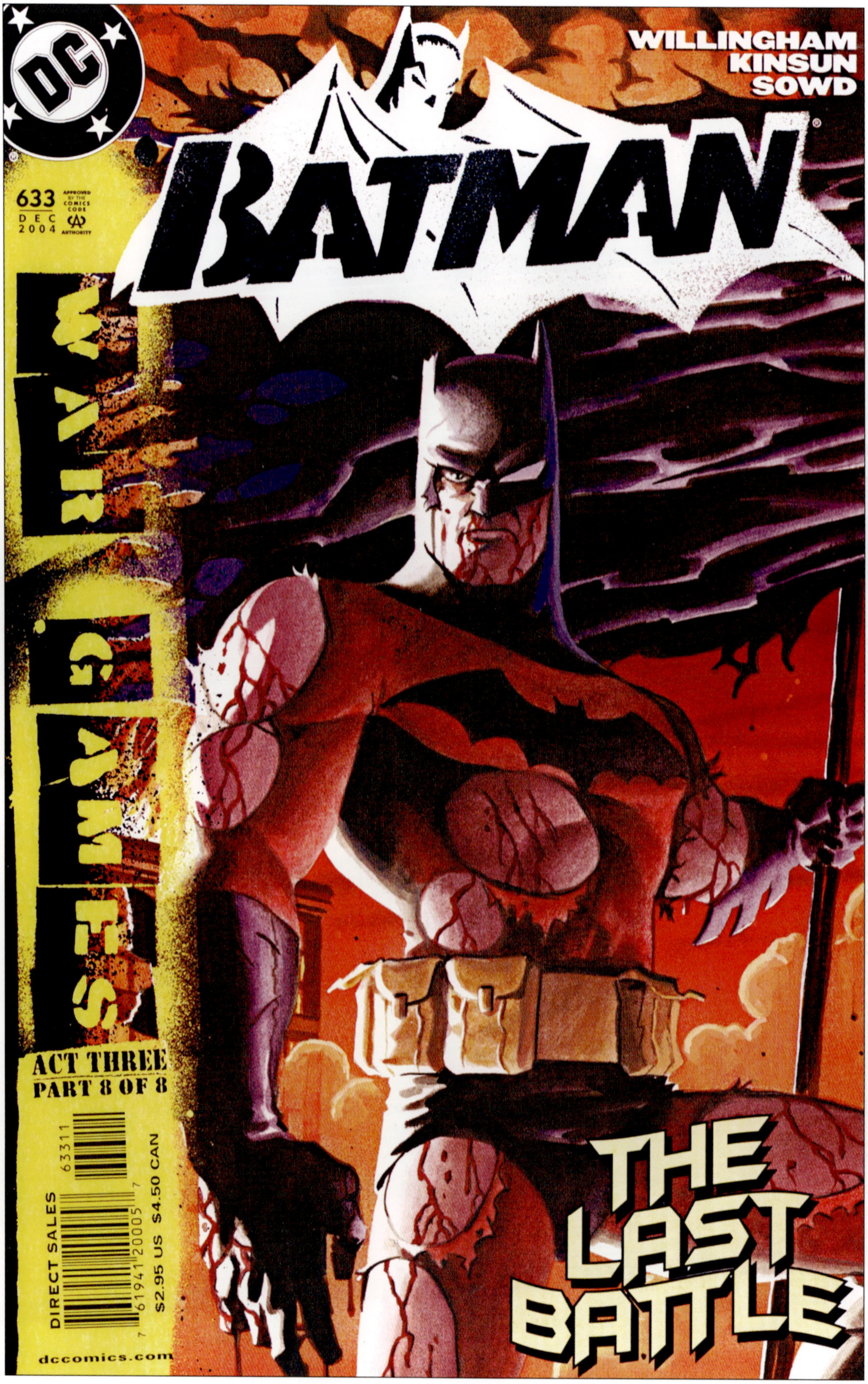

Batman #633

2004

Art by Matt Wagner

This artwork fuses the key elements of Batman that I find most exciting. It's iconic, but still suggesting purposeful action; it's gothic but with a fresh modern slant.

Christopher Nolan *is the respected director of* Memento *and* Insomnia *in addition to the summer 2005 reintroduction of Batman to film,* Batman Begins.

THE DARK KNIGHT RETURNS #1 1986, Art by Frank Miller

Detective Comics #583
1988
Art by Mike Mignola

Page 17:
Limited Collector's Edition C-44
1976
Art by
Carmine Infantino (pencils),
John Wells (painting)

This art hung in the reception area of the DC Comics offices for years before finally being used in print.

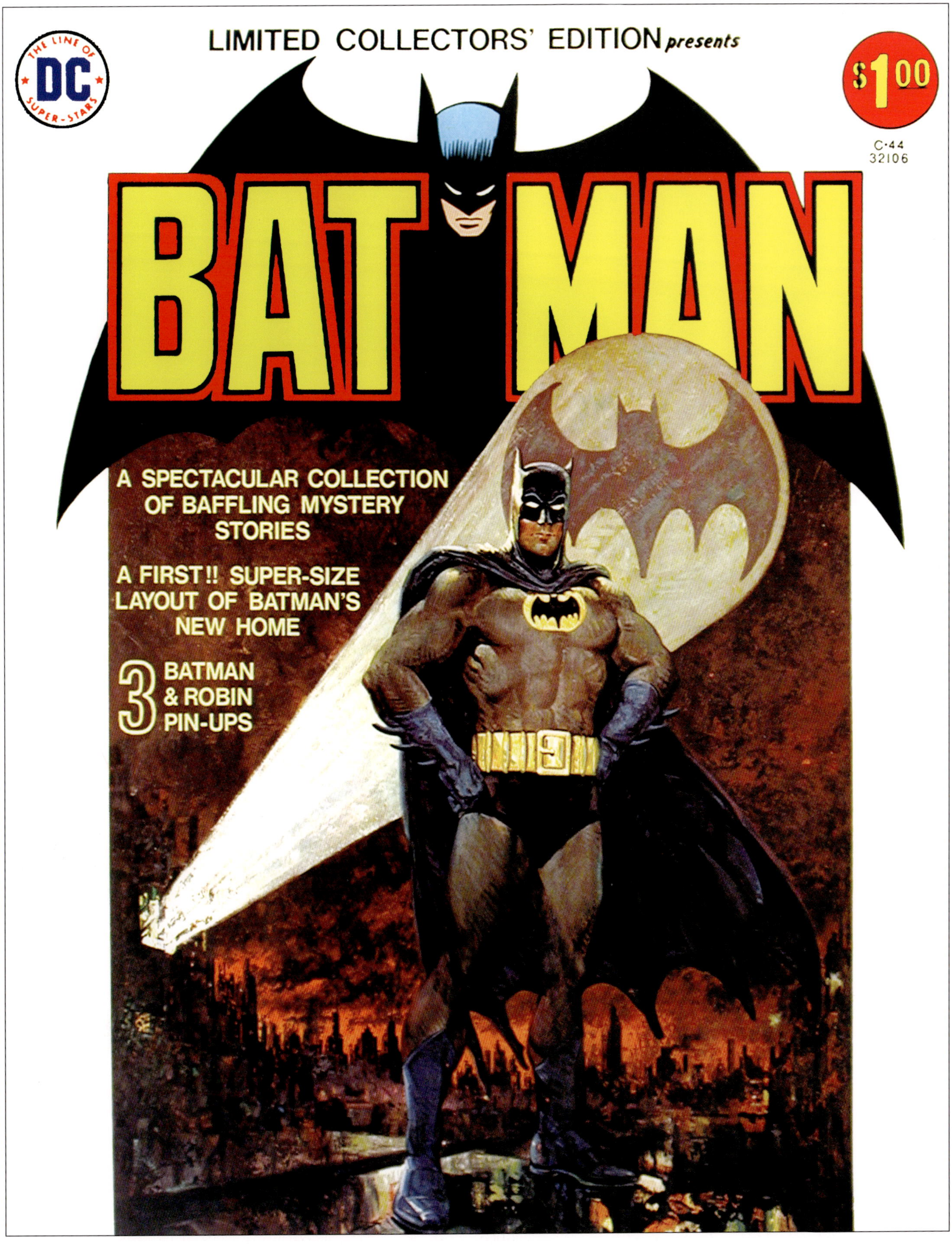
LIMITED COLLECTORS' EDITION presents
THE LINE OF DC SUPER-STARS
$1.00
C-44
32106
BATMAN
A SPECTACULAR COLLECTION OF BAFFLING MYSTERY STORIES
A FIRST!! SUPER-SIZE LAYOUT OF BATMAN'S NEW HOME
3 BATMAN & ROBIN PIN-UPS

Batman #404

1987

Art by David Mazzucchelli

Along with writer Frank Miller, David depicted the first adventures of the costumed Bruce Wayne, providing inspiration for the 2005 feature film Batman Begins.

Detective Comics #457

1976

Art by Dick Giordano

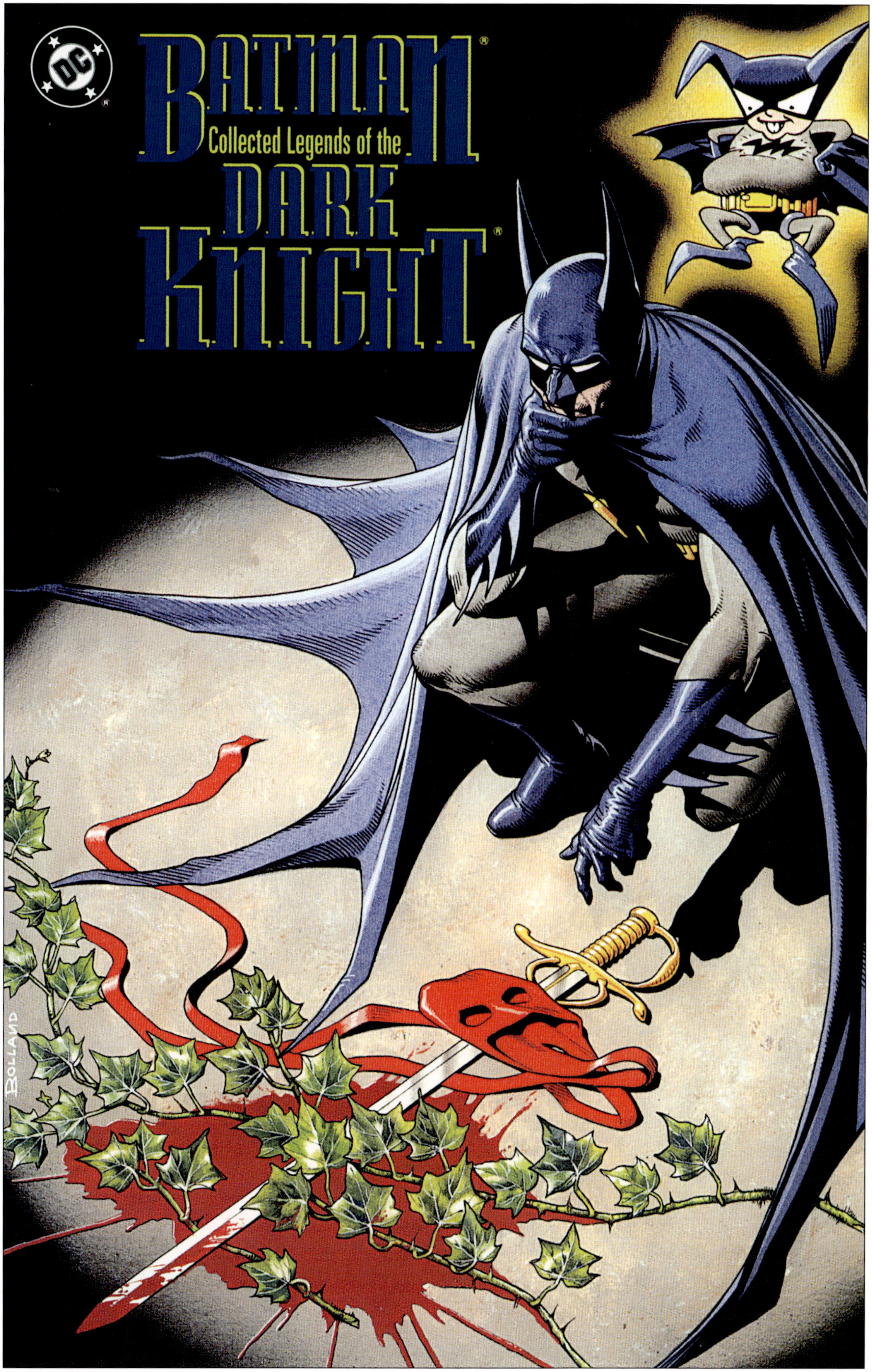

Batman: Collected Legends of the Dark Knight

1994

Art by Brian Bolland

Batman:

The 10-Cent Adventure

2002

Art by Dave Johnson

Batman: Night Cries

1992

Art by Scott Hampton

Batman:
No Man's Land Vol. 1
1999
Art by Alex Maleev

No Man's Land was a year-long story depicting what happened to Gotham City and its citizens after the Federal Government had cut it off. Collected into five volumes, the story shows people at their best and, too often, at their worst.

Batman: Legends of the Dark Knight #177

2004

Art by Jock

Batman #596

2001

Art by Bill Sienkiewicz

Batman #241

1972

Art by Neal Adams & Bernie Wrightson

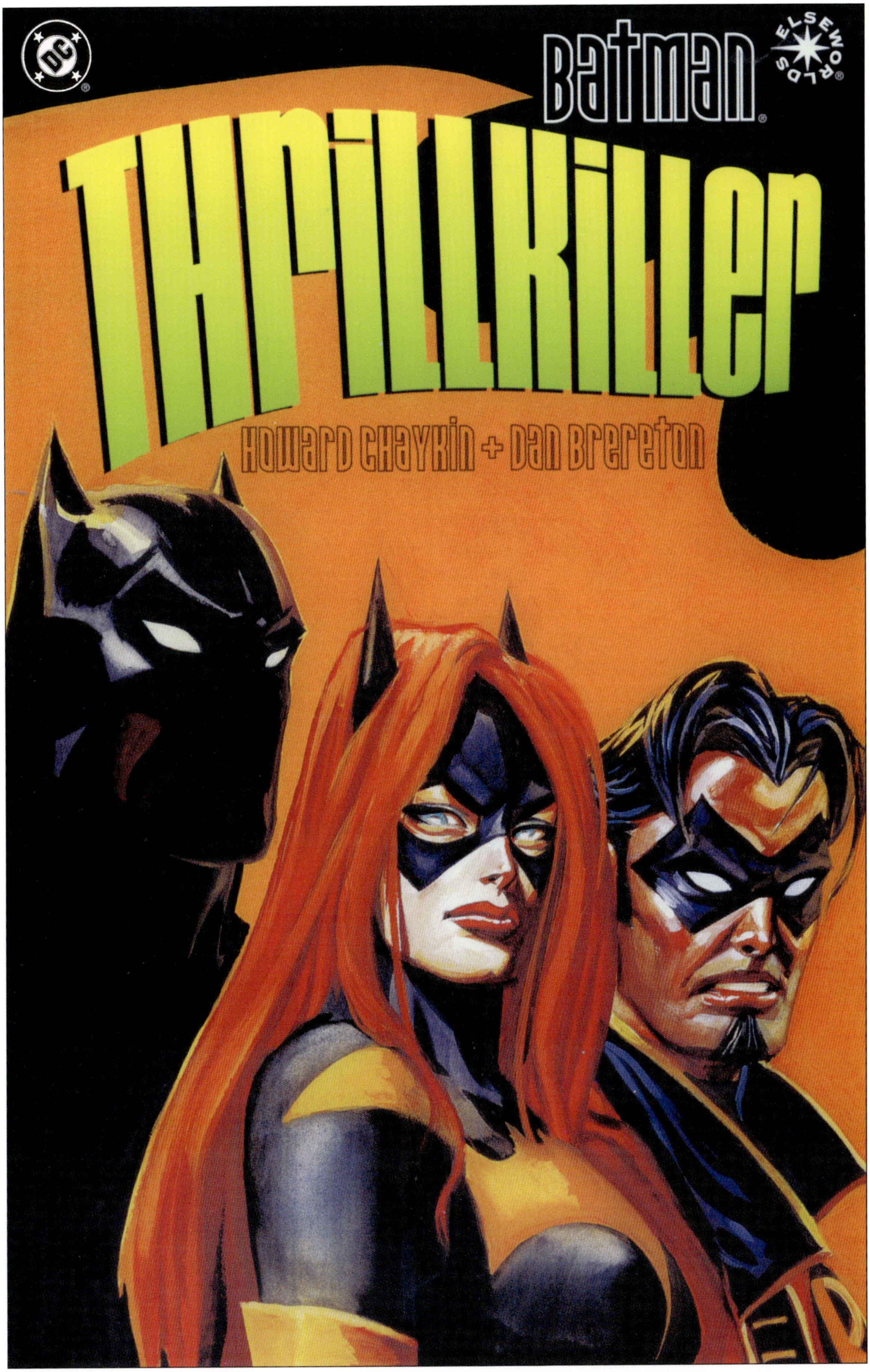

Batman: Thrillkiller

1998

Art by Dan Brereton

Batman: Legends of the Dark Knight #77

1995

Art by Scott Hampton

Batman: The Chalice

1999

Art by John Van Fleet

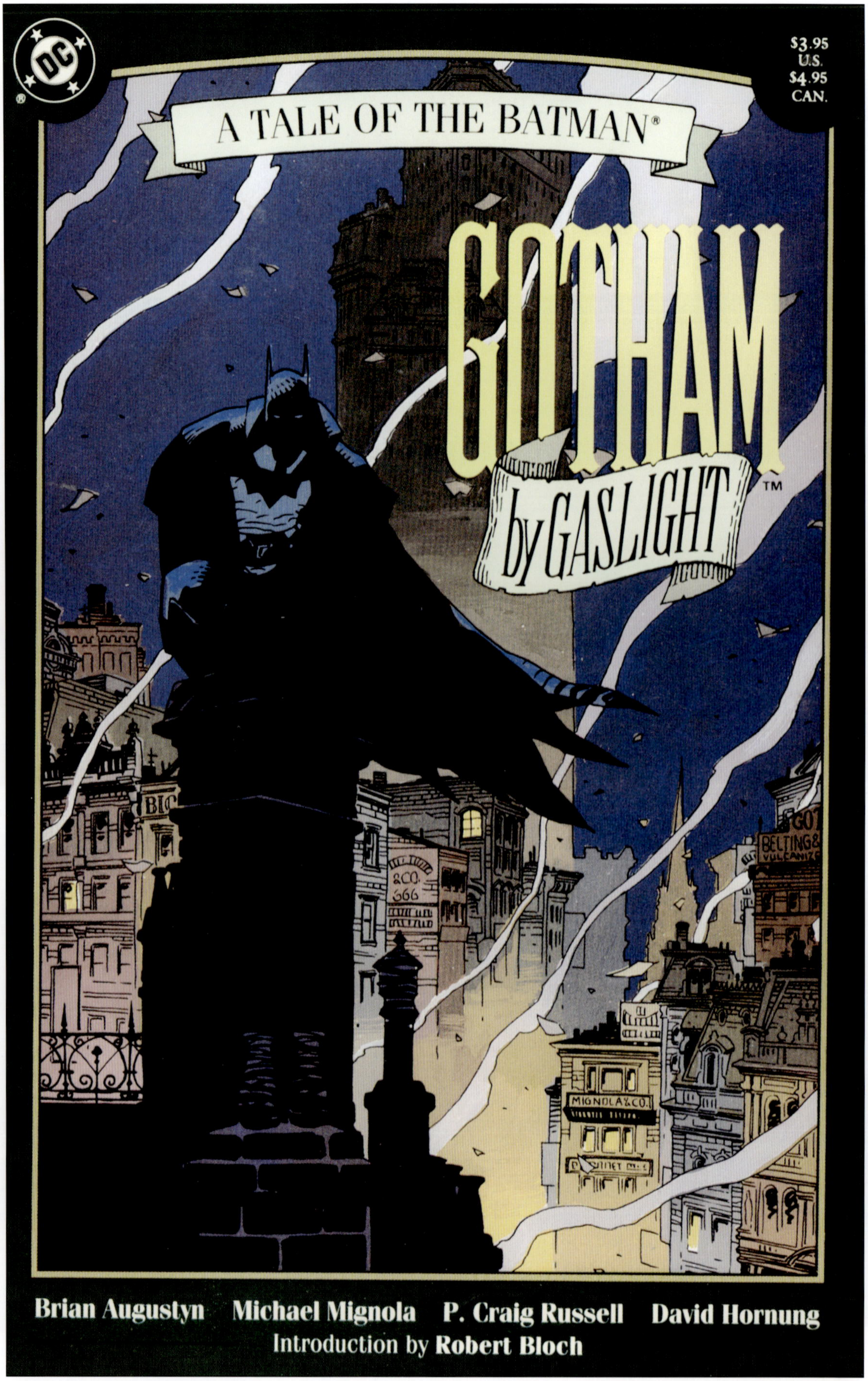

Gotham by Gaslight

1989

Art by Mike Mignola & P. Craig Russell

This story, imagining a 19th-century caped crusader, was successful enough to launch an entire imprint of imaginative tales called Elseworlds.

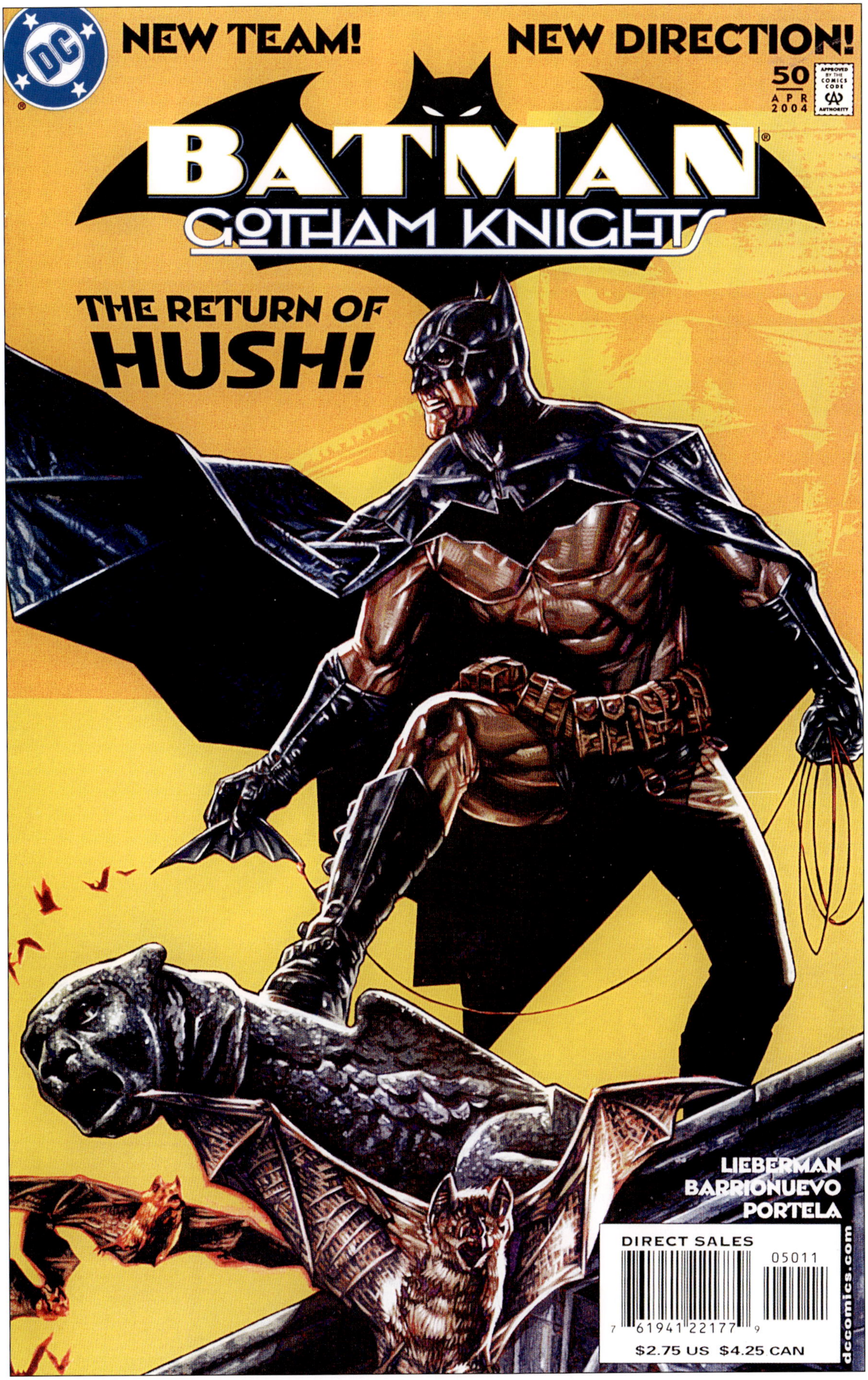

Batman: Gotham Knights #50

2004

Art by Lee Bermejo

Batman: Gotham Knights #1

2000

Art by Dave Johnson

The Batman Chronicles #23

2001

Art by Brian Stelfreeze

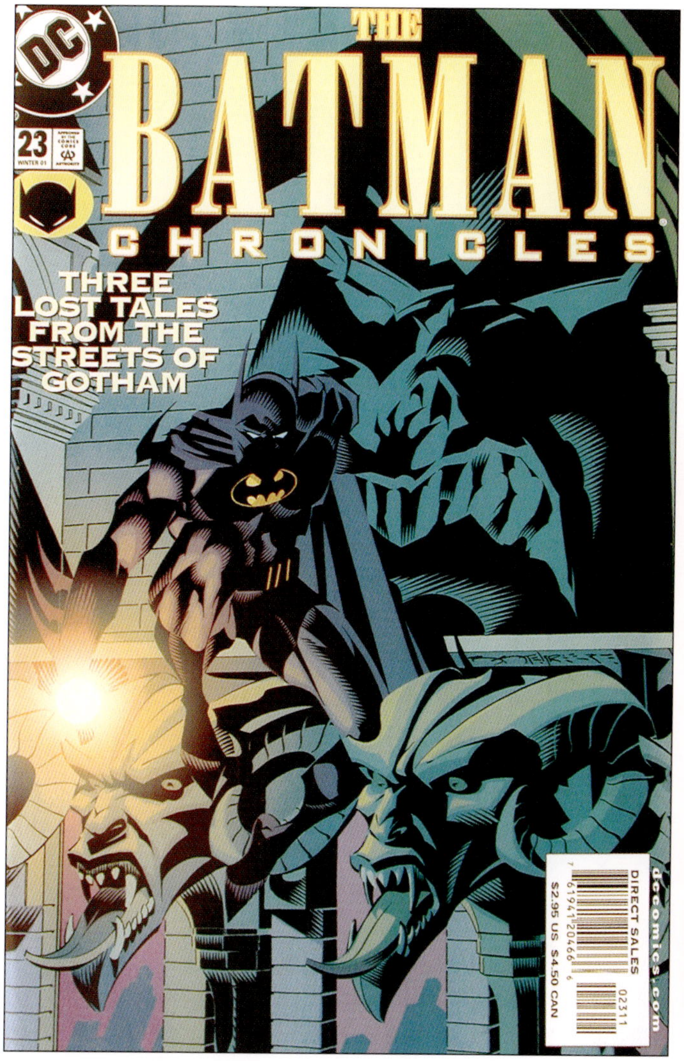

Limited Collector's Edition C-25

1974

Art by Neal Adams

This classic image was actually taken from a story but was used extensively throughout the 1970s.

Batman #520

1995

Art by Kelley Jones

Batman: Hush Vol. 1

2004

Art by Jim Lee

NEIL GAIMAN

BATMAN #181 1966, Art by Carmine Infantino & Murphy Anderson ■ **SWAMP THING #7** 1973, Art by Bernie Wrightson

I've almost never written Batman, but he's what drew me into comics. I was six years old and my father mentioned that, in America, there was a *Batman* TV series. I asked what this was, and was told it was a series about a man who fought crime while dressed as a bat. My only experience of bats at this point was cricket bats, and I wondered how someone could convincingly dress as one of those. A year later the series began to be shown on English TV, and I was caught, as firmly and as effectively as if someone had put a hook through my cheek.

I bought – with my own pocket money – the paperback reprints of old Batman comics: two black and white panels to a page of Lew Sayre Schwartz and Dick Sprang, Batman fighting the Joker, the Riddler, the Penguin and Catwoman (who had to share a book). I made my father buy me *Smash!*, a weekly British comic that reprinted what I now suspect must have been an American Batman daily newspaper strip as its cover feature. I was once thrown out of our local newsagents – literally picked up by the proprietor and deposited on the sidewalk – for spending too much time examining each and every one of the pile of fifty American comics, in order to decide which Batman product would receive the benison of my shilling. ("No, wait!" I said, as they dragged me out. "I've decided!" but it was already too late.)

What got me every time were the covers. DC's editors were masters of the art of creating covers that proposed questions to mysteries that appeared to be insoluble. Why was Batman imprisoned in a giant red metal bat, from which not even Green Lantern could save him? Would Robin die at dawn? Was Superman really faster than the Flash? The stories tended to be disappointments, in their way – the question's sizzle was always tastier than the answer's steak.

You never forget your first time. In my case, the first time Batman cover artist was Carmine Infantino, whose graceful lines, filled with a sly wit and ease, were a comfortable stepping-off point for a child besotted by the TV series. Text-heavy covers, all about relationships – Batman being tugged between two people: look at the first appearance of Poison Ivy (will she ruin Batman and Robin's exclusive friendship? Of course not. Why did I even worry about such trifles?) looking here as if she's just escaped from the label of a tin of sweet corn. Batman thinks she's cute. Robin's not impressed. That was what I needed as a kid from a Batman cover. Bright colors. Reassurance.

While humans tend to be conservative, sticking with what they like, children are *utterly* conservative: they want things as they were last week, which is the way the world has always been. The first time I saw Neal Adams's art in *The Brave and the Bold* (I think it was a story called "...But Bork Can Hurt You") I read it, but was unsure of whether or not I liked it: panels at odd angles, nighttime colors in strange shades of blue, and a Batman who wasn't quite the Batman I knew. He was thinner and odder and wrong.

Still, when I saw Adams's cover for "The Demon of Gothos Mansion" (*Batman* #227-see page 238), I knew that this was something special, and something *right*, and that the world had changed forever. Gothic literature tends to feature heroines, often in their night-dresses, running away from big old houses which always have, for reasons never adequately explained, one solitary light on in a top floor room. Often the ladies run while holding candelabras. Here we have instead a dodgy-looking evil squire running after our heroine, between what look suspiciously like two wolves. The spectral, Robin-less, Batman is not swinging from anything. Instead he is a grey presence, hovering over the image: this tale is indeed a gothic, it tells us, and Batman is a gothic hero, or at least a gothic creature. I may only have been eleven, but I could tell gothic at a glance. (Although I wouldn't have known that the cover that Adams was intentionally echoing, *Detective Comics* #31, was also part of the gothic tradition – an evil villain called The Monk reminds the reader of Matthew "Monk" Lewis's novel *The Monk*, and, as I learned a couple of years later, when the story was reprinted in a *100-Page Super*

Spectacular, the Monk from this story was a vampiric master of werewolves (or possibly vice versa; it's been a long time since I read it. I do remember that Batman opened the Monk's coffin at the end, and, using his gun – the only time I remember him using a gun – shot the becoffined Monk with a silver bullet, thus permanently confusing me as to the Monk's werewolfish or vampiric nature).

By the time I was twelve Len Wein and Bernie Wrightson's *Swamp Thing* was my favorite comic; it was, I think, the comic that made me want to write comics when I grew up. *Swamp Thing* #7, "Night of the Bat," was the comic that sealed Batman in my mind as a gothic figure. The cover only implies what's inside, as Batman, his cloak enormous behind him, swings towards the muck-encrusted swamp monster, inexplicably hanging from the side of a skyscraper. The feeling that this was something happening at night, artificially lit, in the city, was there, almost tangible. But the things that made me remember this cover fondly are really inside – Bernie drew Batman with no pretense of realism. It was as far as one could get from Adam West: behind Batman an unwearably long cloak blew out: was it fifteen feet long? Twenty feet long? Fifty? And the ears, stabbing upward like devil horns, were even longer than Bob Kane's Batman ears on the cover of *Detective* #31. Wrightson's Batman was not a man, obviously; a man would have tripped over that cloak when he walked, the ears would have poked holes in ceilings – he was part of the night. An abstract concept. Gothic.

If there is a joy to the concept of Batman, it's that he isn't one thing, that he contains all the Batmans that have walked the streets of Gotham City in the last sixty-five years, Infantino's elegant Batman, Sprang and Schwartz's big gray boy-scout, Frank Miller's Dark Knight. None of them more real, more valid, more true than any other. But in my heart, he is a spectral presence, a creature straight out of the gothic romances, and that is how he will always remain.

***Neil Gaiman** is the Hugo and Nebula Award-winning author of novels, short stories and many comics including the influential* Sandman.

Batman has the richest and most deadly collection of villains in all of comics. Several are known by all, while others lurk in the shadows, biding their time...

Batman: Legends of the Dark Knight #50

1993

Art by Brian Bolland

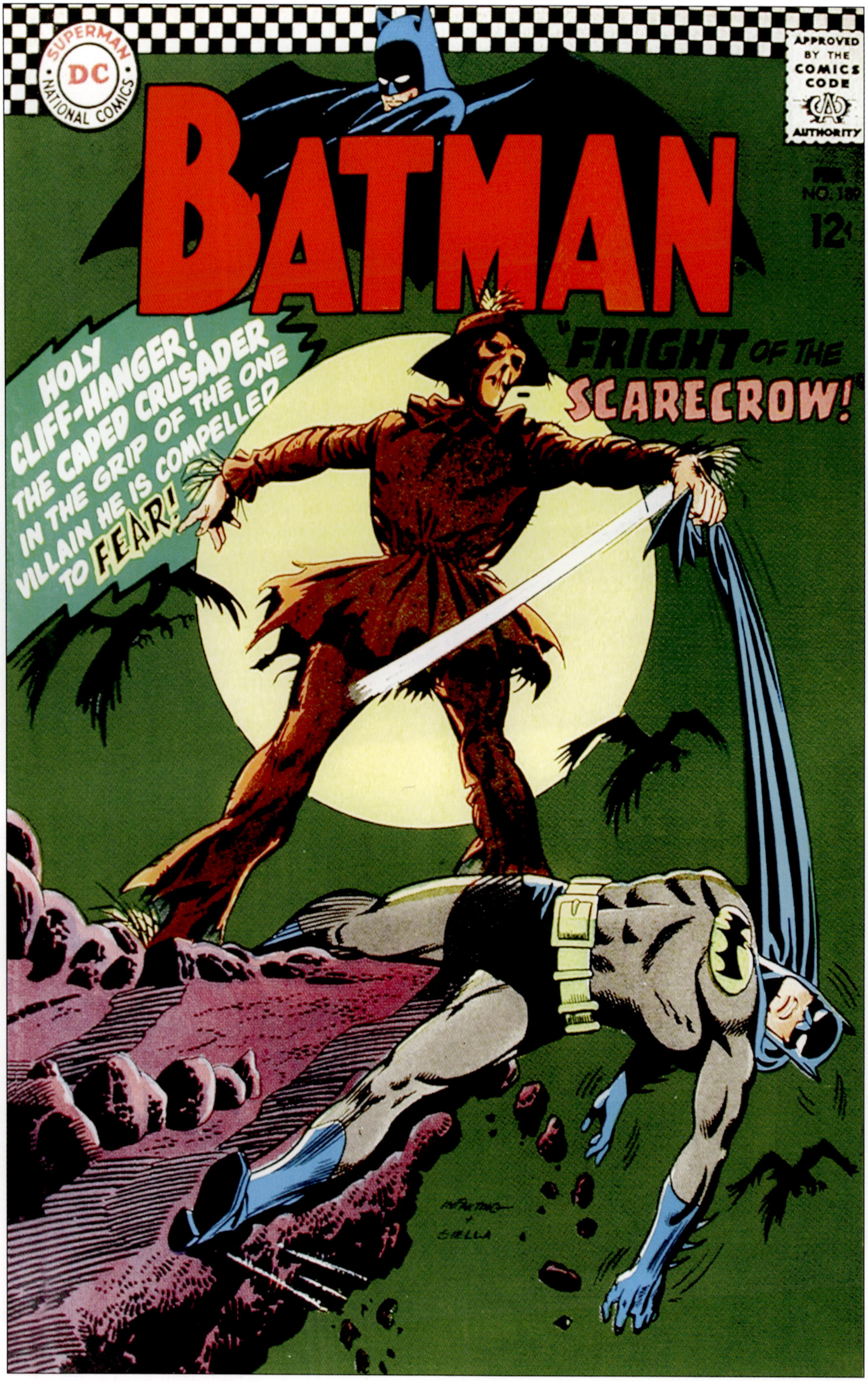

Batman #189

1967

Art by Carmine Infantino & Joe Giella

Page 39:

Batman #50

1949

Bob Kane (figures only), Lew Sayre Schwartz (Pencils) & Charles Paris (Inks)

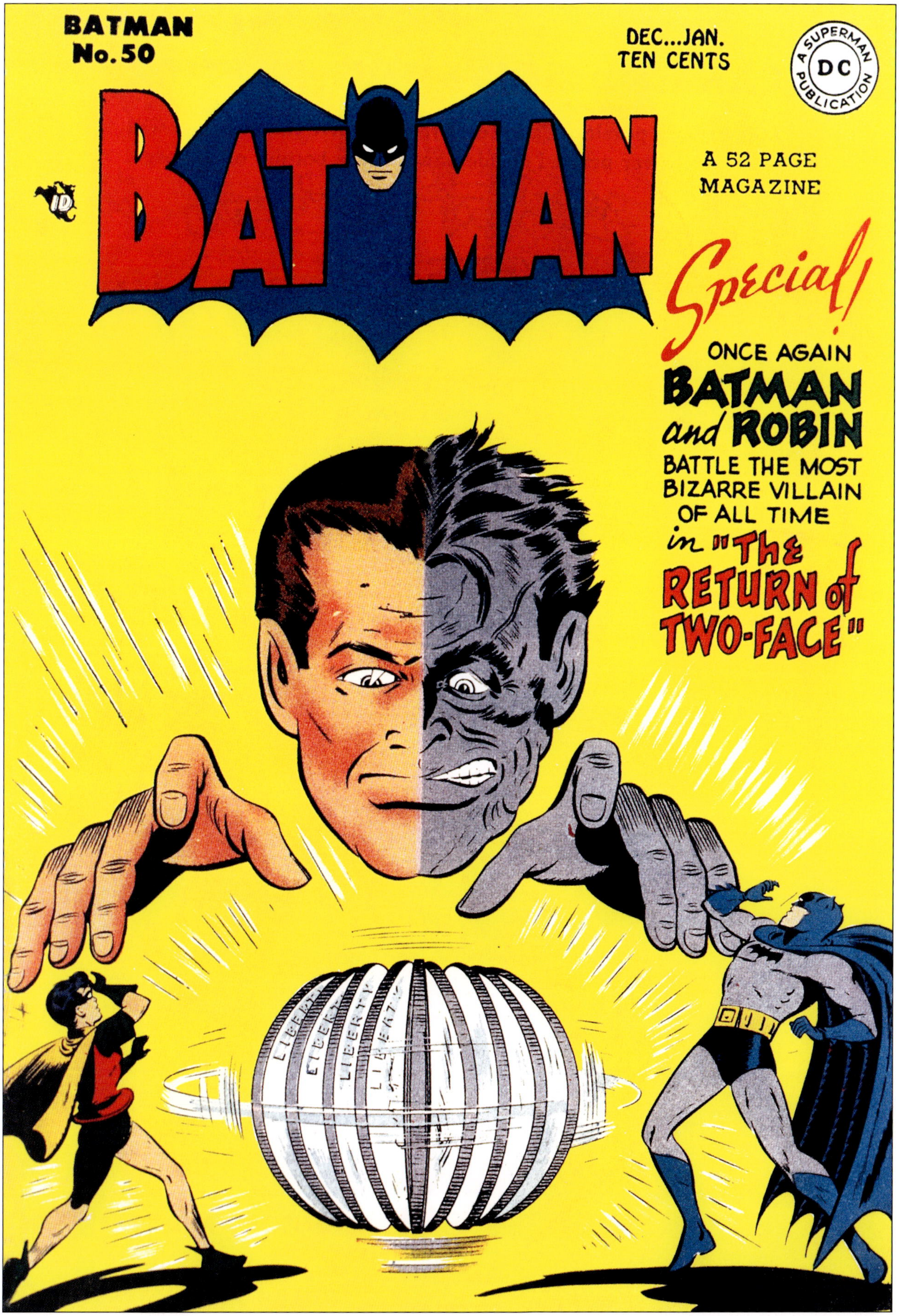
BATMAN
No. 50
DEC...JAN.
TEN CENTS
A SUPERMAN DC PUBLICATION
BATMAN
A 52 PAGE
MAGAZINE
Special!
ONCE AGAIN
BATMAN
and ROBIN
BATTLE THE MOST
BIZARRE VILLAIN
OF ALL TIME
in "The
RETURN of
TWO-FACE"
LIBERTY

The Batman Adventures: Dangerous Dames and Demons
2003
Art by Bruce Timm

This collection won the 2004 Eisner Award for Best Reprint

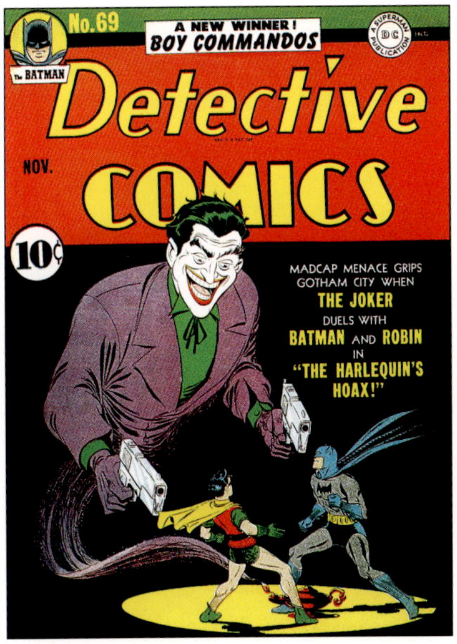

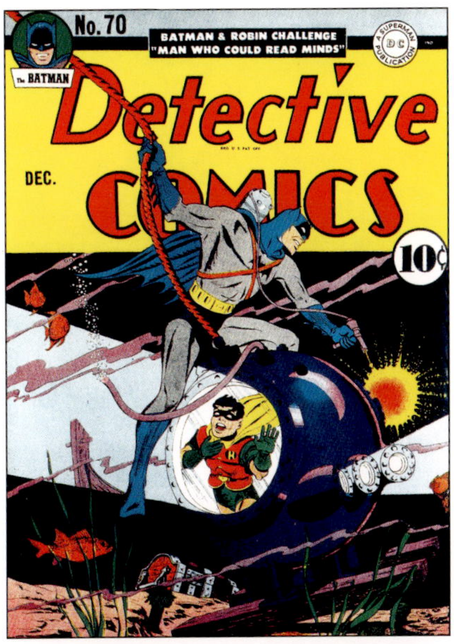

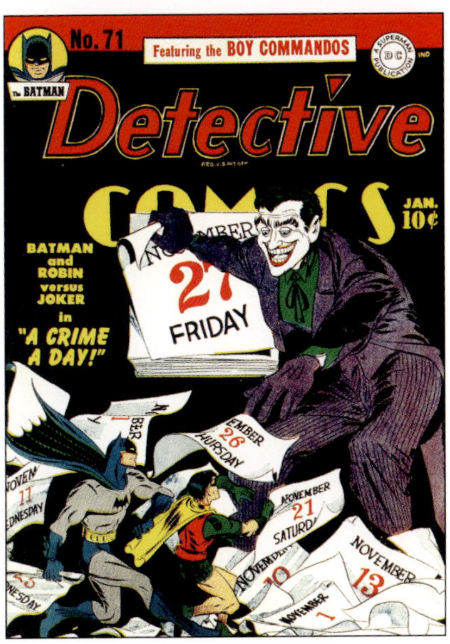

I drew my covers for *Detective Comics* and *Batman* between 1941 and 1947, the early days of what is now known as the Golden Age. It was a time when comic books were proliferating – new titles every month, each competing for attention at the neighborhood candy stores and newsstands.

The covers barely contained their screaming logos featuring all manner of super-heroes in a kaleidoscope of colorful costumes with flowing capes and incredible magic powers. The heroes were locked in battle with sinister evildoers, mad scientists, rampaging monsters and invading aliens, while stopping runaway trains, destroying death turbines and rescuing scantily clad maidens in distress. All in a day's work for the average super-hero. Joining the favorites – Superman, Batman, Captain Marvel and Captain America – were heroes with mythological and biblical derivatives and many with anthropomorphic personas.

To compete in this environment of dazzling images, I strived for flat poster-like shapes and color, dynamic major figures, suspenseful situations and tight composition and design. Not all at one time, of course. Reinforcing the essential image of our heroes and villains was paramount.

My favorite covers and perhaps the most successful in meeting these objectives was the *Detective Comics* series #69, 70 and 71. The intent of #69, one of the earliest Joker covers, was to establish the Joker, seen materializing from Aladdin's lamp, as what I had conceived originally as a larger-than-life menace to Batman and Robin. The simple triangle composition is, I believe, the only version of a gun-toting Joker. Number 70 dramatizes Batman's bond with his protégé Robin in a dangerous undersea attempt to rescue Robin from the exotic-looking bathysphere. The cover for #71 featured a giant Joker (obviously my favorite character). To reinforce Joker as a powerful antagonist, he is depicted overwhelming Batman and Robin with pages of a calendar, symbolic of the lead story "A Crime a Day."

I might mention two others that represent a different approach: *Detective* #67 (see page 73), the first Penguin cover, shows the quixotic villain astride an ostrich that emphasizes his humorous but deadly persona. *Batman* #13 (see page 72) with Batman and Robin parachuting to earth is pure poster design in black and white that literally targets the reader's eye.

***Jerry Robinson** started working with Batman creator Bob Kane as a teenager, moving from inking to fully illustrating numerous covers and stories. He's credited with helping define the look of the Joker among other familiar figures.*

Batman:

The Long Halloween

1998

Art by Tim Sale

Page 43:

Batman #42

1947

Art by Jack Burnley & Charles Paris

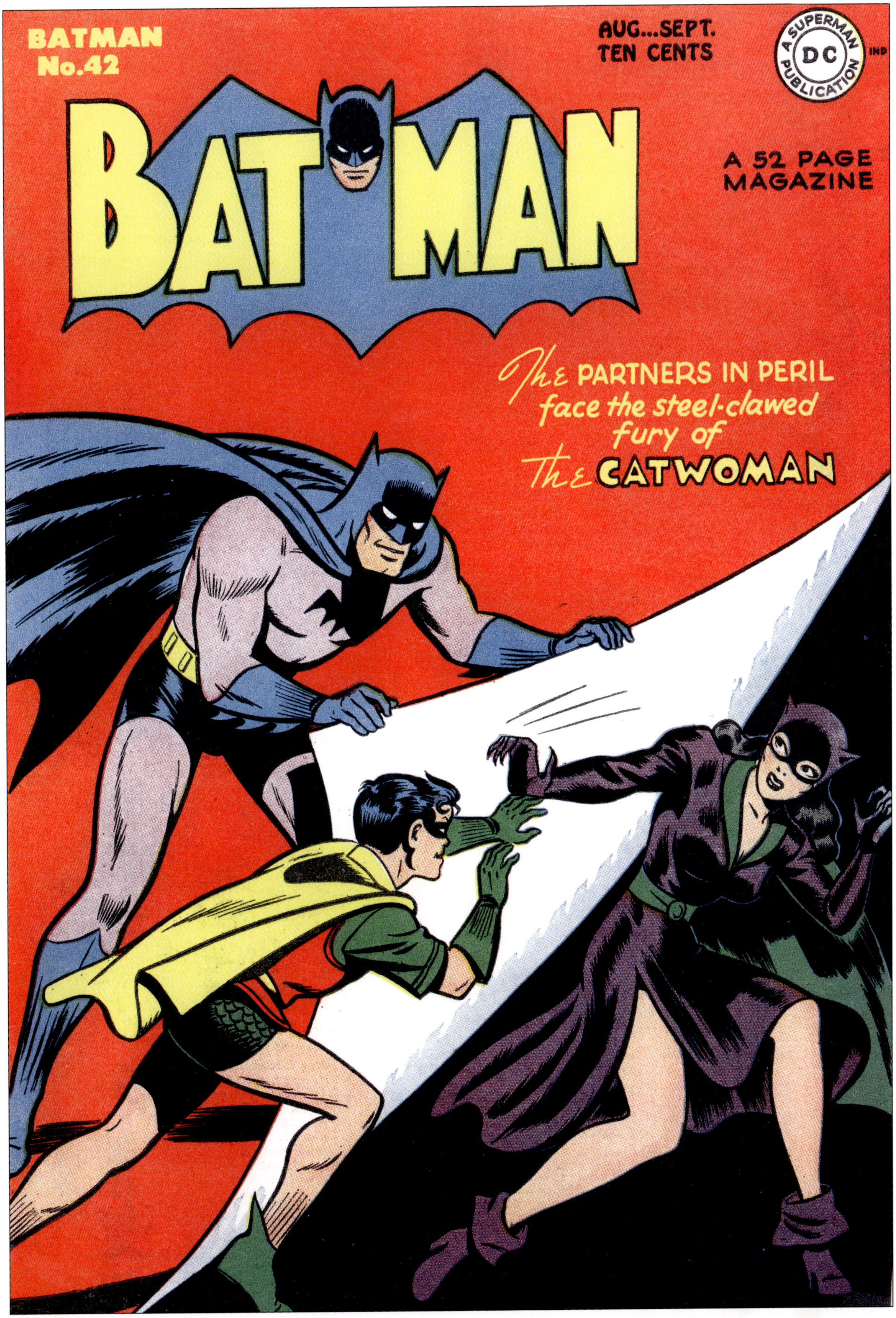
BATMAN
No.42
AUG...SEPT.
TEN CENTS
A SUPERMAN DC PUBLICATION
IND
BATMAN
A 52 PAGE
MAGAZINE
The PARTNERS IN PERIL
face the steel-clawed
fury of
The CATWOMAN

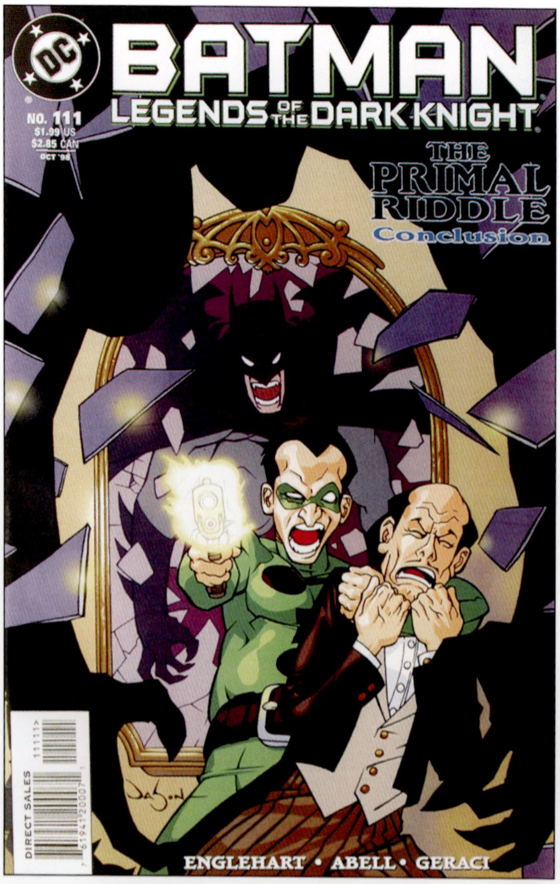

Batman: Legends of the Dark Knight #111

1998

Art by Jason Pearson

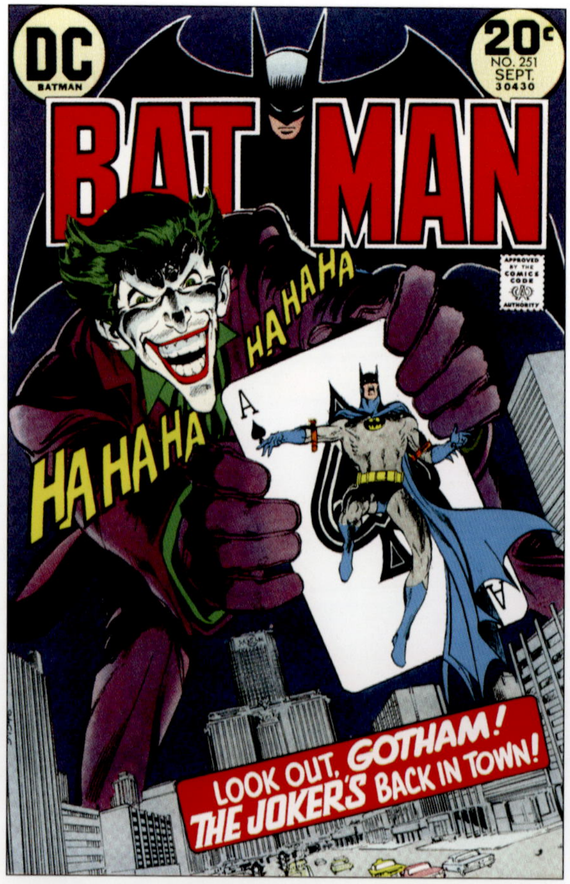

Batman #251

1973

Art by Neal Adams

Batman #68

1952

Art by Win Mortimer

Batman: Gotham Knights #15

2001

Art by Brian Bolland

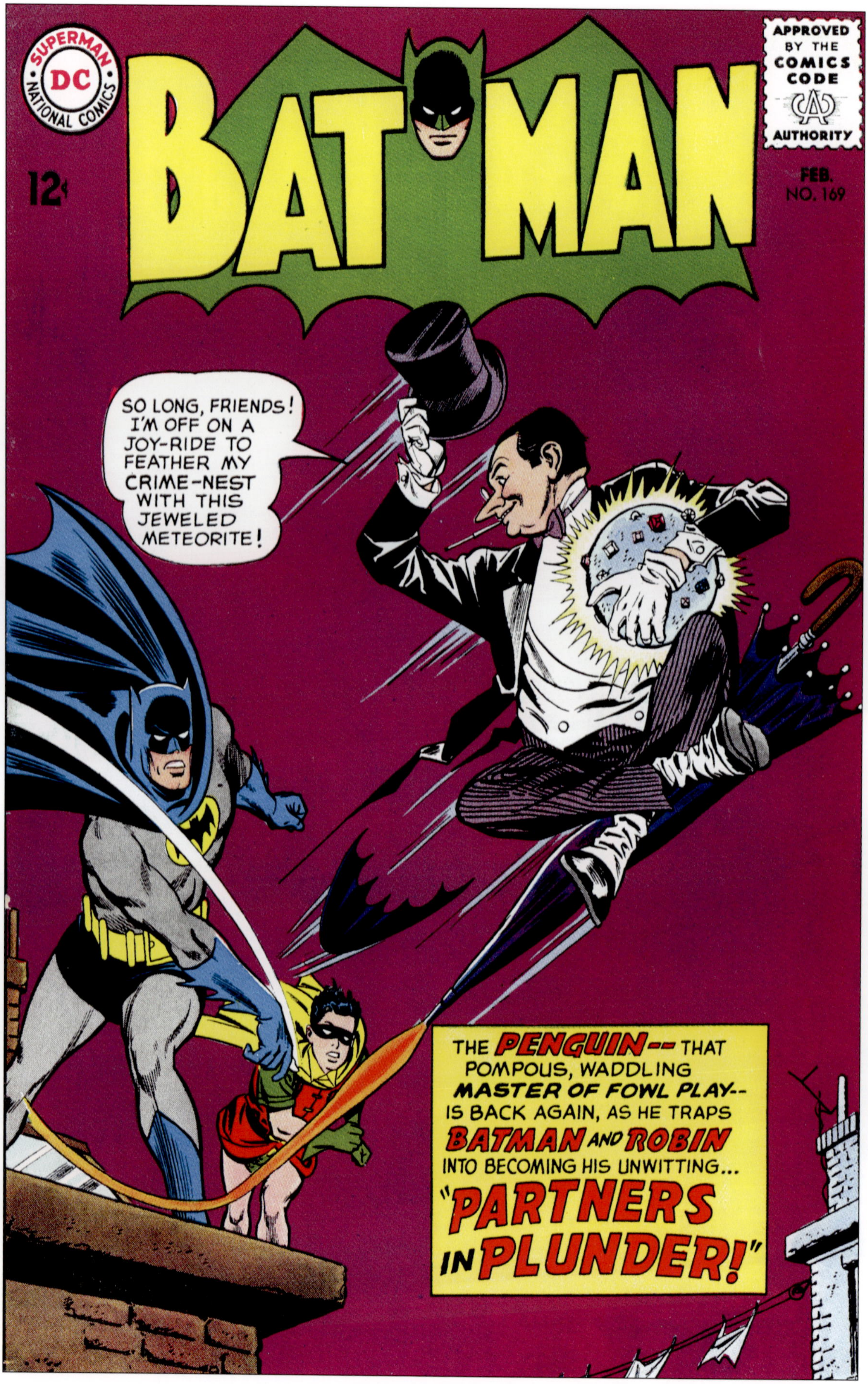

Batman #169

1965

Art by Carmine Infantino & Joe Giella

Detective Comics #705

1997

Art by Graham Nolan & Karl Story

Detective Comics #400

1970

Art by Neal Adams

Detective Comics #569

1986

Art by Alan Davis & Paul Neary

Secret Origins Special

1989

Art by Brian Bolland

Batman: Legends of the Dark Knight #119

1999

Art by Brian Bolland

Batman: Legends of the Dark Knight #139

2001

Art by Paul Gulacy & Jimmy Palmiotti

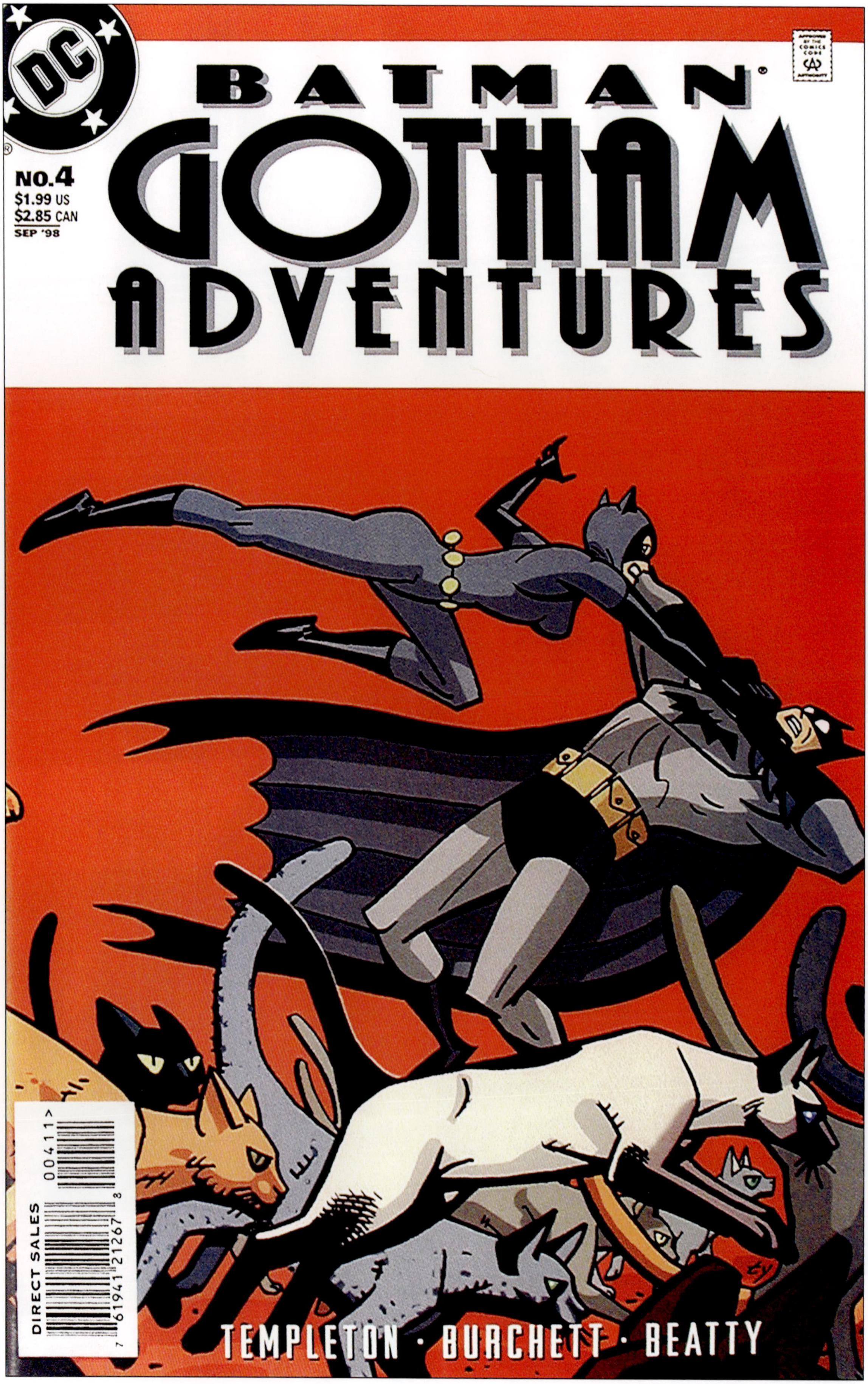

Batman: Gotham Adventures #4

1998

Art by Ty Templeton

Batman: Gotham Adventures #32

2001

Art by Bob Smith & Terry Beatty

Page 55:

Batman #121

1959

Art by Curt Swan & Stan Kaye

Introduced here as Mr. Zero, he was renamed Mr. Freeze when he was used on the ABC television series.

The Brave and the Bold #111

1974

Art by Jim Aparo

Detective Comics #120

1947

Art by Win Mortimer

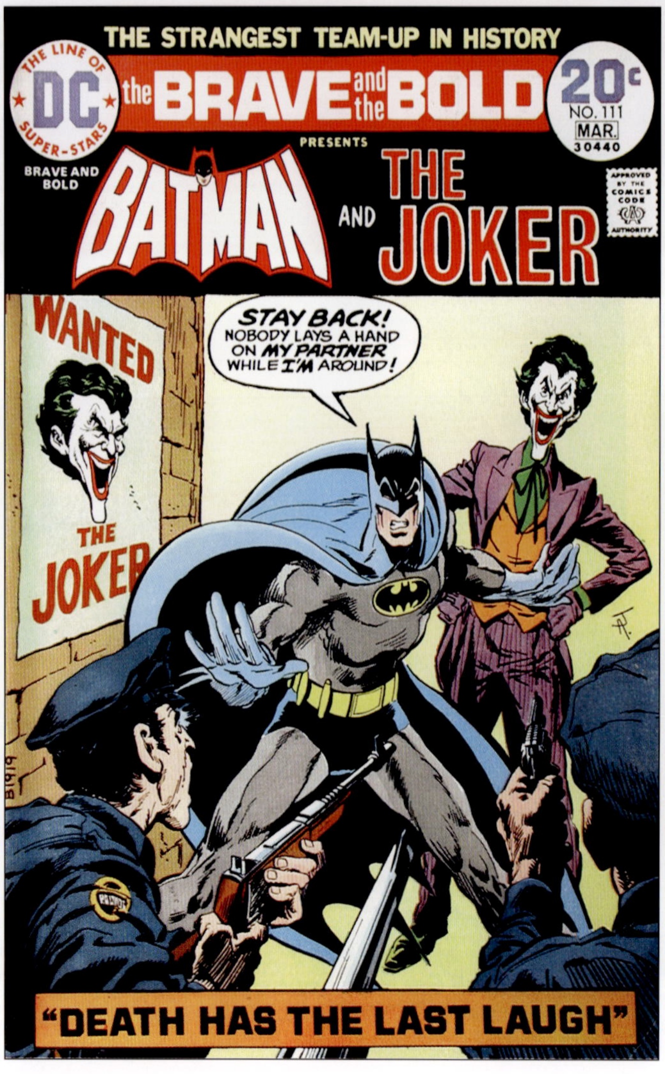

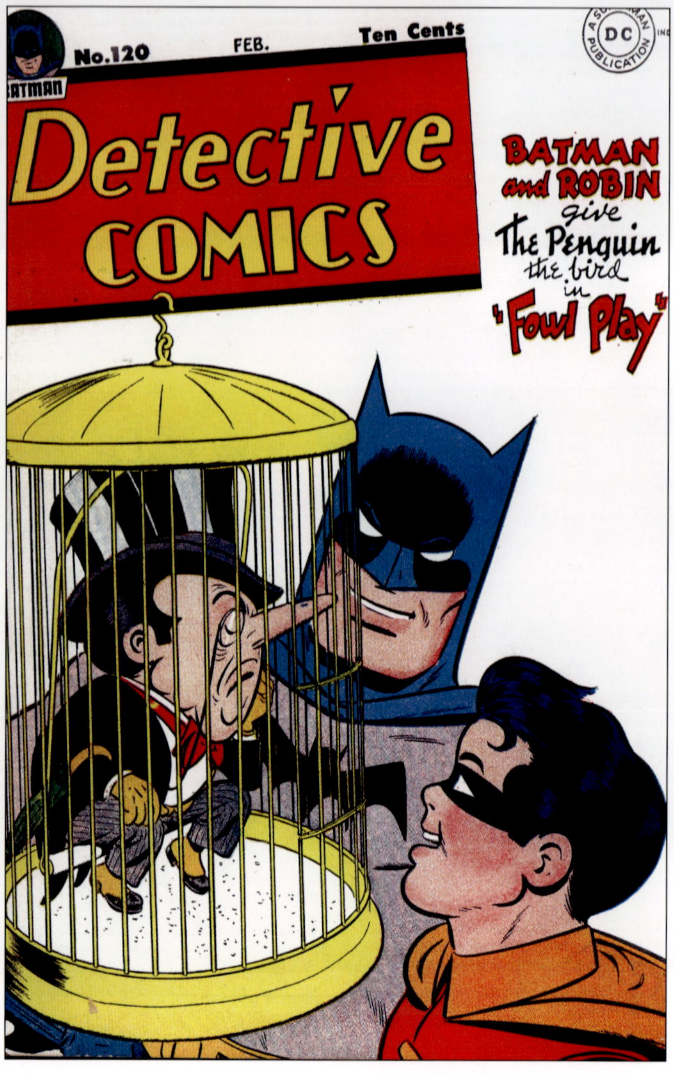

10¢
SUPERMAN DC NATIONAL COMICS
FEB. NO. 121
APPROVED BY THE COMICS CODE AUTHORITY
BATMAN
AND NOW I'LL HAVE THE MOST VALUABLE LIVE TROPHIES IN THE WORLD-- BATMAN AND ROBIN FROZEN IN BLOCKS OF ICE!
Featuring "The ICE CRIMES of MR. ZERO!"

Batman #591

2001

Art by Scott McDaniel

Batman #610

2003

Art by Jim Lee & Scott Williams

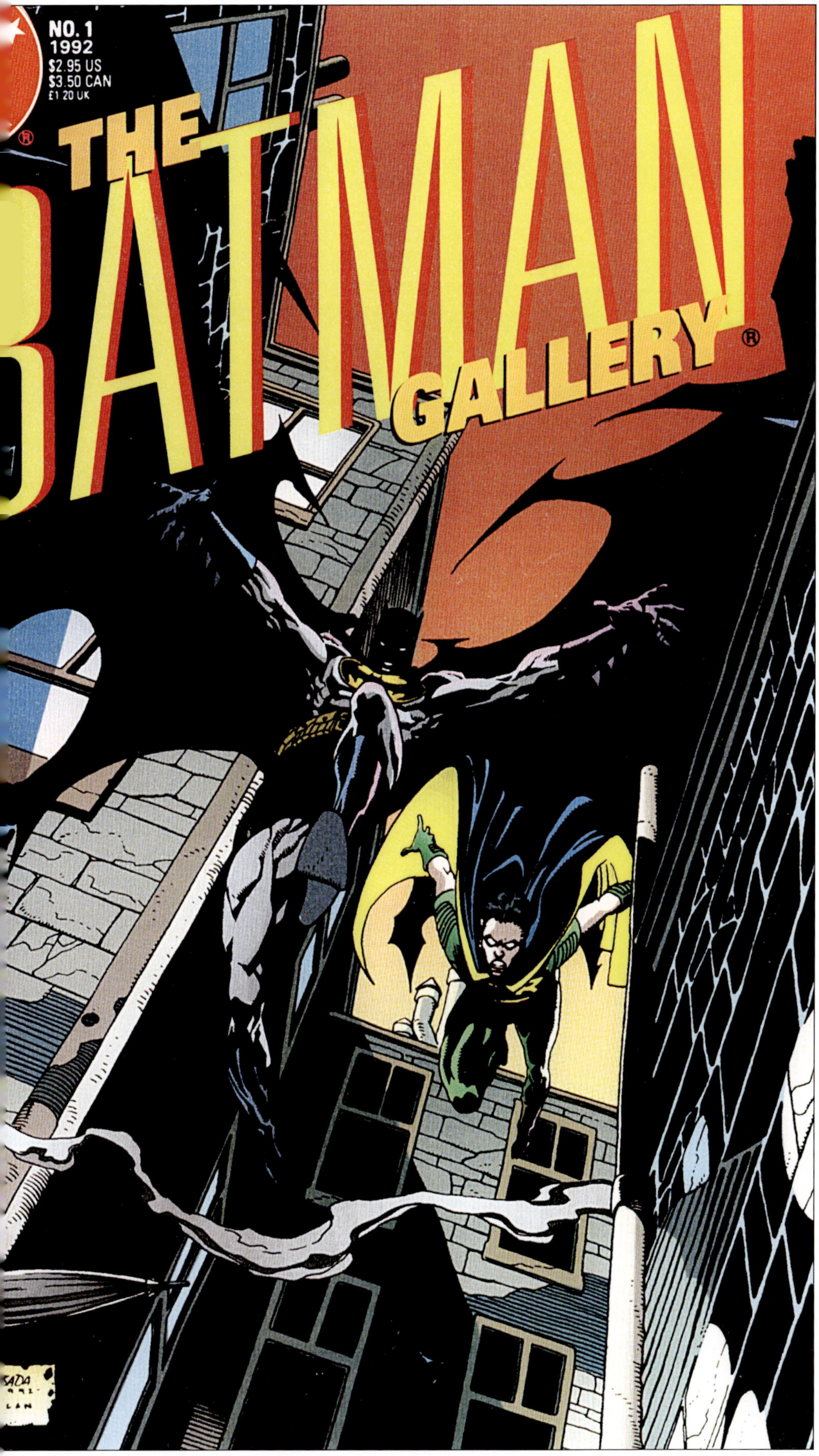

The Batman Gallery #1

1992

Art by Joe Quesada & Kevin Nowlan

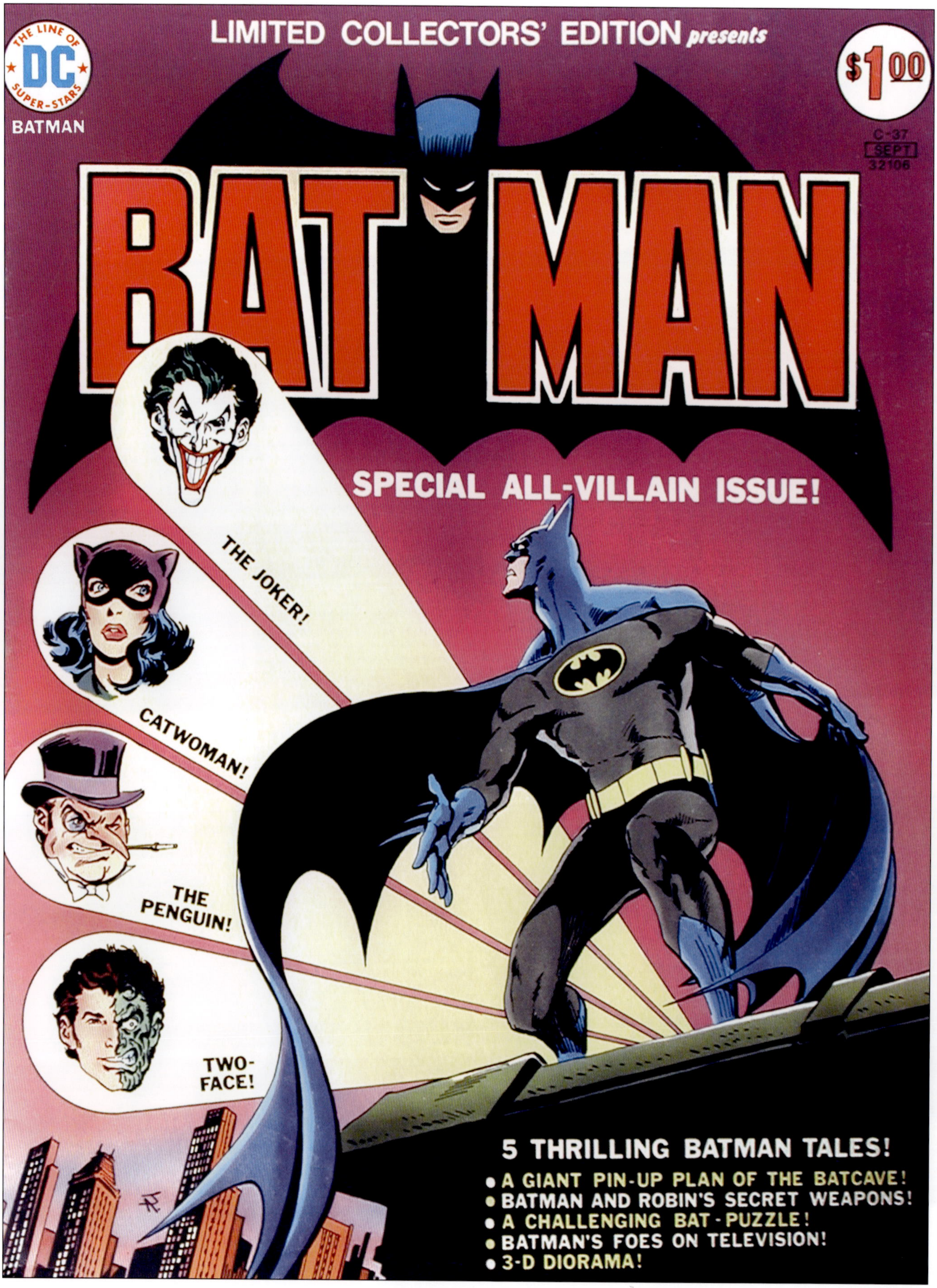
LIMITED COLLECTORS' EDITION presents
THE LINE OF DC SUPER-STARS
BATMAN
$1.00
C-37
SEPT
32106
BATMAN
SPECIAL ALL-VILLAIN ISSUE!
THE JOKER!
CATWOMAN!
THE PENGUIN!
TWO-FACE!
5 THRILLING BATMAN TALES!
• A GIANT PIN-UP PLAN OF THE BATCAVE!
• BATMAN AND ROBIN'S SECRET WEAPONS!
• A CHALLENGING BAT-PUZZLE!
• BATMAN'S FOES ON TELEVISION!
• 3-D DIORAMA!

Page 60:

Limited Collectors' Edition C-37

1975

Art by Jim Aparo

DETECTIVE COMICS #475 1977, Art by Marshall Rogers & Terry Austin

This was it — my first super-hero comic. But it wasn't the first I read. In fact, I didn't read it for years. I just kept it hidden. Why? Look at the cover. I was a kid. And a wuss. It scared the hell out of me. The Joker's haunting eyes. Twin fish (with that same look in their eyes) being used as guns. *And* they were wearing lipstick. To be honest, this thing should've put me in therapy. Instead, it's where my addiction was born. Most boys want baseball cards. I just wanted more comics. And Count Chokula.

***Brad Meltzer** is the best-selling author of five thrillers as well as the co-creator of the WB television series* Jack & Bobby. *For comics, he has written the critically acclaimed* Green Arrow: Archer's Quest *and the best-selling miniseries* Identity Crisis.

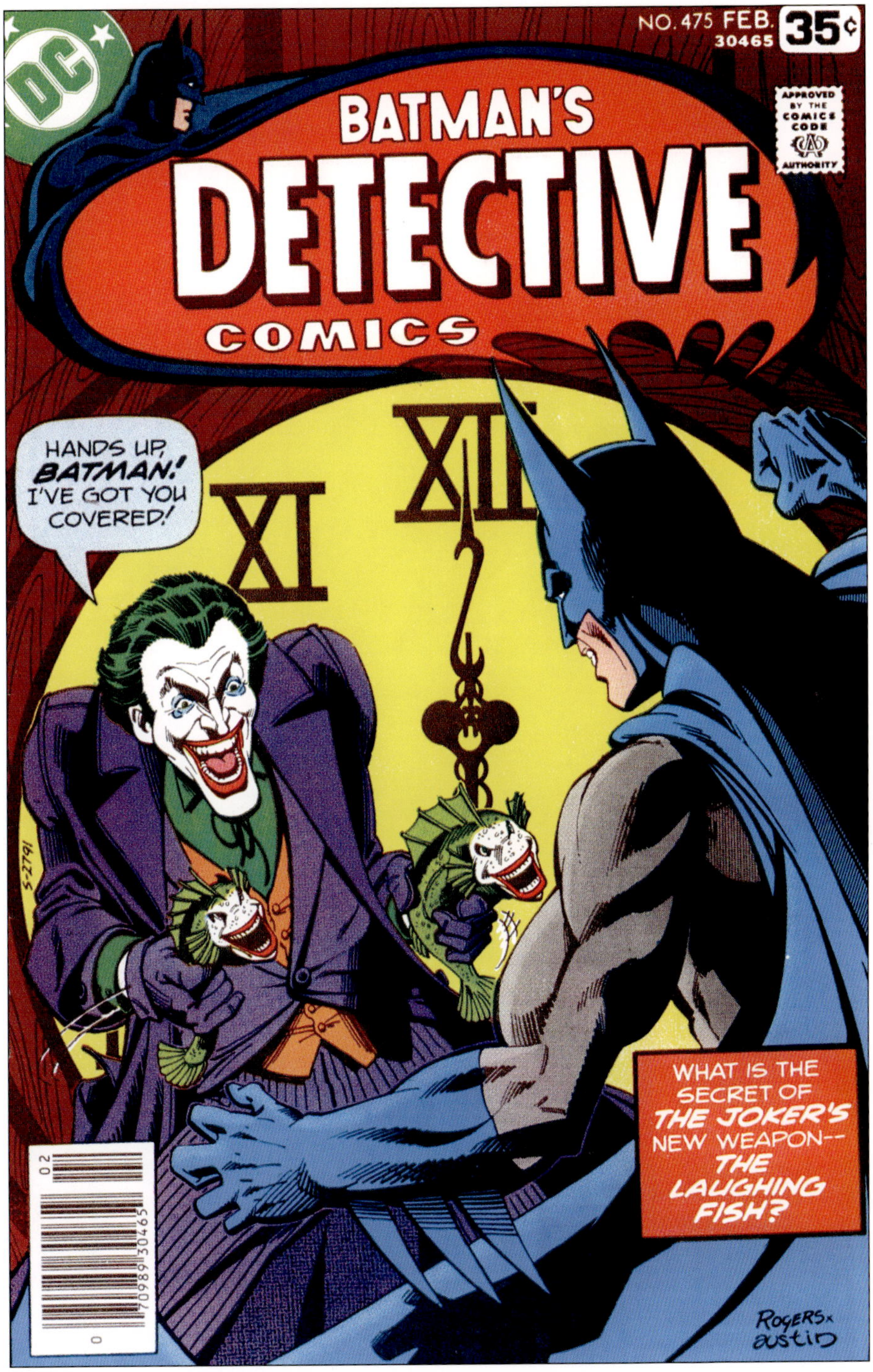

Detective Comics #474

1977

Art by Marshall Rogers & Terry Austin

Batman: Gotham Adventures #44

2002

Art by Bob Smith & Terry Beatty

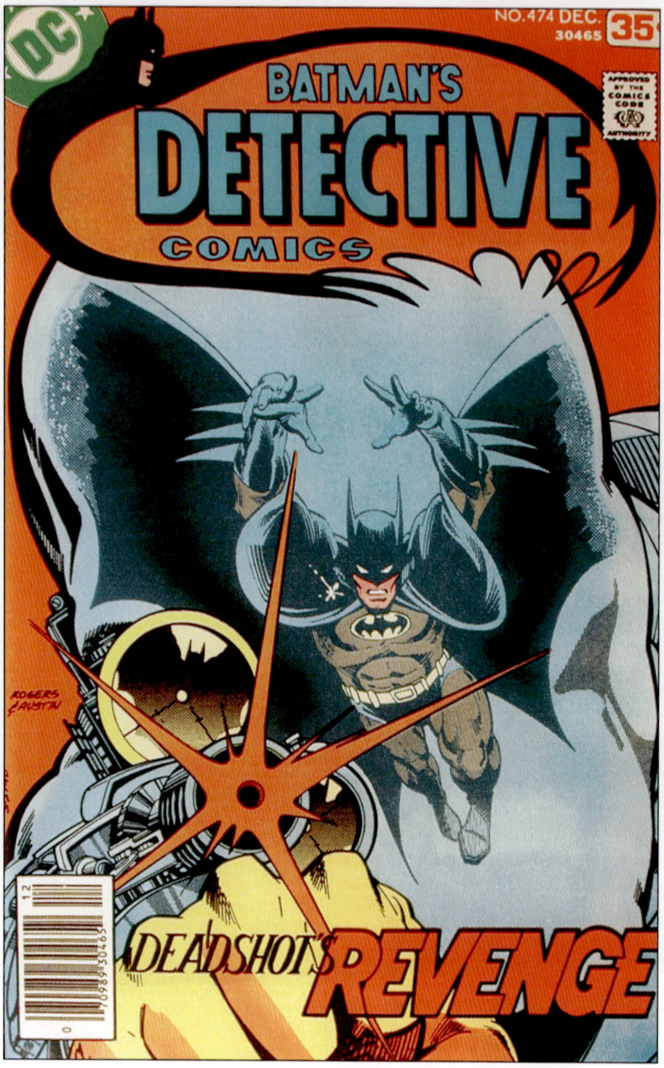

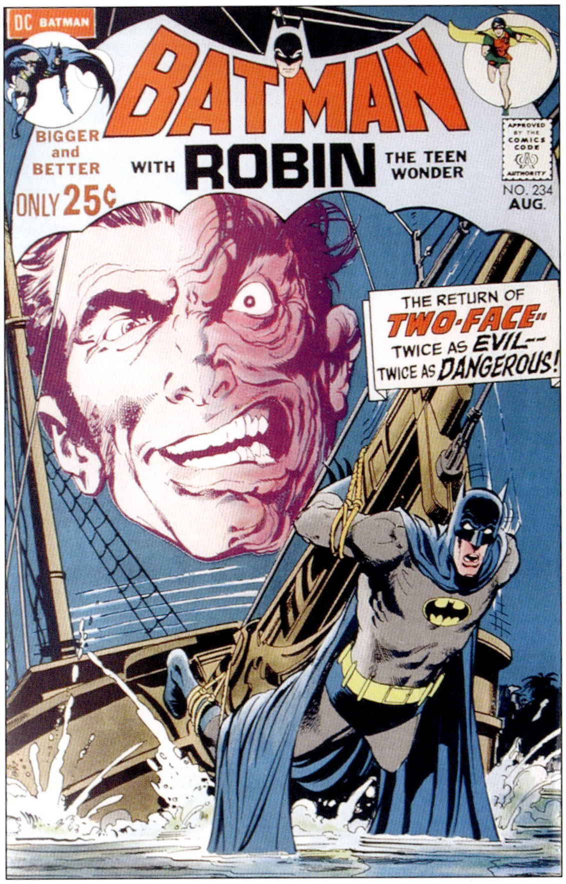

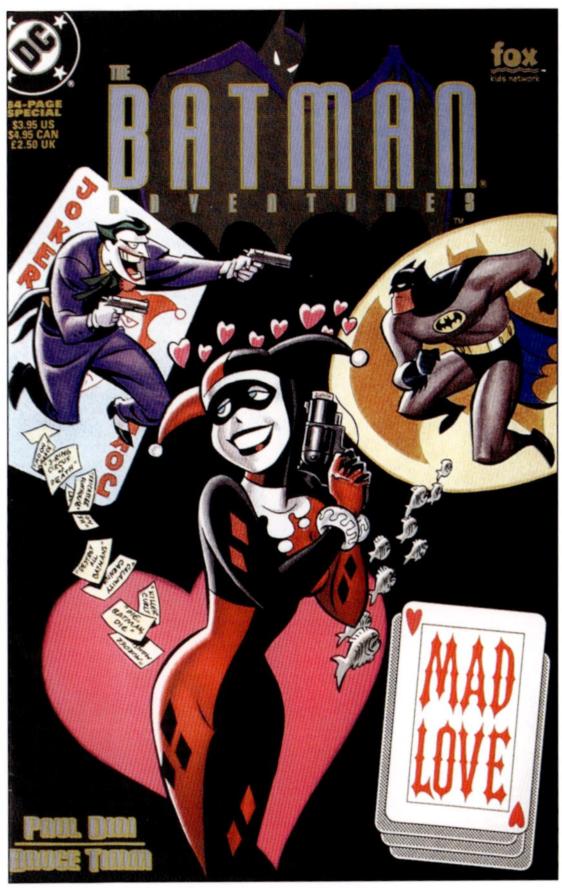

Batman #234

1971

Art by Neal Adams

Batman #171

1965

Art by Carmine Infantino & Joe Giella

The Batman Adventures: Mad Love (newsstand edition)

1994

Art by Bruce Timm

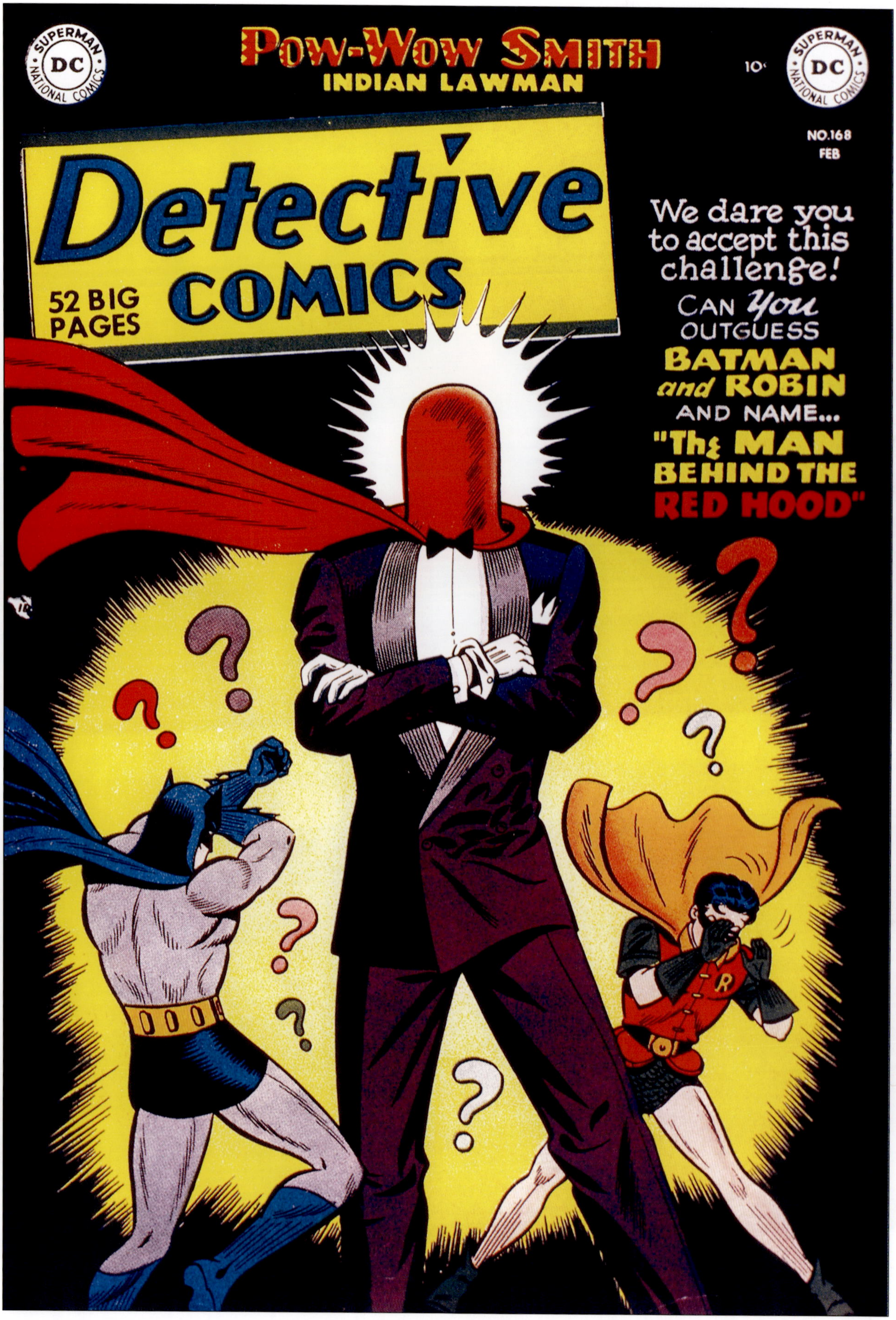

Detective Comics #168
1951
Art by
Lew Sayre
Schwartz &
Charles Paris

Detective Comics #187
1952
Art by
Win Mortimer

Also: A NEW MYSTERY with ROY RAYMOND, TV DETECTIVE
SUPERMAN DC NATIONAL COMICS
SUPERMAN DC NATIONAL COMICS
Detective COMICS
JAN. NO. 203
10c
BATMAN AND ROBIN DUEL THE QUEEN OF THE UNDERWORLD IN "CRIMES OF THE CATWOMAN!"

Page 66:

Detective Comics #203

1954

Art by Win Mortimer

Batman #497

1993

Art by Kelley Jones

Bane breaking Batman's back was one of the most monumental events of the 1990s. The Knightfall storyline spanned the line of Batman titles and was turned into a successful novel by editor Denny O'Neil.

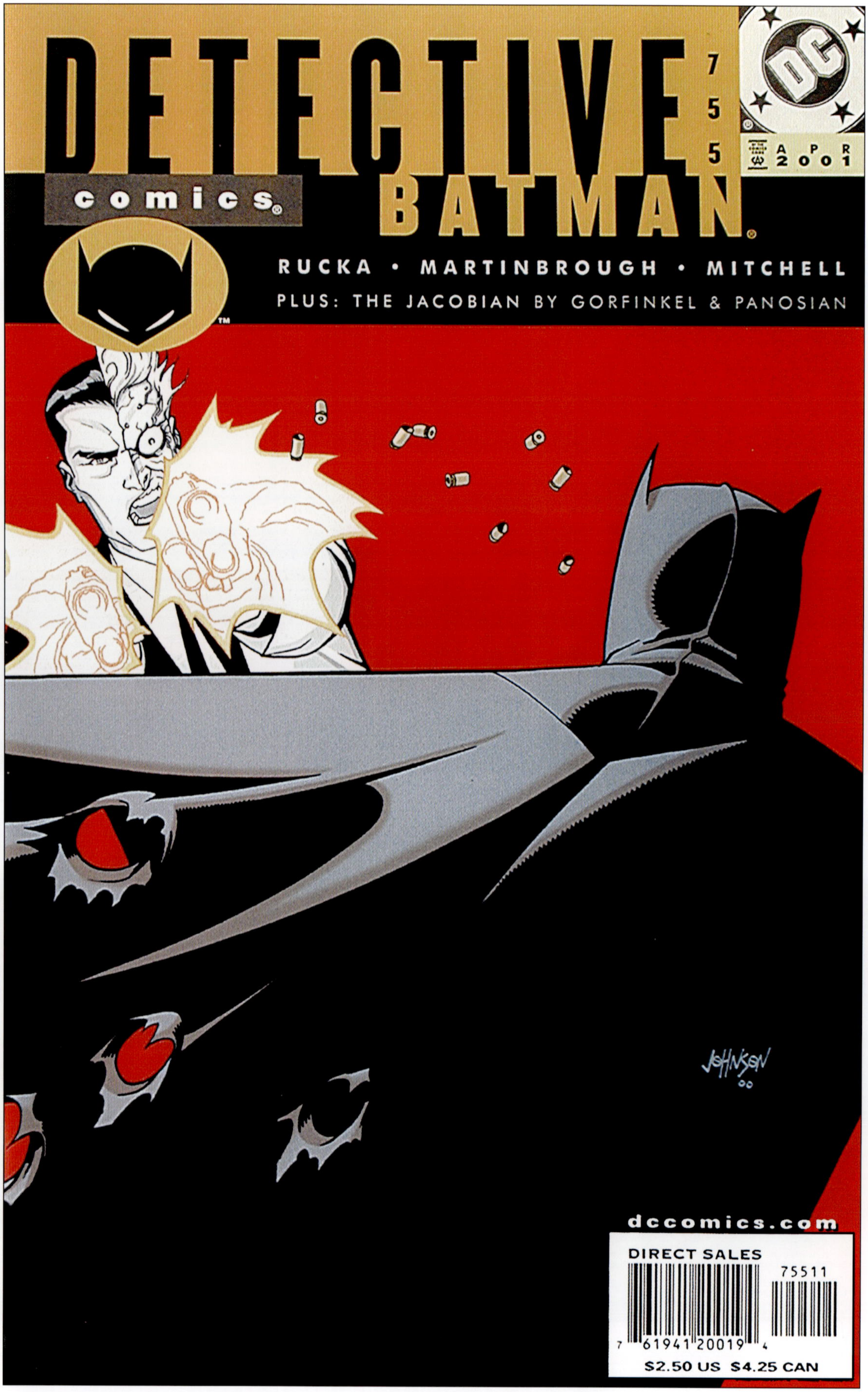

Detective Comics #755

2001

Art by Dave Johnson

Batman #619

2003

Art by Jim Lee & Scott Williams

This was the cover for the second printing of the concluding chapter of the Jeph Loeb/Jim Lee "Hush" story. Collector's editions featured gatefold covers, one spotlighting the heroes, the other the villains.

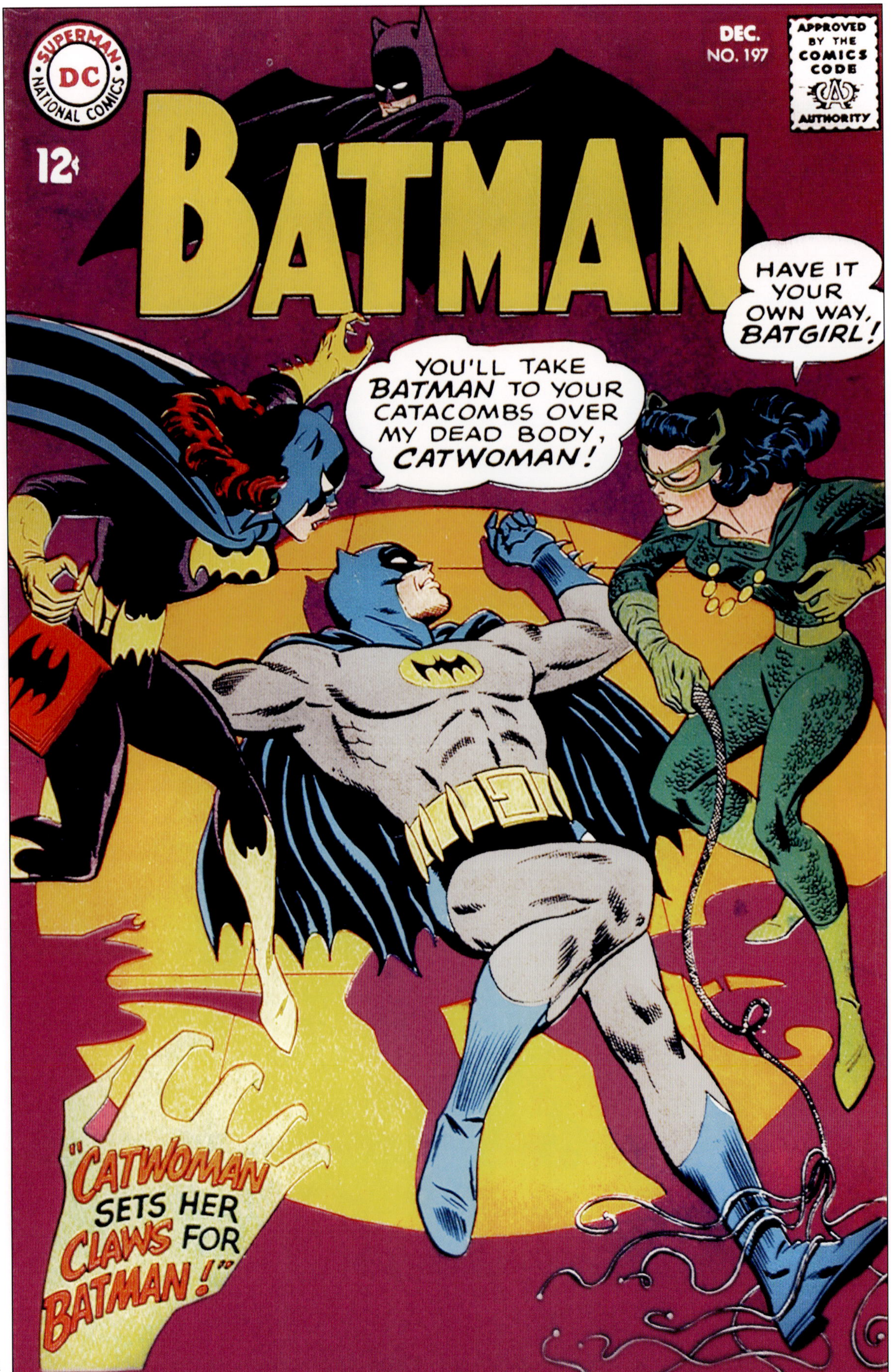

Batman #197

1967

Art by Carmine Infantino & Mike Esposito

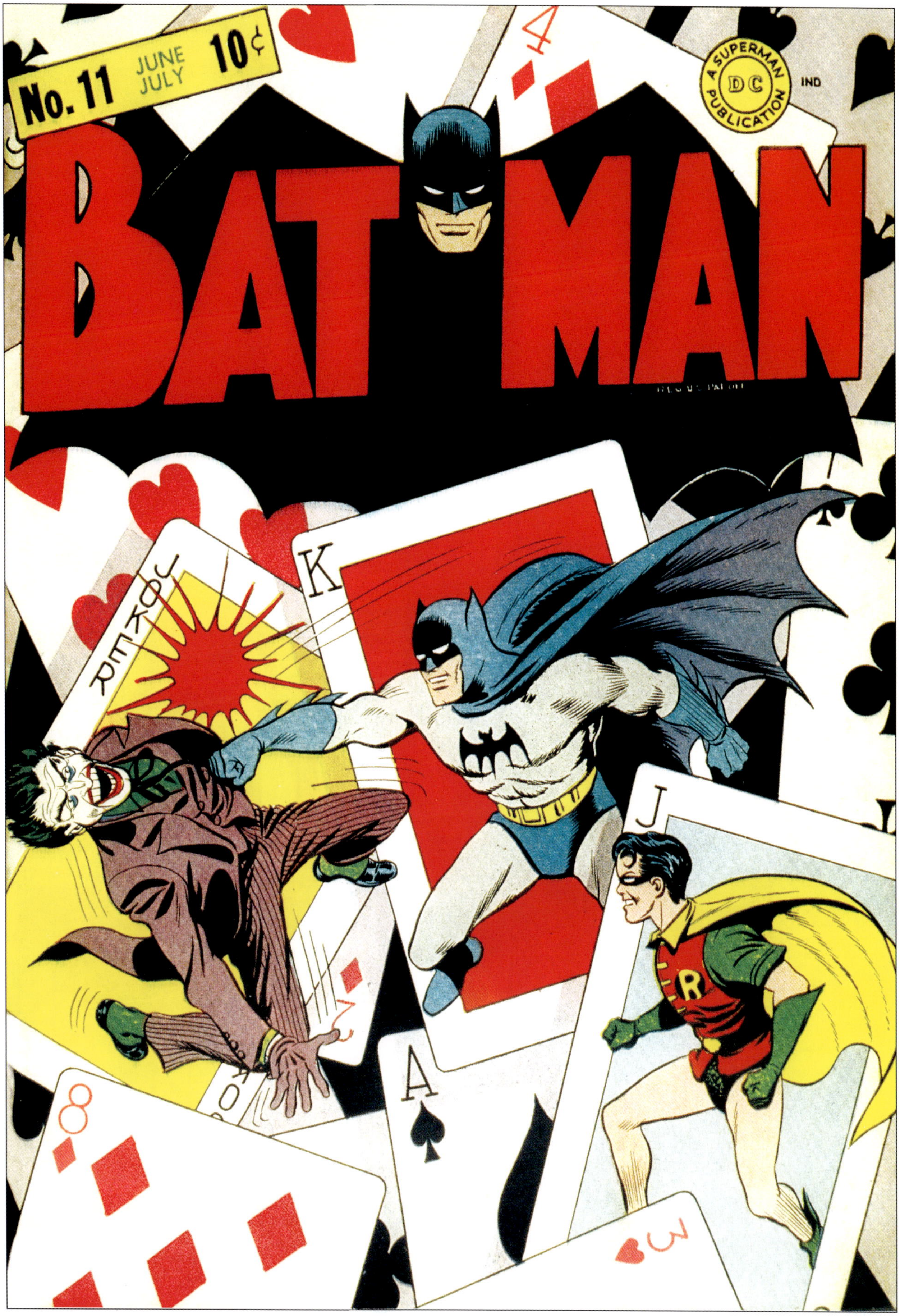

Batman #11

1942

Art by Fred Ray

When working with Bob Kane, how were the cover chores done?

When I first joined the Batman of [Bob] Kane and [Bill] Finger, Bob did the pencil roughs and I would do the finishes and inking (and for some time, the lettering). Bob worked in his apartment and I worked in my own space a few blocks away. We would get together almost daily and several times a week with Bill to discuss ideas. Bob would deliver the finished art to DC. When George Roussos joined us, he would ink most of the backgrounds.

Later, when Bill and I worked directly for DC, Bill worked with Jack Schiff and Mort Weisinger and I worked with my editor, Whit Ellsworth. Then I was able to do many of the covers myself – layout, complete pencils and inks, which needless to say, I much preferred. Sometimes, when there was time, I would also do the color.

How was cover design decided? What steps were employed?

Whit Ellsworth didn't usually require sketches. Generally I would describe to Whit my idea for a cover or perhaps do rough layout for the design. Sometimes on deadline, Whit wouldn't see the art until it was complete. I worked next to Whit so he was able at times to make suggestions during the process. I enjoyed working with Whit. I guess mostly because if he had confidence in you, he let you do your own thing.

As Batman became increasingly popular, we quickly had to go from one thirteen-page story and cover a month to adding the *Batman* quarterly of four stories and a cover. Soon after, *World's Finest* required another story and a cover on which I often collaborated with Fred Ray, a great Superman cover artist. We enjoyed working together, developing the ideas. At one time our desks were literally adjoining one another. The covers combined Batman, Robin and Superman and we pencilled and inked our respective characters. During World War II, Whit suggested some of the patriotic covers.

The *Detective Comics* and *Batman* covers were not often coordinated with the interior stories. I recall one cover that did, featuring the Joker masquerading as a florist. I finished the lead story and the cover was a variation of the splash page.

Was the approach to BATMAN any different than for DETECTIVE?

The *Batman* covers were more symbolic, not as story driven. That *Batman* was a quarterly may have been a factor. *Batman* contained four stories and we didn't want to feature one story over the others on the cover. We went with a symbolic concept to give a sense of the Batman persona, whereas *Detective* covers were more likely to be coordinated with that issue's story.

Early on, the covers were not always story specific. Did you prefer that?

I think they were both a challenge. I preferred a symbolic rather than a literal interpretation. Remember, this was the beginning of the comic book genre so one of my objectives was to round out the persona of Batman and Robin and establish the menacing, bizarre nature of the Joker character, and exploit the concept of the super-villain.

It was easier to focus on one character, Batman, before Robin was introduced. On the other hand, it made for a more dramatic situation with the two of them, such as *Detective #70* (see page 41). That image of the bathysphere didn't appear in any story. However, it was in the news. I think Jacques Cousteau used one in his deep sea explorations. I liked its unique shape and worked out a dramatic and suspenseful situation in an exotic setting. Among the villains, the Joker was of course my favorite. Later, the Penguin, an intriguing character, was fun to do.

Did you get feedback from DC in terms of which covers seemed to help sell titles?

I can't recall. Batman was so growing in popularity I don't think any issue was disappointing in sales. I think we all knew a great cover regardless of sales.

Who did the cover coloring? You or National?

A wonderful man, Raymond Perry, did most of the color at the time. He was a well-known illustrator in his heyday. He seemed quite advanced in years to a teenager like me, although he was probably in his 50s. I was always in awe of him and always called him Mr. Perry. It was sad that he was reduced to coloring comics in his declining years. He did beautiful, thoughtful coloring. We frequently walked home together after work. We lived just a few blocks from each other. I learned a lot from him. When I wanted some special color scheme on a story, I would discuss it with him. He always got just the right effect. Occasionally, if I had time, I liked to do the color myself. We used Dr. Martin dyes on a silver print reproduction of the art, a surface that was able to absorb the dye. From there the color separations were done by the engraver.

Incidentally, I designed the logo that I believe first appeared on *Batman* #1. I knew nothing about lettering styles or fonts, so I just made up my own that I thought worked.

Gotham City is as much a character in Batman stories as any living being. The city's look is gothic; its skyline casts deep shadows over citizens and criminals alike.

Batman Chronicles #10

1997

Art by Phil Winslade

Detective Comics #362

1967

Art by Carmine Infantino & Murphy Anderson

Detective Comics #368

1967

Art by Carmine Infantino & Murphy Anderson

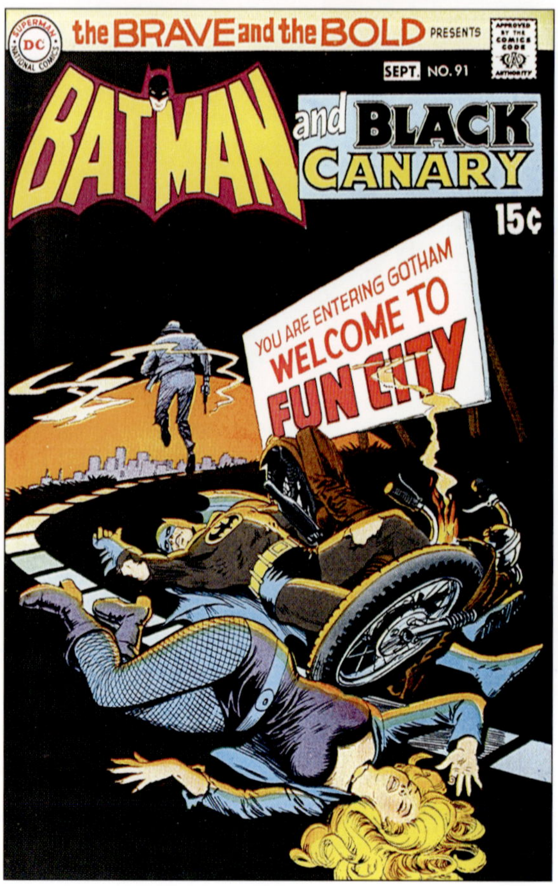

Batman #485

1992

Art by Michael Golden

Batman #566

1998

Art by Jon Bogdanove

The Brave and the Bold #91

1970

Art by Nick Cardy

DETECTIVE COMICS #629 1991, Art by Michael Golden

Michael Golden, in the early 1990s, created a series of *Detective* covers that, to me at least, seemed to appear as if from nowhere to speak to the character of Batman in a way that no one since Neal Adams had been able to do. Furthermore, he did it the opposite way from Adams — instead of starring the figure of Batman, the hero of the book, he chose to emphasize the hugely compelling milieu of Gotham City, sometimes almost losing the image of Batman altogether, as on this cover. This approach served two purposes: to show how much a creature of mystery and his environment Batman is in the way that he can slip in and out of the shadows, and for Golden to showcase his excellence at pattern and *stuff*. Objects. Buildings, guns, cars, rockets, fish, bones, *stuff*, piling on top of each other visually to create pattern, all carefully rendered, then using color and contrast to keep the image from being too busy and cluttered.

Golden's technique is second to none; he is a meticulous craftsman, exacting and thoughtful, and in his use of his tools remains as accomplished as anyone working today. But his lasting impact, I believe, is in his ability to look at what is needed to tell his story, what, besides the figures, is important to the hero's world and the moment to be depicted, and then drawing the hell out of it. This cover does that in spades.

***Tim Sale,** in collaboration with writer Jeph Loeb, has produced* Batman: Haunted Knight, Batman: The Long Halloween, Batman: Dark Victory, *which have been named by* Wizard Magazine *three of the most important graphic novels to own. Additionally, Tim has produced a series of covers for* Detective Comics.

Detective Comics #626

1991

Art by Michael Golden

Batman #452

1990

Art by Mike Mignola & Joe Quesada

Detective Comics #745

2000

Art by Dave Johnson

Batman: Gotham City Secret Files & Origins

2000

Art by John Van Fleet

Batman: Gotham Noir

2001

Art by Sean Phillips

Detective Comics #722

1998

Art by Brian Stelfreeze

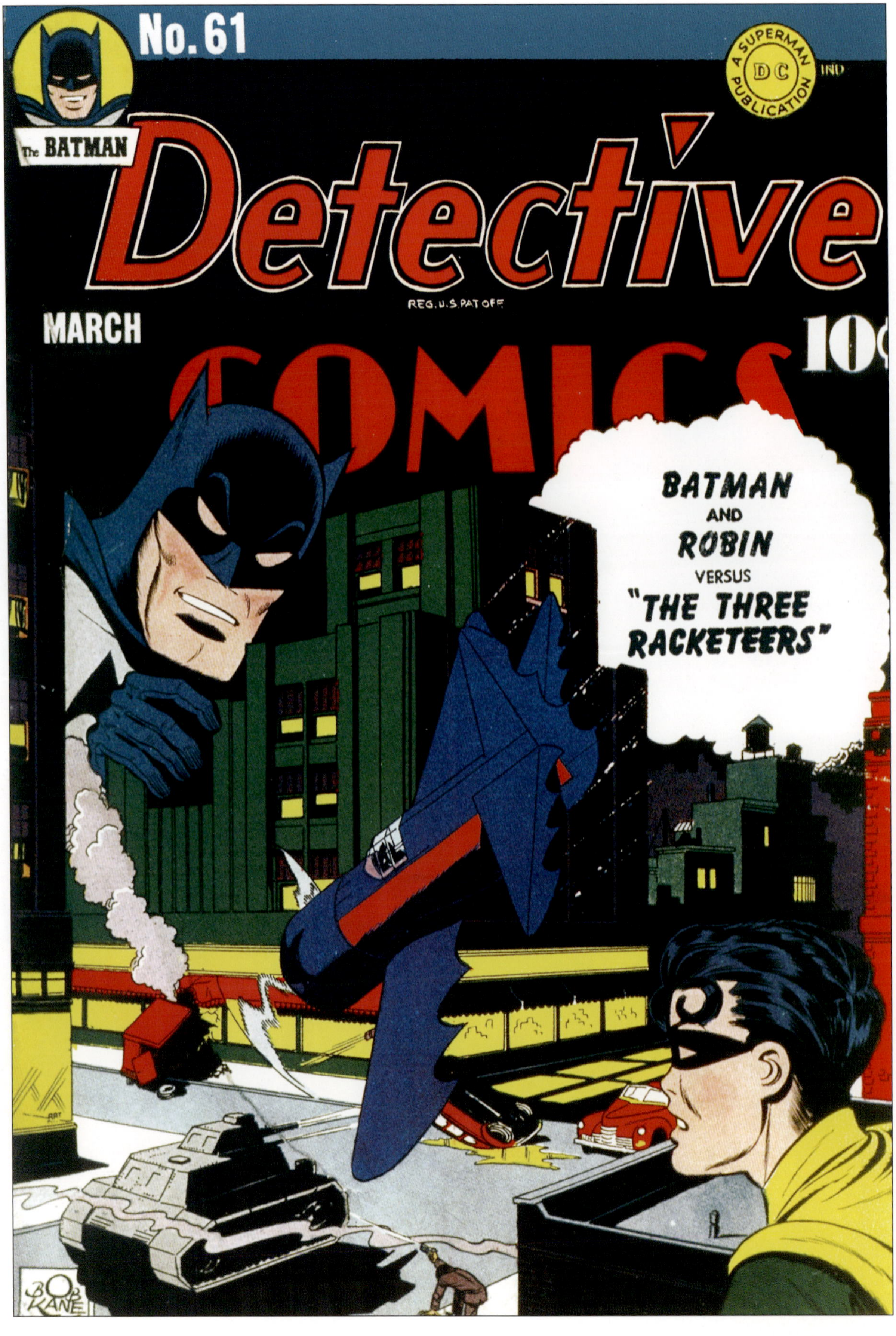

Detective Comics #61

1942

Art by Bob Kane, Jerry Robinson & George Roussos

The presence of an optimistic ally has kept Batman from tumbling into the dark realms of obsession. Meet the original boy sidekick, Robin.

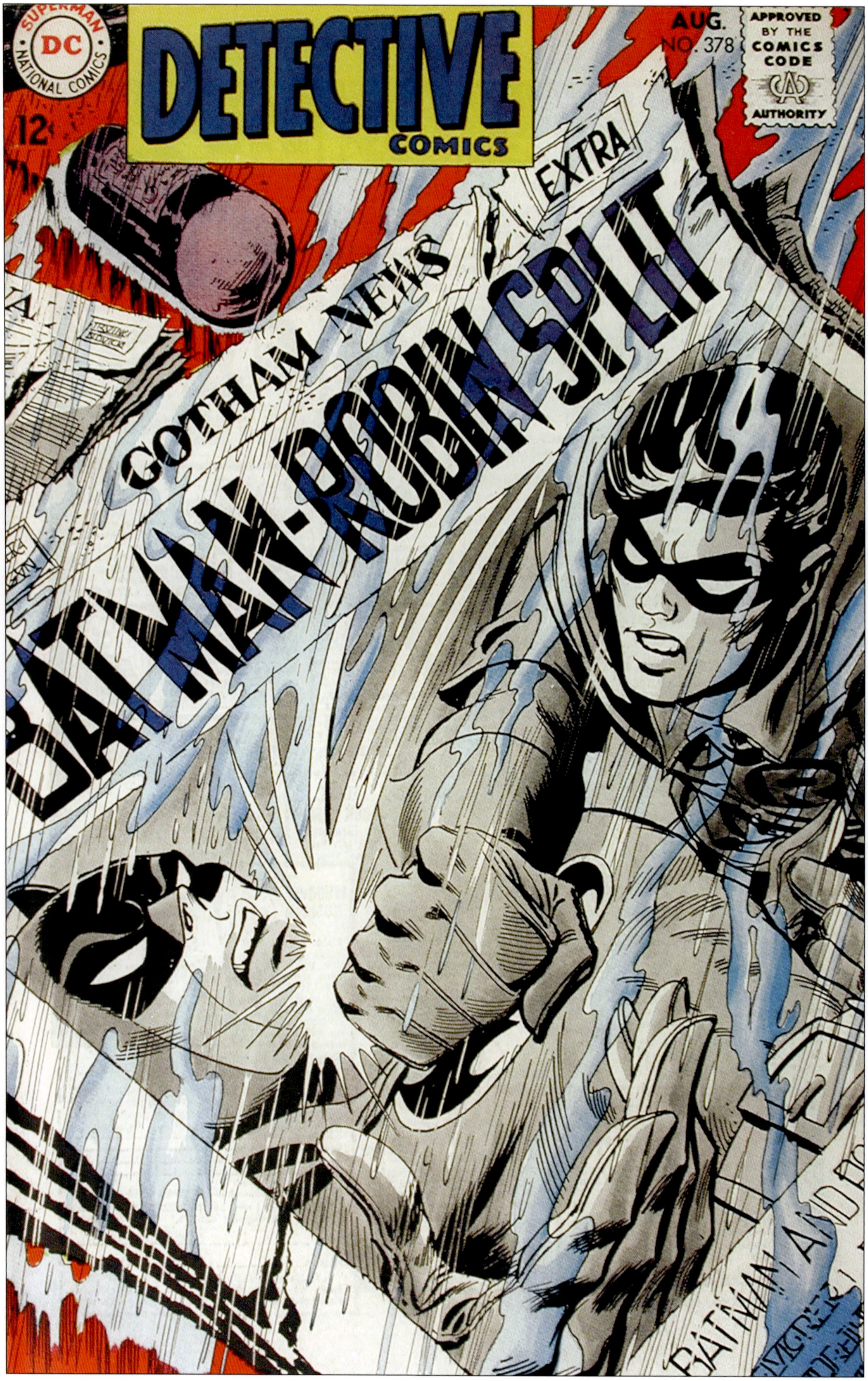

Detective Comics #378

1968

Art by Irv Novick

Batman #465

1991

Art by Norm Breyfogle

Batman #437

1989

Art by George Pérez

Batman #183

1966

Art by Carmine Infantino & Joe Giella

DC Comics Presents: Batman

2004

Art by Adam Hughes

Legendary comic book editor Julius Schwartz passed away in February, 2004. To celebrate his accomplishments, DC Comics published eight comics, each featuring two stories inspired by classic cover images. Modern day artists also offered their own interpretation.

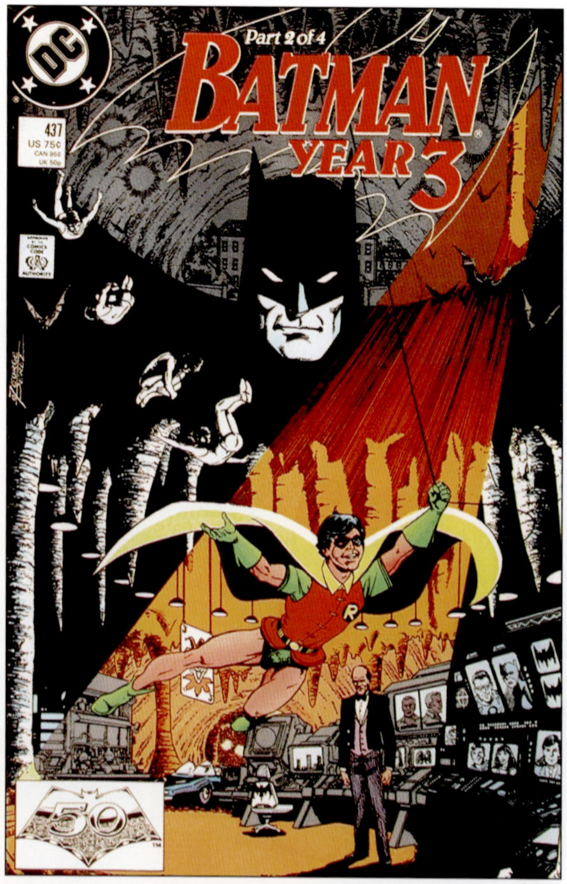

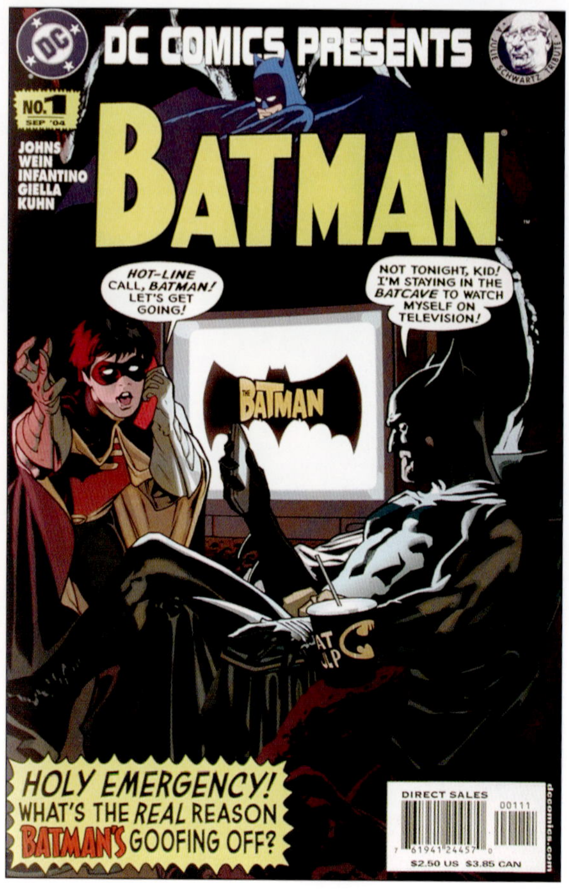

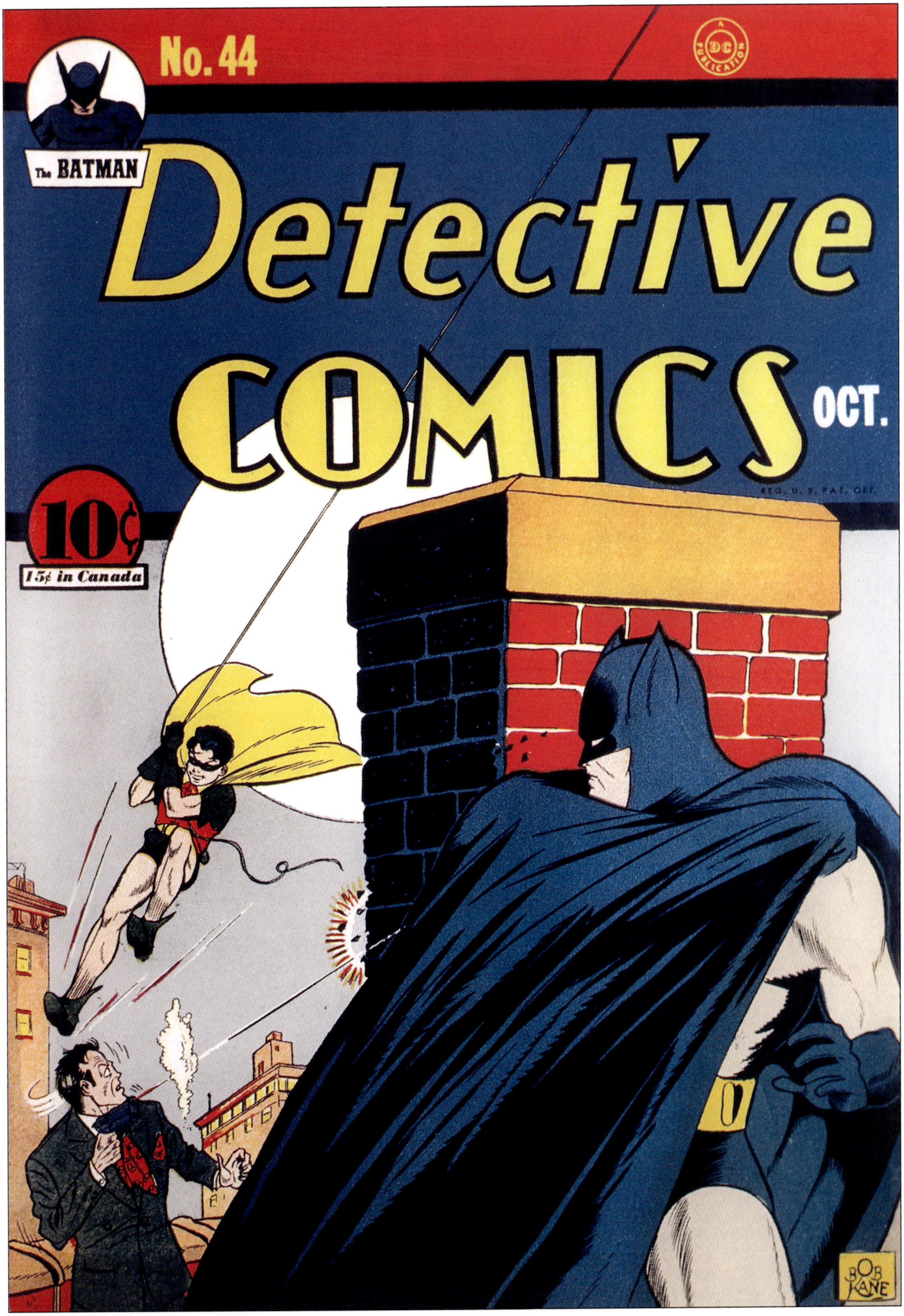

Detective Comics #44
1940
Art by
Bob Kane,
Jerry Robinson &
George Roussos

Batman: Legends of the Dark Knight #100

1997

Art by Alex Ross

Robin #1

1991

Art by Brian Bolland

Not until the third Robin, Tim Drake, did the character receive his own title. He starred in three miniseries before graduating to his own monthly.

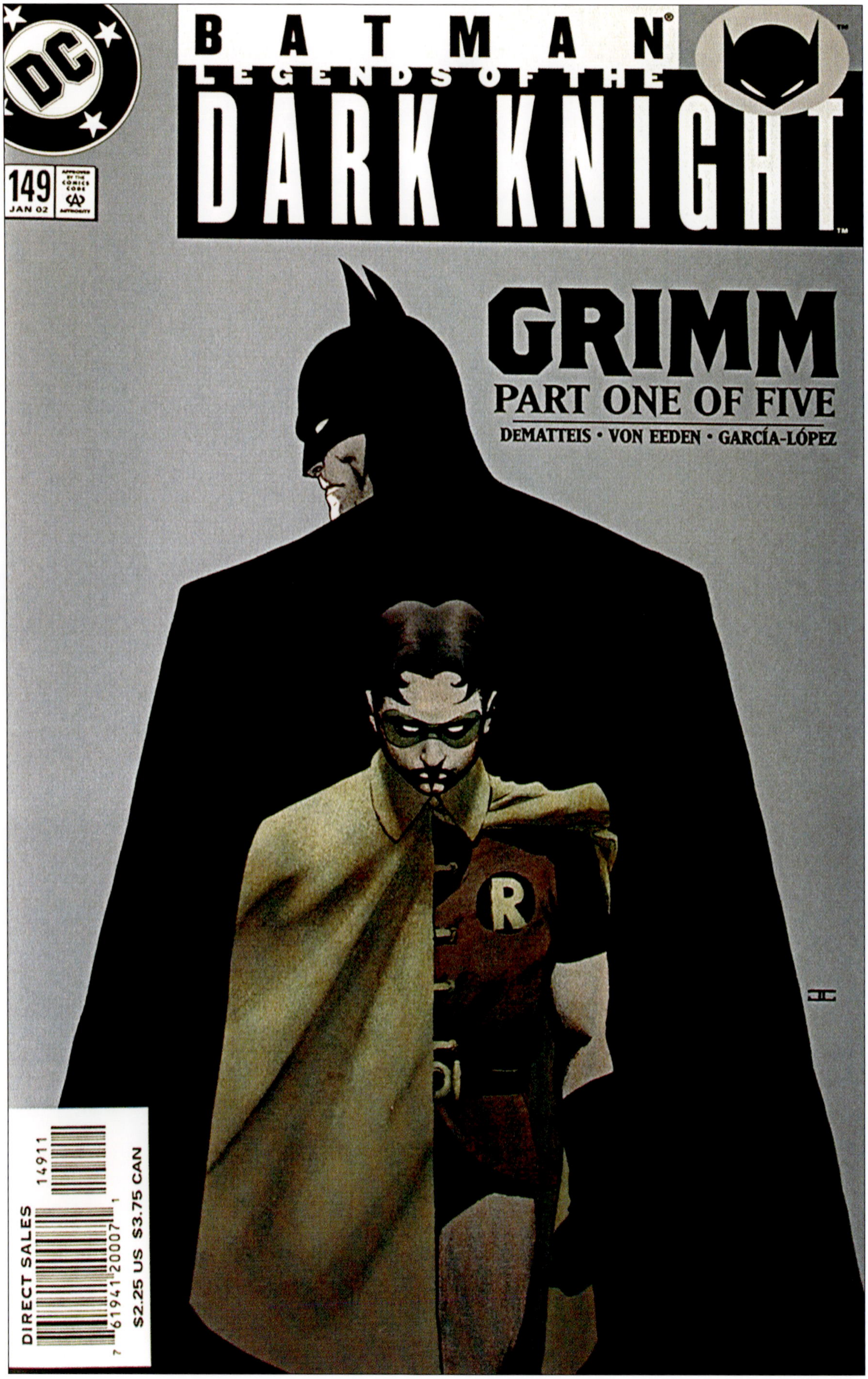

Batman: Legends of the Dark Knight #149

2002

Art by John Cassaday

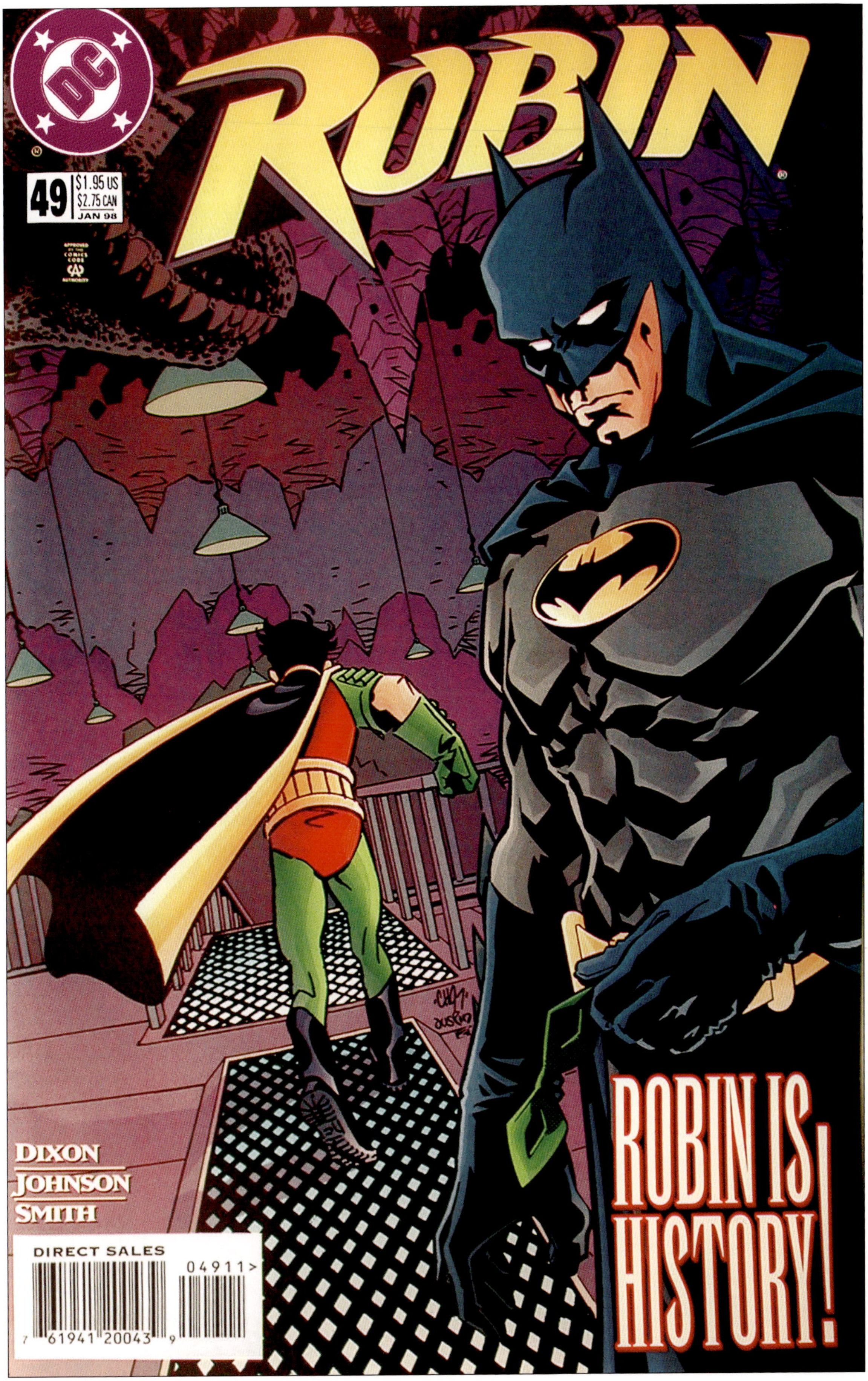

Robin #49

1998

Art by Cully Hamner & Terry Austin

Robin #127

2004

Art by Damion Scott

Stephanie Brown was a popular supporting character using the costumed identity of Spoiler. For a brief time, she actually trained to be the fourth Robin but was fired by Batman for disobeying orders.

Batman & Robin Adventures #1

1995

Art by Ty Templeton

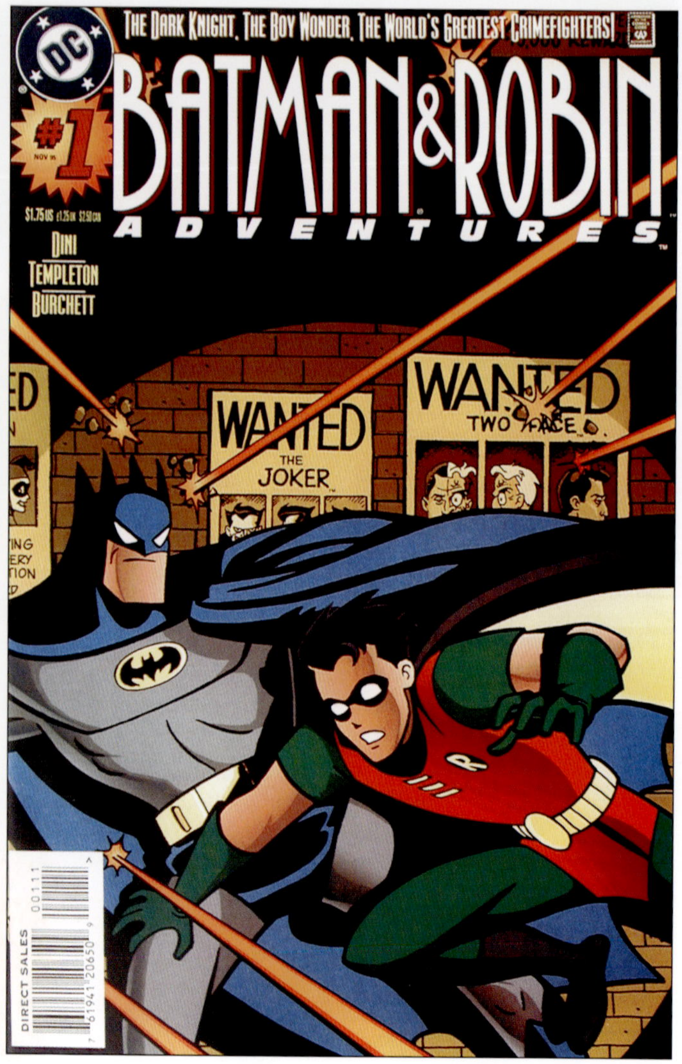

Batman Chronicles:

The Gauntlet

1997

Art by Lee Weeks

No. 38
The BATMAN
Detective COMICS
APRIL
10¢
THE Sensational CHARACTER-
FIND OF 1940....
Robin-
THE BOY WONDER
BOB KANE

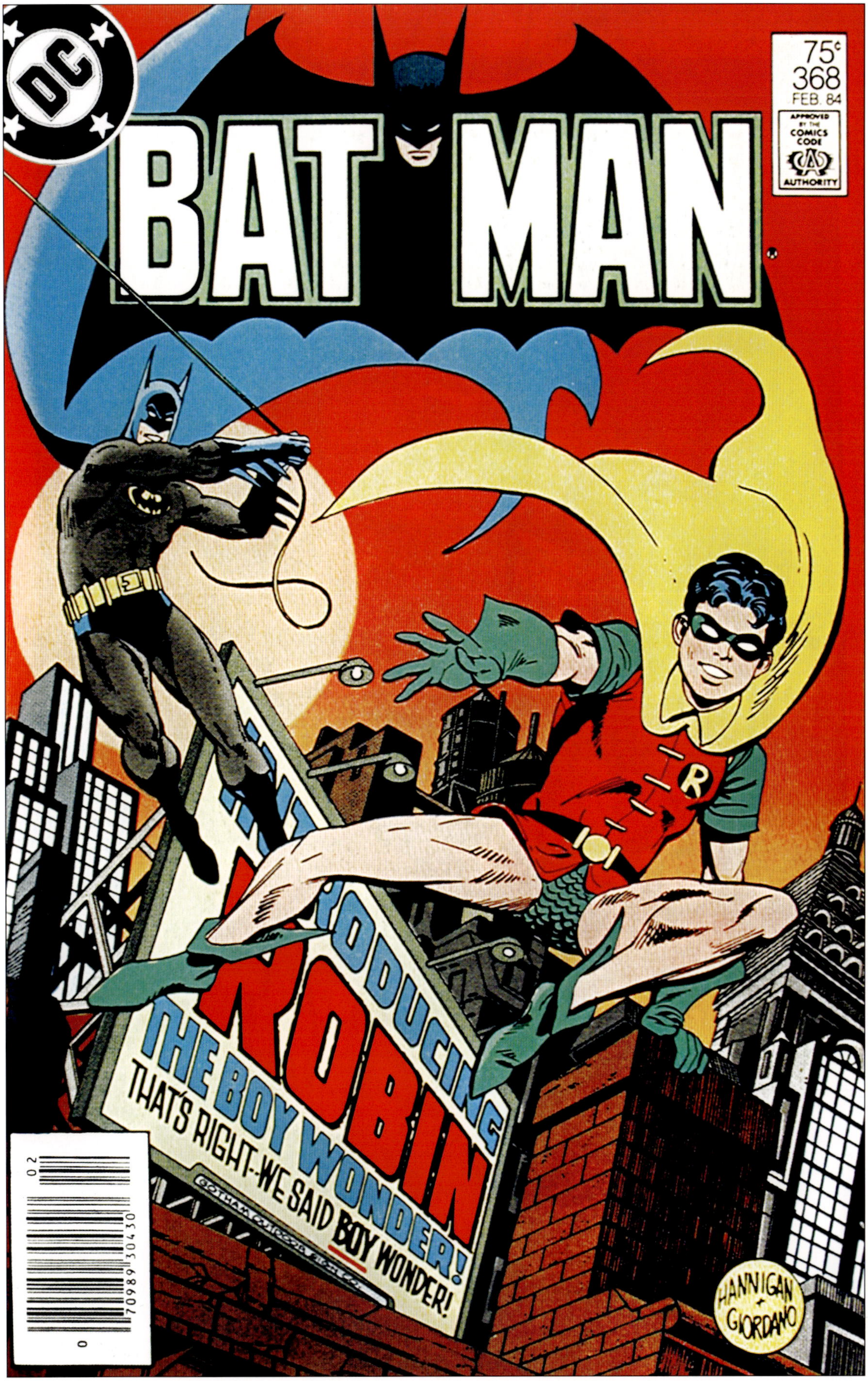

Page 96:

Detective Comics #38

1940

Art by Bob Kane & Jerry Robinson

Inspired by Robin Hood, Bob Kane introduced the first teen sidekick for a costumed crimefighter.

Batman #368

1984

Art by Ed Hannigan & Dick Giordano

After Dick Grayson gave up the Robin uniform to become Nightwing, Jason Todd became the second Boy Wonder. Fans rejected him, having Jason killed during a phone-in vote stunt.

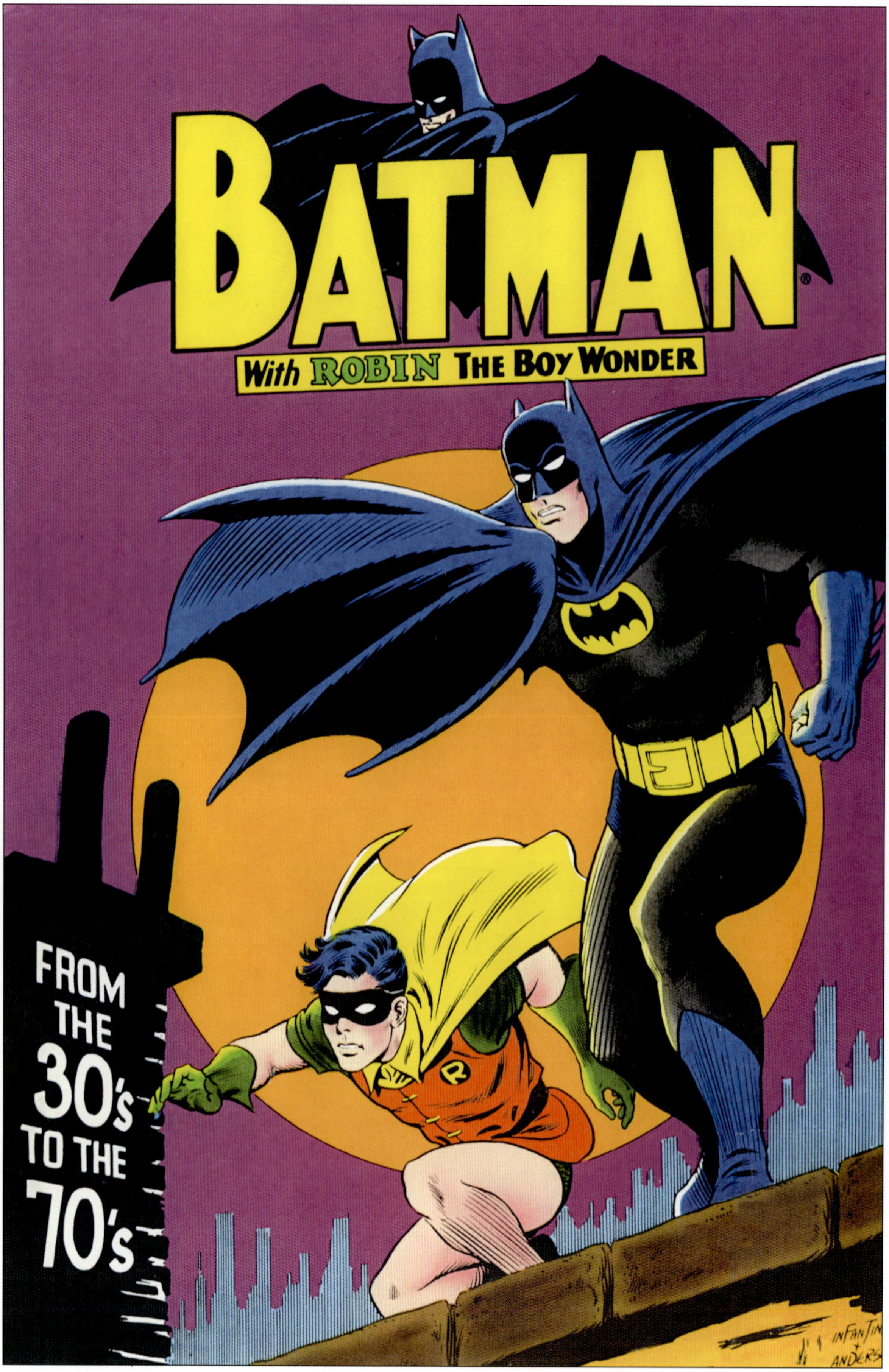

Batman from the 30's to the 70's
1971
Art by Carmine Infantino & Murphy Anderson

This piece originally was a pinup included in the comics and has become one of the definitive depictions of the duo, often imitated.

Batman #27

1945

Art by Jack Burnley

Star-Spangled Comics #88

1949

Art by Jim Mooney & Win Mortimer

Robin had his own solo feature for several years, although Batman did make the occasional guest appearance.

Batman: Turning Points #2

2001

Art by Ty Templeton

This cover is an homage to the giant props found in many stories from the late 1940s through the 1950s.

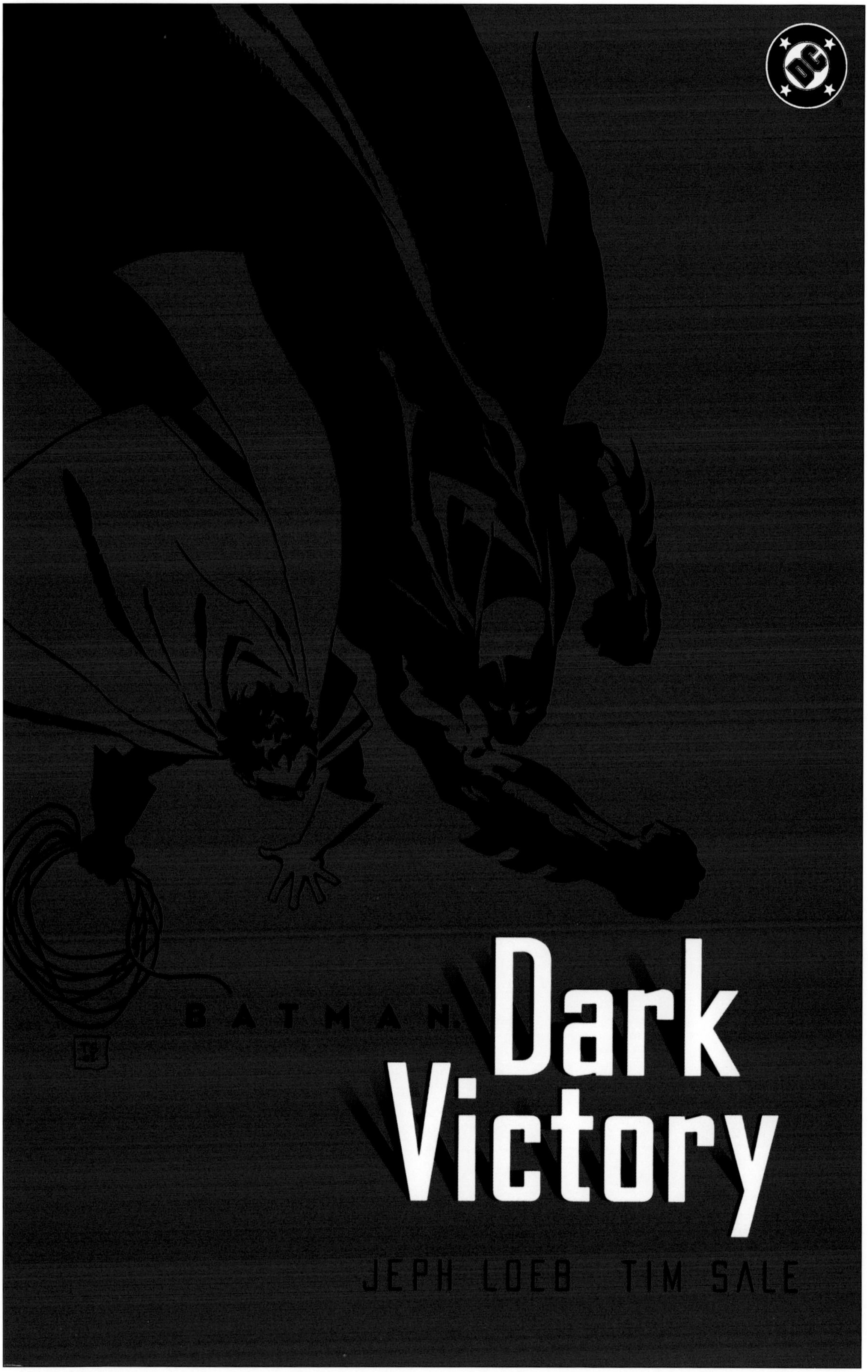

Batman: Dark Victory

2001

Art by Tim Sale

The cape and cowl, the bat-signal and city skyline...these elements and more have inspired artists to create uniquely designed covers over the years.

Batman #194

1968

Art by Carmine Infantino & Murphy Anderson

This is the first time the cover logo was absent in favor of integrating the title into the artwork.

Batman: Gotham Adventures #3

1998

Art by Ty Templeton

On the animated series, the Grey Ghost was seen as Bruce Wayne's inspiration. He was voiced by Adam West, television's first Caped Crusader.

Batman Adventures #6

2003

Art by Kelsey Shannon

Detective Comics #765

2002

Art by James Hodgkins & John McCrea

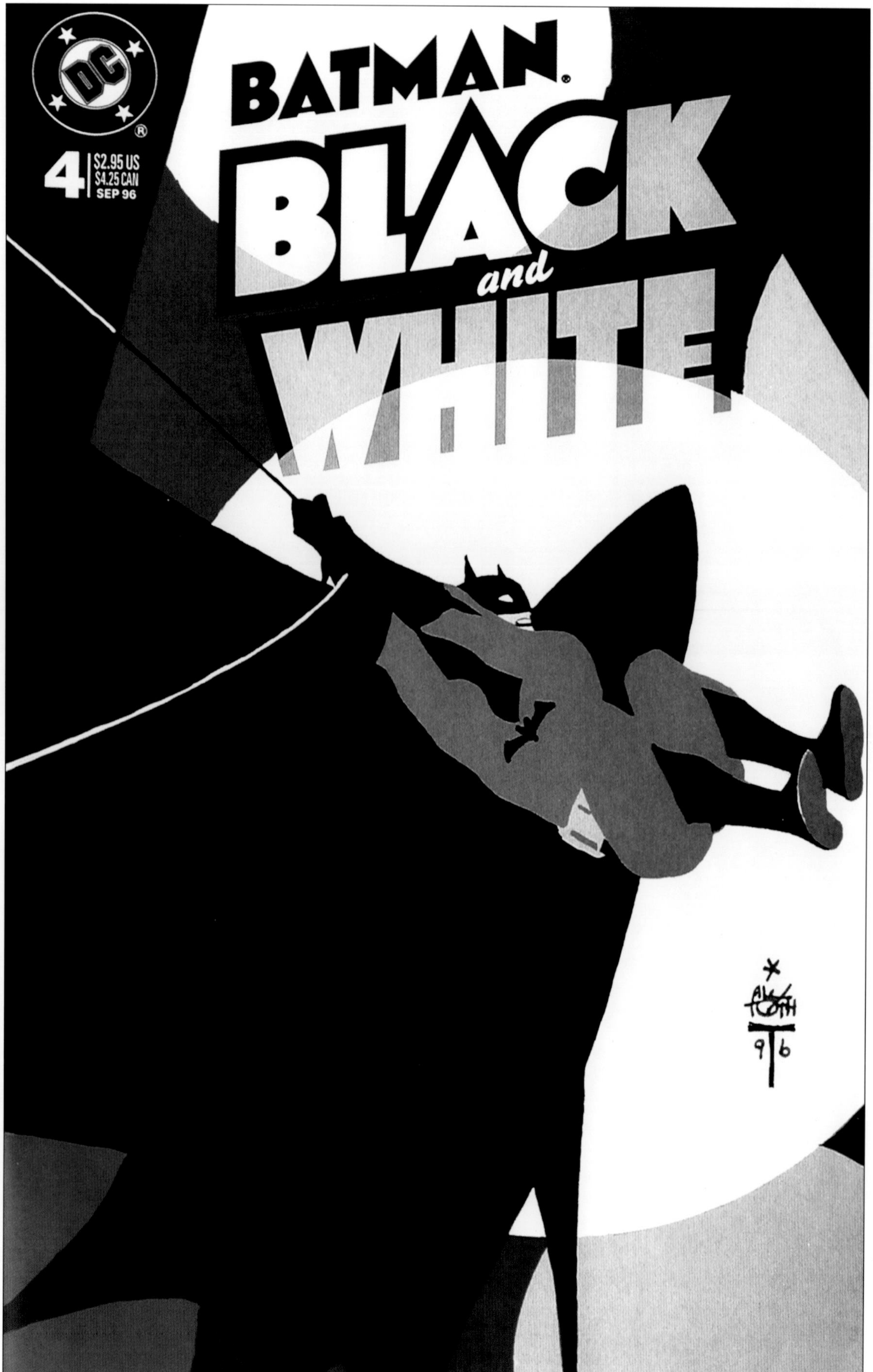
BATMAN
BLACK
and
WHITE
4
$2.95 US
$4.25 CAN
SEP 96
DC

I was recently riding on a bus from Heathrow Airport in London and I got to talking to a young lady sitting next to me. She was a Russian from Moscow studying English and Russian literature in Cambridge University. She wanted to know what I did for a living. "I'm a cartoonist," I said. She was attractive and very bright and I wanted to impress her. Later we exchanged emails. She'd visited my website and she told me that while she could appreciate the skill that probably goes into what I did, wasn't the subject matter all just macho violence and ultimately quite harmful to children? As yet I haven't thought up a reply that might convince her, or me, that she's wrong. When I'm not in the company of people who are into comics, which is most of the time, I'm not absolutely certain that the medium I work in isn't just a lot of worthless vulgar tat.

So here I am looking at a bit of comic art that I've chosen and I'm trying to think what, exactly, it is that gave my heart a jolt when I first saw it, and what it is about any bit of comic art that makes me believe that this stuff is more than just worthless tat. I chose a Batman cover by an artist who, as far as I can remember, only did the one.

From an early age I always thought there was something special about Alex Toth. His work popped up sporadically, so my liking for it didn't come as a result of a liking for any particular character. There was something in the drawing. The sardonic face of *Eclipso*. The interestingly different but very well observed poses of the Flash and the Atom as they faced the "Challenge of the Expanding World." "The Case of the Curious Classic" in *Hot Wheels*. The ingenious use of black and white and the daring compositions in his work for Warren magazines. The brilliant *Bravo for Adventure*. His career, like that of many of the great artists, has been a taster for what might have been. Just when we might have thought Alex's contribution was over, along comes his cover for *Batman Black & White* #4. It's minimal even by the standards of an artist who people consider to be the ultimate minimalist. People have summed up Alex Toth's work by calling it "simple," but to me the fact that he has pared his work down to the bone means he doesn't have the luxury of disguising weak and poorly thought out work behind the veneer of flashy but seductive inky noodlings, the way many of the rest of us do it. If you don't know Alex's work, this cover may look like not very much at all. If you do, you'll see in it echoes of all the great work he's ever done.

When people hear what I do for a living they often assume I'm really interested in whether the Hulk could knock Superman through a wall or whether the new super-hero movie is better than the last one. Well, I'm not! I'm interested in lines drawn beautifully on paper. In the interplay of black and white and gray, in the expressive depiction of human anatomy and movement and character, in the pleasure I get from looking at the work of an artist who is infinitely superior to me, and Alex Toth's cover has me believing that he is an artist working at the very pinnacle of his field and that comics are a medium into which great talent is poured...and are, dare I say it, deserving of the word "Art."

As to whether comics are violent and harmful to children. Well, look at me. I've been reading comics all my life and I'm about the least violent person I know, so I think they're probably perfectly harmless...and I'll kill anyone who says otherwise!!

Brian Bolland *gained fame in America for the series* Camelot 3000 *and* Batman: The Killing Joke *in addition to his 350+ covers for the company.*

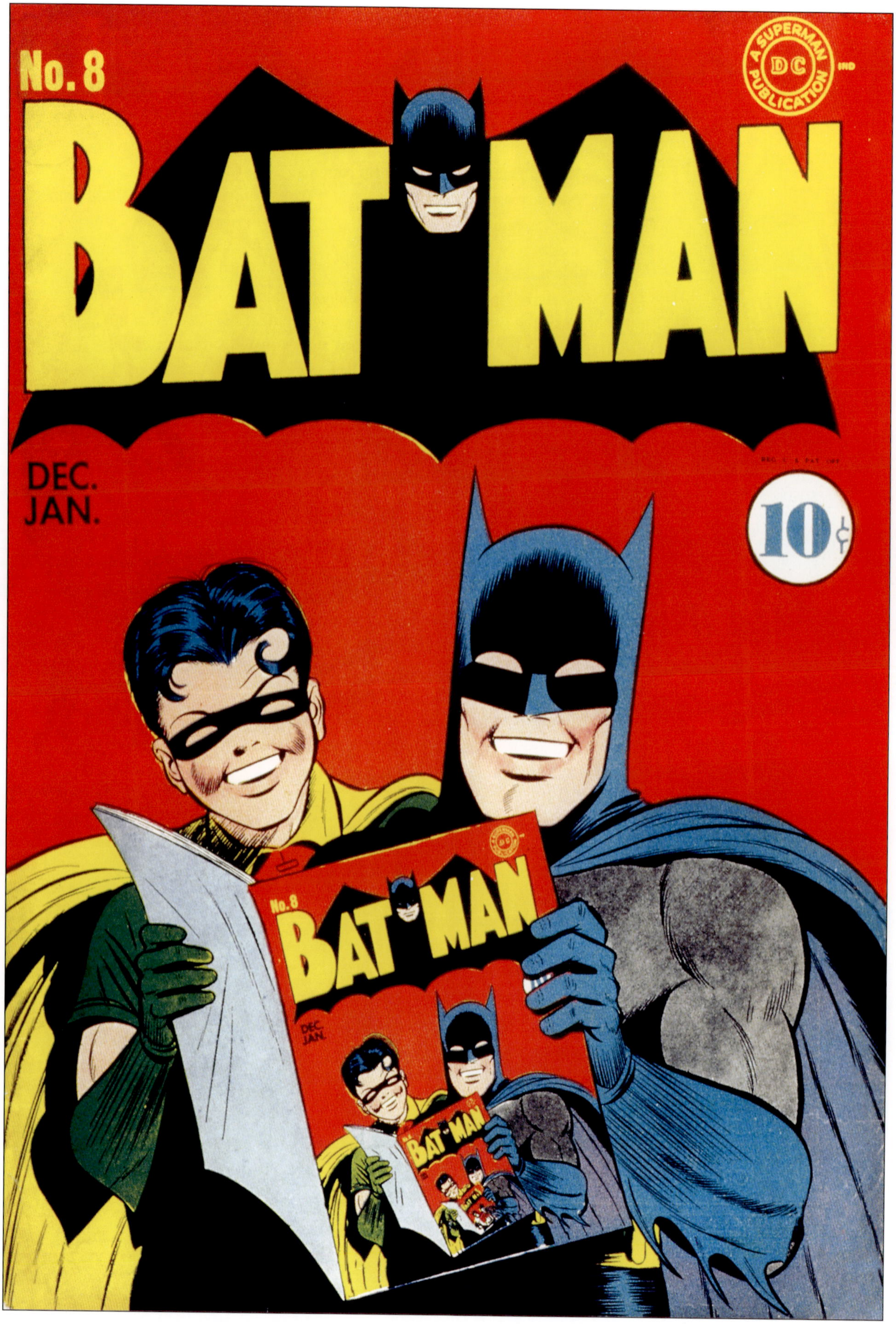

Batman #8

1942

Art by

Fred Ray &

Jerry Robinson

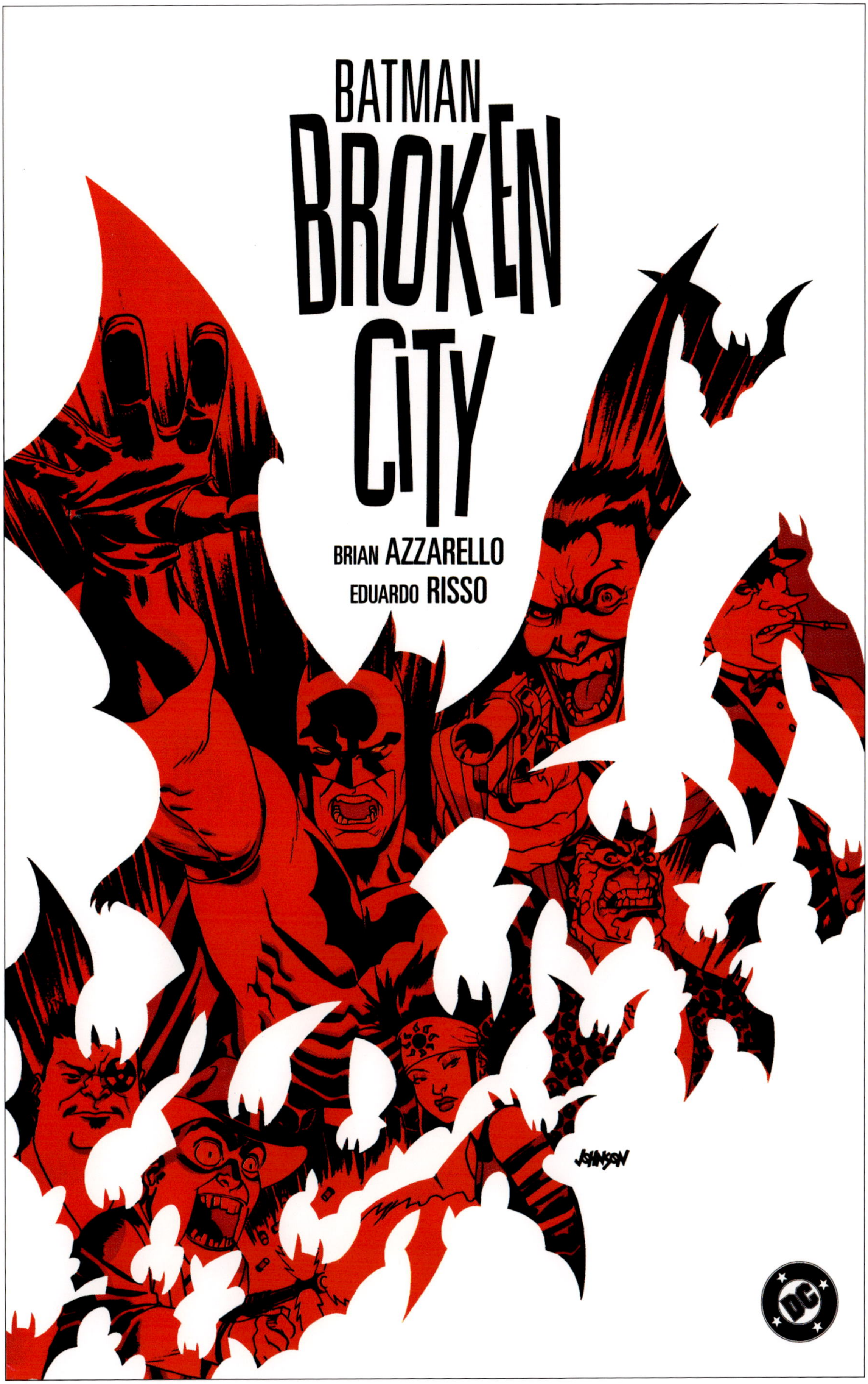

Batman: Broken City

2004

Art by Dave Johnson

Detective Comics #797

2004

Art by Jock

DARK KNIGHT RETURNS #2 1986, Art by Frank Miller

Dark.

Mysterious.

Brooding.

Batman has always been a creature of the night, and while all the great Batman artists have been able to capture these elements of the Dark Knight, few have evoked the intensity at his core: his resolute will to survive and indomitable need to overcome. And none have done it better than Frank Miller.

I was 21 when his epic — the *Dark Knight Returns* — debuted; and while I loved the first book, I often felt Miller's version of Batman didn't leap off the page until I saw this cover to book two. It was visceral, brutish, electric...alive. You could see Batman's breath coming off his torn, ripped cheeks; hear the sound of his wheezing, punctured lungs; the crack of his broken, dislocated bones; the squishing sounds of blood pooled within his boots — all so painfully human.

Yet with this cover, Miller's Batman had metamorphosed into something more than human. An irresistible force of nature, he was chunky, squared off, barely contained by the physical edges of the paper itself. Gone were the brushy shadows; replaced by tiny rivulets of ink, they formed scratchy tributaries of intricate line work. And for the first time, the color added a whole new dimension to the art. Lynn Varley's colors and hues lay not within the borders of the lines, but on top of them, often boldly independent of them, as her painted work staked new ground, asserting its rightful place and role within the new, emerging art form of graphic novels. An incredible collaboration — this image was a complete departure from all previous interpretations of the Dark Knight and managed to say more to me about who Batman was than a million shots of him standing on a gargoyle above Gotham City could not: Batman was a bad mofo not to be messed with, human or not.

***Jim Lee** is the founder of WildStorm Studios and co-creator of numerous features notably* WildCATS, Gen 13, Divine Right *and* The Intimates. *As an artist, he has drawn virtually every major hero at DC and Marvel with recent year-long runs on both* Batman *and* Superman.

Batman #208

1969

Art by Nick Cardy

Batman: Master of the Future

1991

Art by Eduardo Barreto

Gotham Central #11

2003

Art by Michael Lark

Batman: Gotham Knights #19

2001

Art by Brian Bolland

Batman #621

2004

Art by Dave Johnson

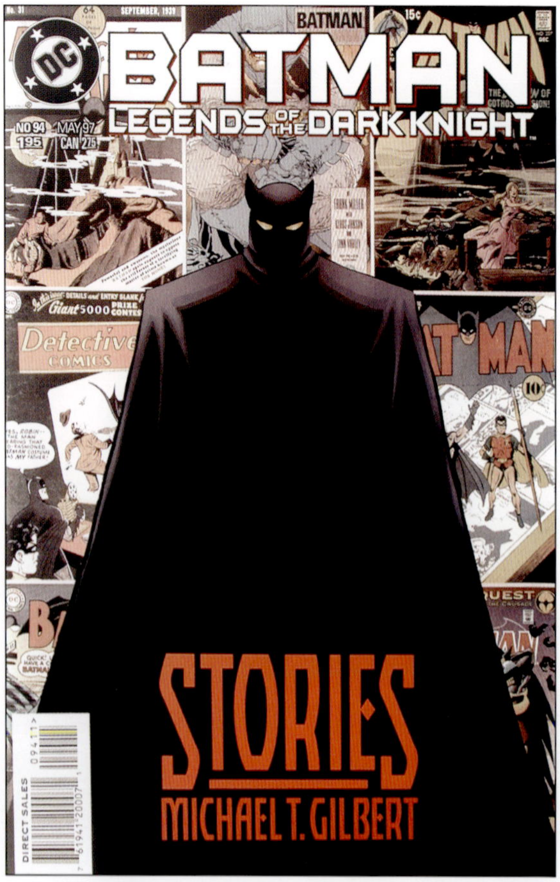

Batman: Legends of the Dark Knight #94

1997

Art by Michael T. Gilbert

Batman: Legends of the Dark Knight #150

2002

Art by John Cassaday

Batman #199

1968

Art by Carmine Infantino & Murphy Anderson

Jim Aparo is a man whose very name is synonymous with Batman. He first drew the character in *The Brave and the Bold* #97, beginning a lengthy run on that title. However, his first Batman cover was *Detective Comics* #430 in 1972.

"Most of the covers I did on Batman in the 1970's were designed by then Editorial Director Carmine Infantino," Aparo recalls. He had no problem with Infantino's cover designs. As for a preference between drawing covers or interiors, Aparo notes, "As long as I was presented with an artistic challenge, that was all I needed." He added, "The challenge was always to make Batman the icon he is: intense, dark and grim while still telling a story that fans would want to see and read.

"*Brave and Bold* #184 is a cover that particularly sticks out in my mind as an iconic image of Batman. This image of Batman standing in a graveyard in front of a tombstone unmasking himself said the whole story in one picture."

The Brave and the Bold, among his many assignments, was a favorite because "it allowed me to play with the rest of the DCU and still in my own universe."

Aparo said, "Two other covers stick right out in my mind…one was the cover to *Brave and Bold* #124 where I drew myself on the cover with Sgt. Rock. It was for a joke and it worked." The other cover that sticks out to Aparo was issue #134, "the story where Green Lantern was thought to be brainwashed and had defected to the other side. Obviously he didn't, but it was a story that was a lot of fun to draw."

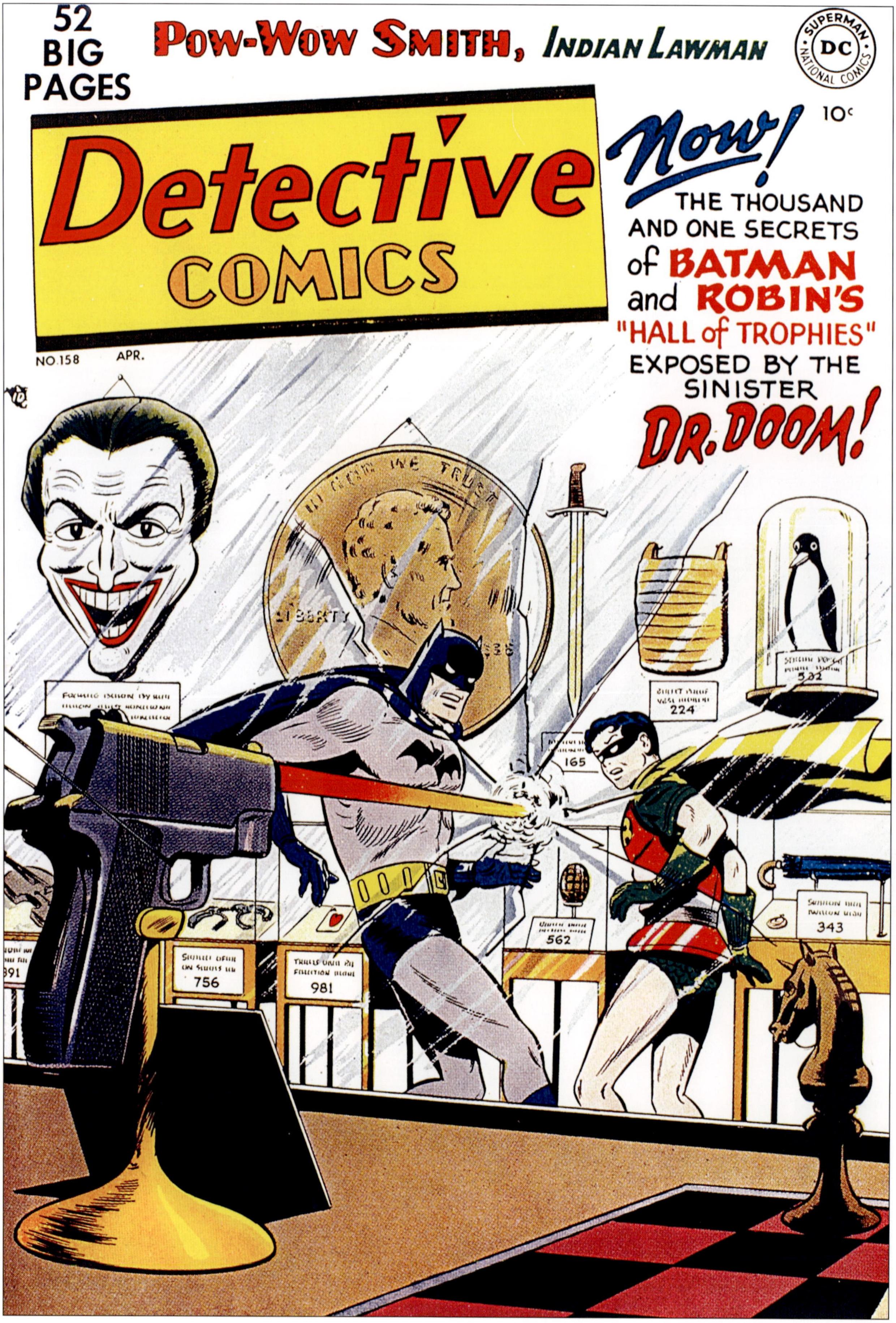
52 BIG PAGES
POW-WOW SMITH, INDIAN LAWMAN
SUPERMAN DC NATIONAL COMICS
10¢
Detective COMICS
NO.158 APR.
Now! THE THOUSAND AND ONE SECRETS of BATMAN and ROBIN'S "HALL of TROPHIES" EXPOSED BY THE SINISTER DR. DOOM!
IN GOD WE TRUST
LIBERTY
224
165
532
562
343
756
981
391

Page 118:

Detective Comics #158

1950

Art by Win Mortimer

Detective Comics #716

1997

Art by Brian Stelfreeze

Batman #575

2000

Art by Scott McDaniel

Batman:

Gotham Adventures #45

2002

Art by Darwyn Cooke

BATMAN: DARK VICTORY #1 1999, Art by Tim Sale

There are so many that are favorites... hard to pick just one. However, from the first time I saw the cover to DARK VICTORY #1 I knew that Tim [Sale] had done something extraordinary. Much of that came from Mark Chiarello's suggestion that he color it red. To our knowledge, there hadn't been a red Batman, certainly not the only figure on the cover. What makes it so striking is that the red seems right even though there is no red in Batman's costume. The way the image POPPED from the black set the tone of the series — that there was a darkness surrounding the figure. This would lead off the rest of the series' covers, with all the figures coming out of the black.

***Jeph Loeb** has been working on the WB's* Smallville *series as both writer and Supervising Producer. His Batman projects with artists Tim Sale and Jim Lee have been best-selling events.*

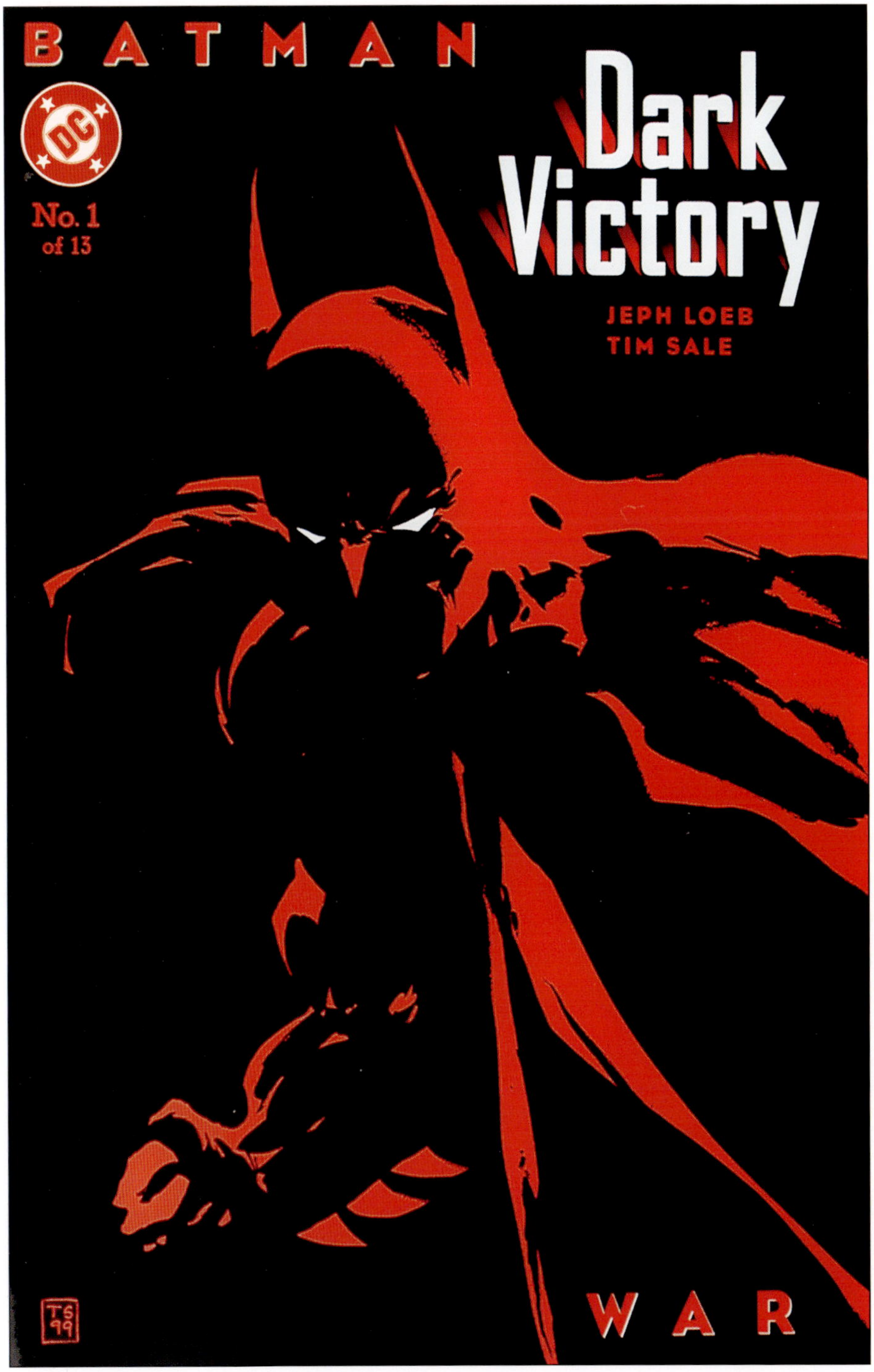

BATMAN
No.31
A 52-PAGE MAGAZINE
A SUPERMAN DC PUBLICATION
IND
BATMAN
OCT...NOV
TEN CENTS

Detective Comics #476

1978

Art by Marshall Rogers & Terry Austin

Batman #196

1968

Art by Carmine Infantino & Murphy Anderson

Detective Comics #353

1966

Art by Carmine Infantino & Joe Giella

Page 122:

Batman #31

1945

Art by Dick Sprang

Batman:

Gotham Knights #24

2002

Art by Brian Bolland

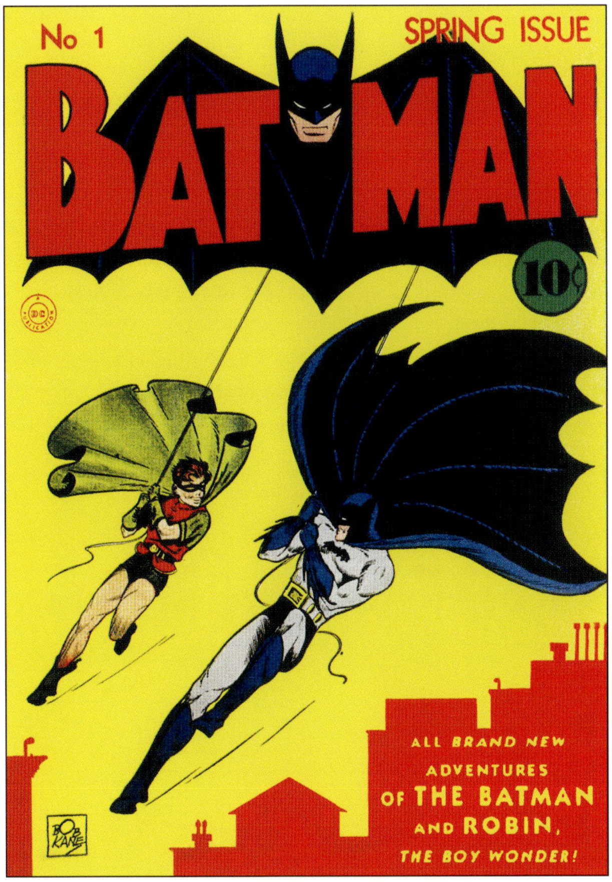

BATMAN #1 1940, Art by Bob Kane & Jerry Robinson ■ **BATMAN #184** 1966, Art by Carmine Infantino & Murphy Anderson

The amazing covers are tantalizing when they come at you all at once. It's a little like looking into a spinning kaleidoscope of the finest pop culture art of the last several decades. The Batman comic book cover artists have given us years of memorable pop art. When I was a young boy I couldn't wait to see what the next cover looked like. It would be a window into wondrous adventures with my favorite super-hero. I could open these pages and become Batman, the Caped Crusader, leaping from the darkness into danger.

I was the unexpected avenger making the world a safer place. It gave my friends and me athletic hours of high adventure emulating Batman and Robin. Little did I know that some twenty years later I would again be playing Batman, that I would become the Caped Crusader himself in *Batman the Movie* and in our classic television series. Is this not a wonderful world? As an actor, Batman really became my signature role, and I am grateful for it. There are few actors who get a chance to create a classic character. I salute DC for the opportunities and the inspiration they have given me with their magnificent creation. It has been an ongoing pleasure and a challenge to have given Batman flesh and blood and my own unique interpretation. Thank you, DC.

Of all the engaging Batman cover art, I have an affection for #1, the first cover. It is simple, it communicates the relationship and derring-do of the lead characters, and it was my first look. And I especially like #184 because the cover is so like our television show. And, of course, he said modestly, because Batman looks like me.

Adam West *is recognized around the world as the first television Batman. He has also voiced the character for various animated incarnations.*

Dramatic and angular, silhouetted against a Gotham moon, Batman has always been a graphic designer's dream: the kind of iconic character that lends himself to an equally iconic graphic representation. Like the bat-signal or the chest emblem, the Batman logo itself has become an integral and recognizable part of the Bat-mythos.

Batman is unusual in that he is one of the few characters in comics to actually feature in his own masthead; his grim demeanor glowered out from the cover of the first issue, announcing his presence in his own title in no uncertain terms.

Unlike the Superman logo, which, though tweaked and polished, has remained relatively unchanged and stayed true to its original conception, the Batman logo has evolved as the Batman himself has evolved through 65 years and over 600 issues.

1

1A

2

3

4

5

1
The original logo remained relatively unchanged for over one hundred and fifty issues.

1A
The "ears" became shorter, the jaw more angular, but the idiosyncratic thick-thin stroke stresses on the "A"s, the reverse of the typographic norm, remained unchanged.

2
Even in the comic's camp era that preceded the Adam West TV show, first aired on January 12, 1966 on ABC, Batman retains an air of menace and mystery, here clenching his cape to cover his face.

3
The original typographic quirk had been ironed out when the traditional logo returned with issue 215, for which the designer has obviously referenced and updated the original version.

4
Only around issue 220 does he lose his composure for a moment — this Batman looks more perplexed than vengeful. The type has been shaped to fit inside the bat shape for the first time, possibly inspired by the TV show's version of the logo. This encapsulation presents an interesting design problem in the curving of the right upright of the "N" and the left upright of the "B."

5
Later, Robin briefly graduates to team billing on the early '70s run. "With" and "The Teen Wonder" provide the anonymous designer with a difficult problem in balance and symmetry, which is not entirely elegantly resolved.

6

With a bat shape resembling the original in many respects, albeit with sharper points to the cape and curls on the top of the wings, the '70s logo first introduced on issue 241 and lasting until issue 403 was initially outlined square block capitals. Like the original logo, these burst out of the confines of the silhouette and would feature in the logo in a chunkier and squatter fashion for several years and iterations to come.

7

By the time we arrive in 1987 and Frank Miller's "Year One" storyline, Batman's face has been appropriately blacked out — in fact the logo would remain this way until features were reintroduced in 2003.

8

The later '80s versions of the logo moved towards a simpler, elegant, serifed and less illustrative graphic approach, and for a while the bat shape disappeared from the background entirely. However, it was soon back.

9

With the release of the Batman movies beginning in 1989 and through the 1990s, the lettering was again redesigned, this time to tie in to the publicity and marketing surrounding the films.

10

For the new century, Chip Kidd, designer of *Batman Collected*, simplified the design to a spaced heavy gothic sans serif.

11

The current logo takes it full circle back to the illustrative roots of the original — this version is probably the most complex interpretation yet, well-suited to Jim Lee's intricate art style. Batman, face in darkest shadow, again glowers from behind the type as he did on that first issue in 1940.

__Rian Hughes__ is an award-winning creator of logos, type fonts and designs. His work can be found in animation, on Hawaiian shirts and bicycle helmets and CD cases. He has crafted the look for numerous DC Comics publications and won the Campaign Press Awards Silver and the New York Art Director's Club Merit Award.

6

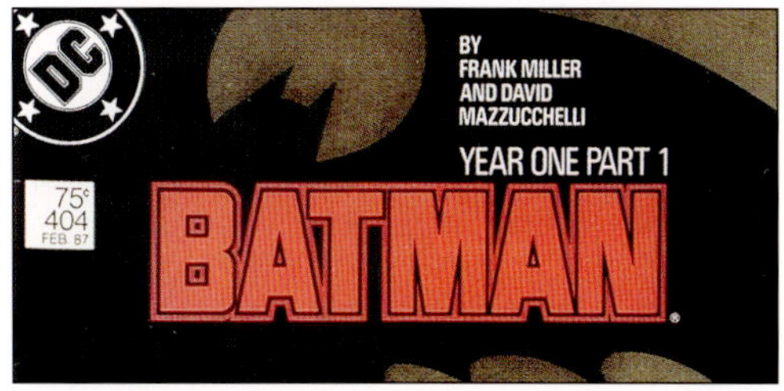

7

8

9

10

11

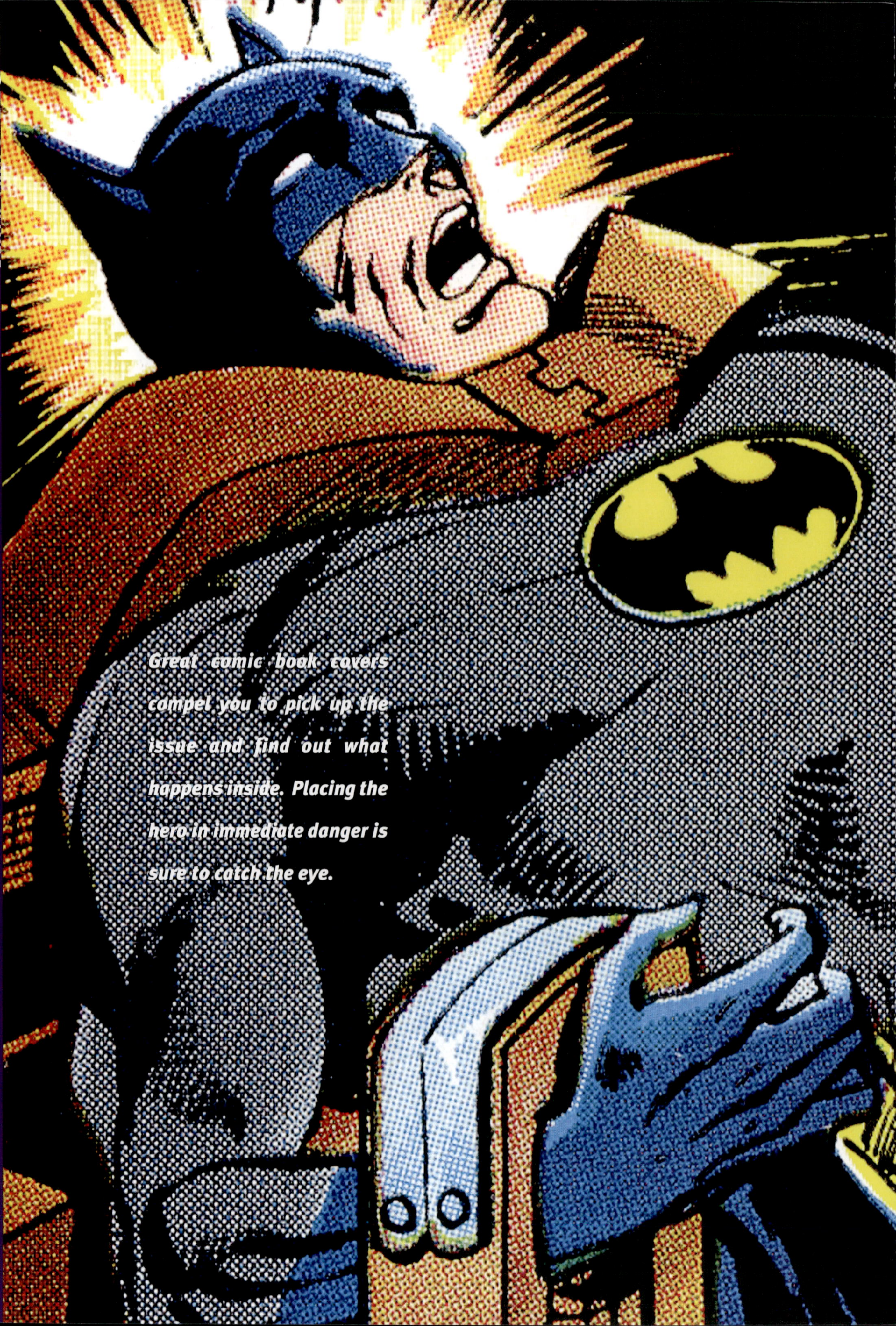

Great comic book covers compel you to pick up the issue and find out what happens inside. Placing the hero in immediate danger is sure to catch the eye.

Detective Comics #93
1944
Art by
Dick Sprang

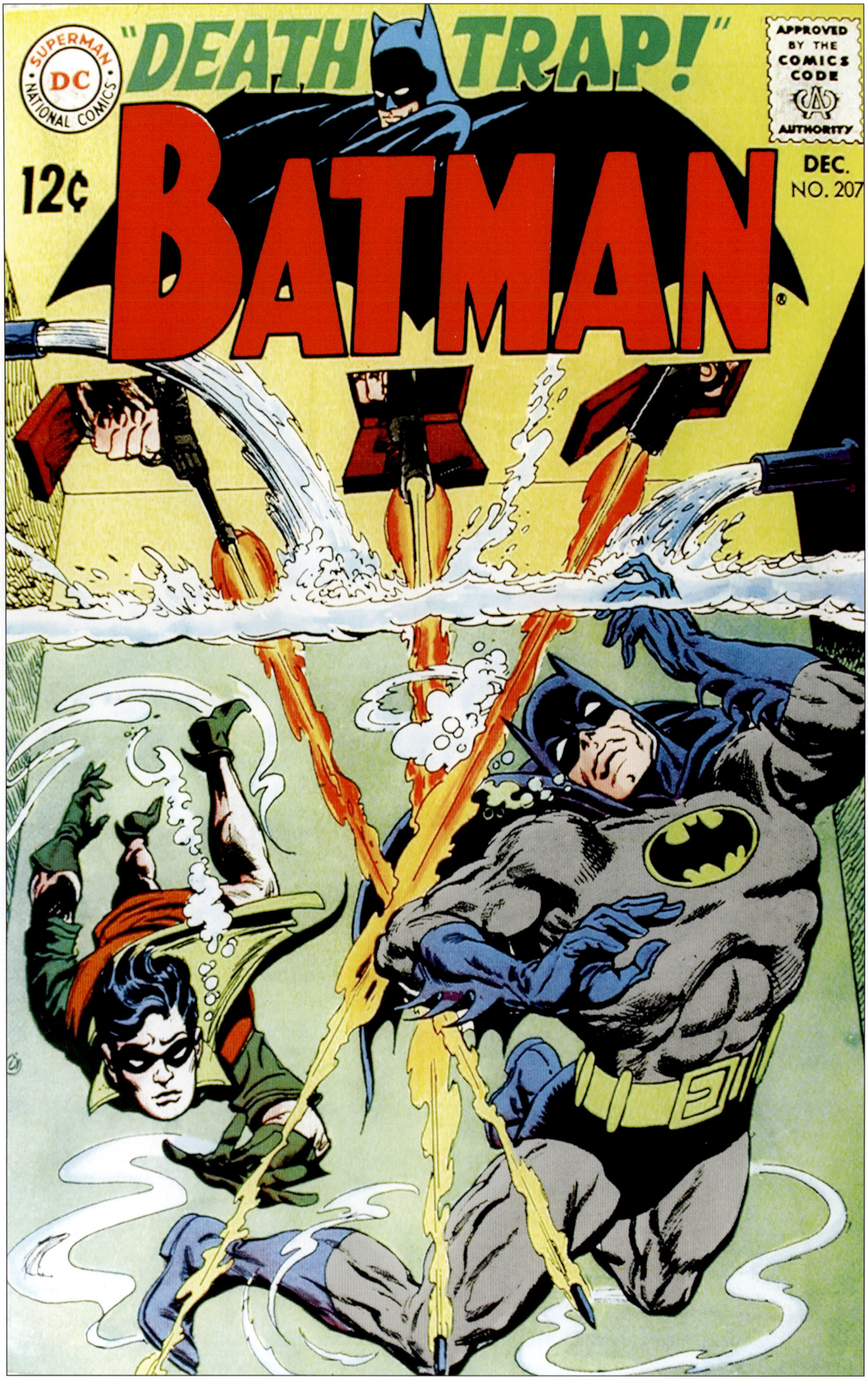

Batman #207

1968

Art by Irv Novick

Page 131:

Detective Comics #324

1964

Art by Sheldon Moldoff

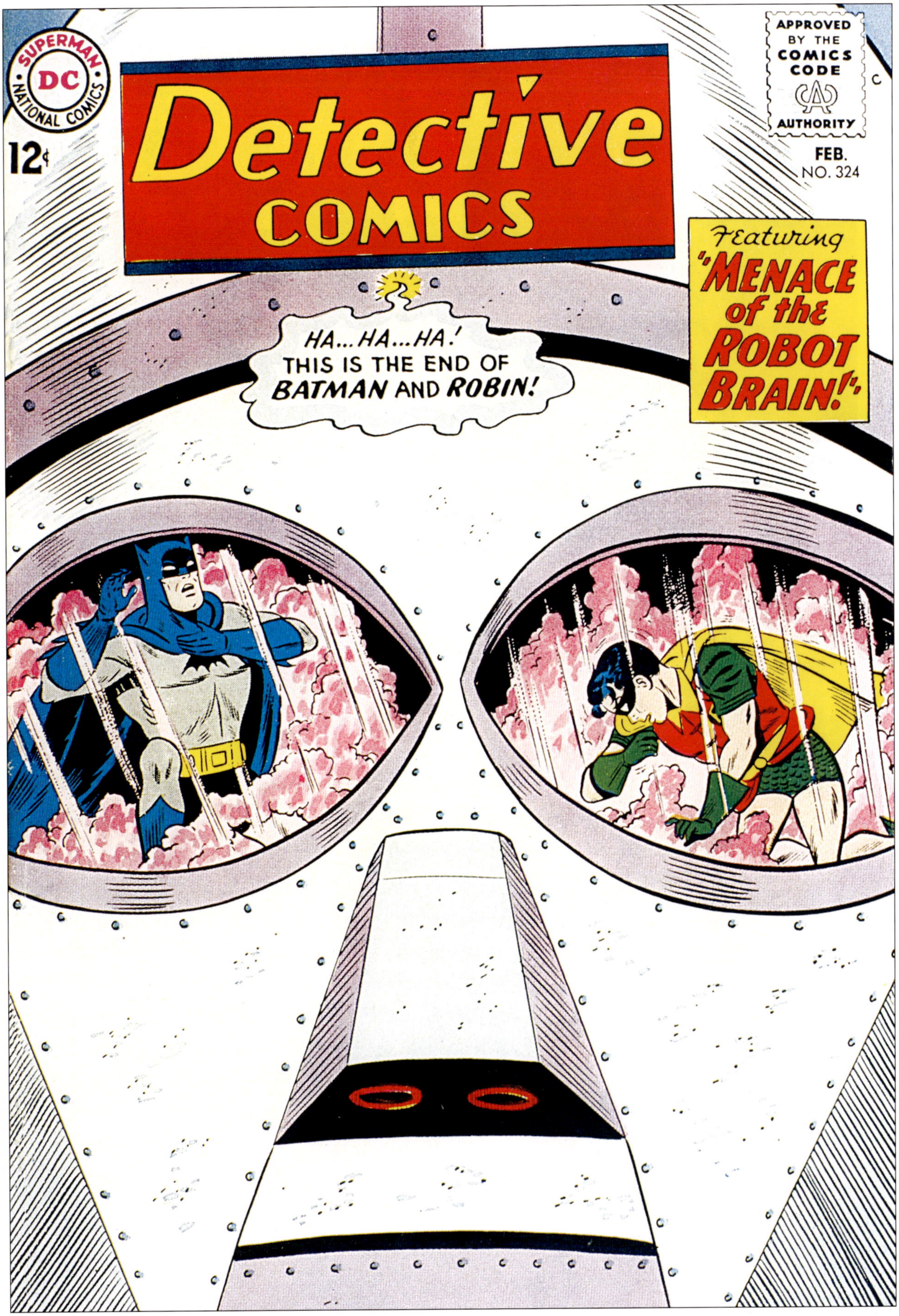
SUPERMAN DC NATIONAL COMICS
12¢
Detective COMICS
APPROVED BY THE COMICS CODE AUTHORITY
FEB. NO. 324
Featuring "MENACE of the ROBOT BRAIN!"
HA...HA...HA! THIS IS THE END OF BATMAN AND ROBIN!

Batman: Shadow of the Bat #50

1996

Art by Carl Critchlow

BATMAN #166 1964, Art by Carmine Infantino & Joe Giella

There's a very simple reason why I absolutely love this cover. Why every time I see it, it reminds me of why I love comic books and how I fell in love with them. As my brother, Jeremy, and I went through my uncle's old collection of comic books up in my grandmother's attic, flipping past *The Brave and the Bold* and *Fantastic Four*, this one more than any of the others caught my twelve-year-old eyes. It made me want to read this story. The look of shock on Batman's face, and the deadly two-way trap confronting the caped crusader, it all screamed at me – "Read this!" I had to see Batman in action! I guess back then, the covers were more story oriented. You look at any of them and it tells you a basic story idea. Without anything like *Wizard* or *Previews*, you didn't know what was going on in the comic books until you saw them on the stand. This reminds me why I love comic books, and Batman. I want to see him escape and beat the bad guy. It doesn't get much simpler than that.

***Geoff Johns** shifted from a production career in Hollywood to comics, gaining acclaim for his work on* The Flash, JSA, Hawkman *and* Teen Titans.

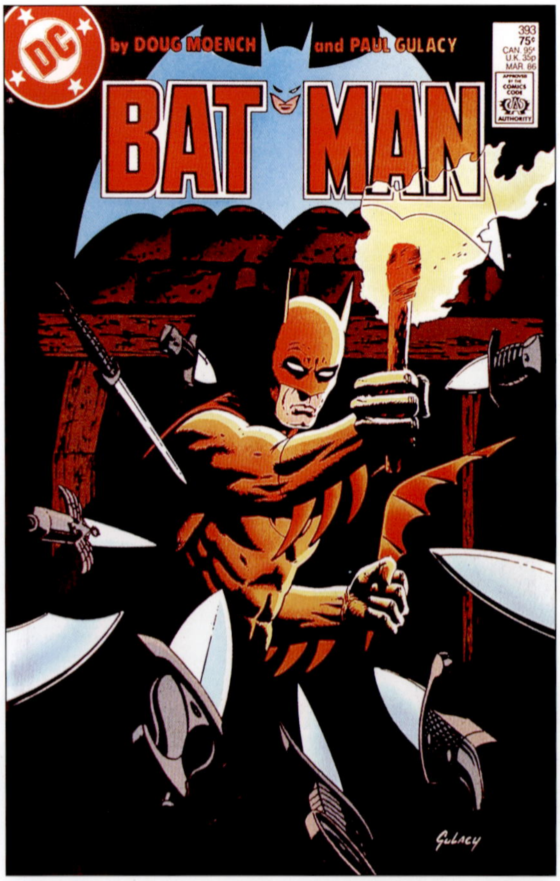

Batman #393

1986

Art by Paul Gulacy

Batman Beyond #17

2001

Art by Brian Stelfreeze

Batman & Robin Adventures #20

1997

Art by Ty Templeton

The Batman Chronicles #16

1999

Art by Jason Pearson

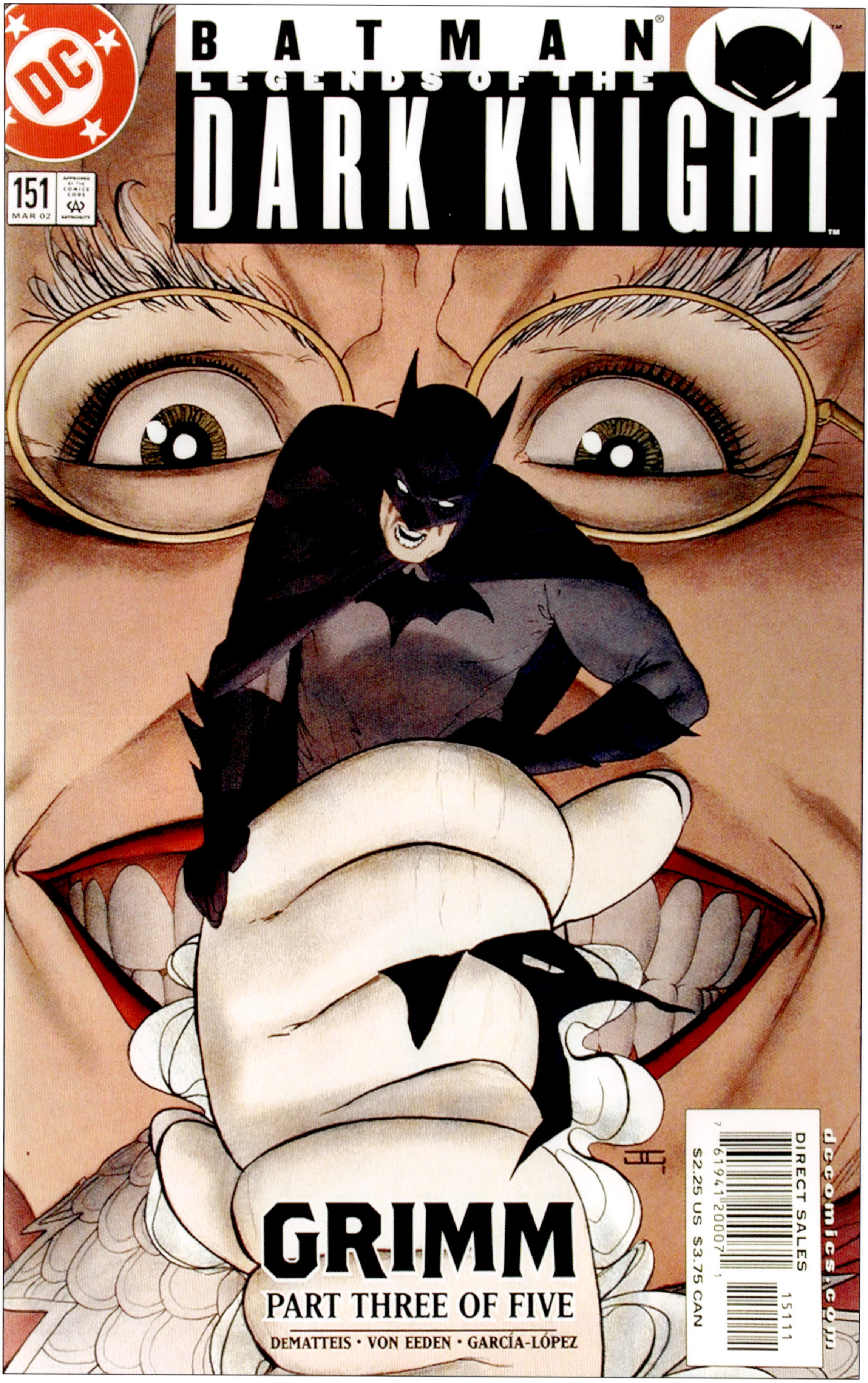

Batman: Legends of the Dark Knight #151

2002

Art by John Cassaday

DETECTIVE COMICS #395 1970, Art by Neal Adams

"Secret of the Waiting Graves" was not the first Batman story I wrote. But it was the one that really began a long, fruitful, and generally satisfying symbiosis between writer and character — the one that helped redefine a hero who had, at that point, existed for thirty years and gave me a costumed do-gooder with whom, in some twisted way, I could identify. Part of the redefinition happened in the graphics work of Neal Adams, both the cover art and the interior visual narrative; this was a Batman a person could almost believe existed — or at least *should* exist.

***Denny O'Neil** first wrote Batman in 1969, establishing himself as one of the character's most influential creators. He also edited the family of titles for over a decade, guiding Batman through a harrowing series of adventures that redefined the Dark Knight Detective.*

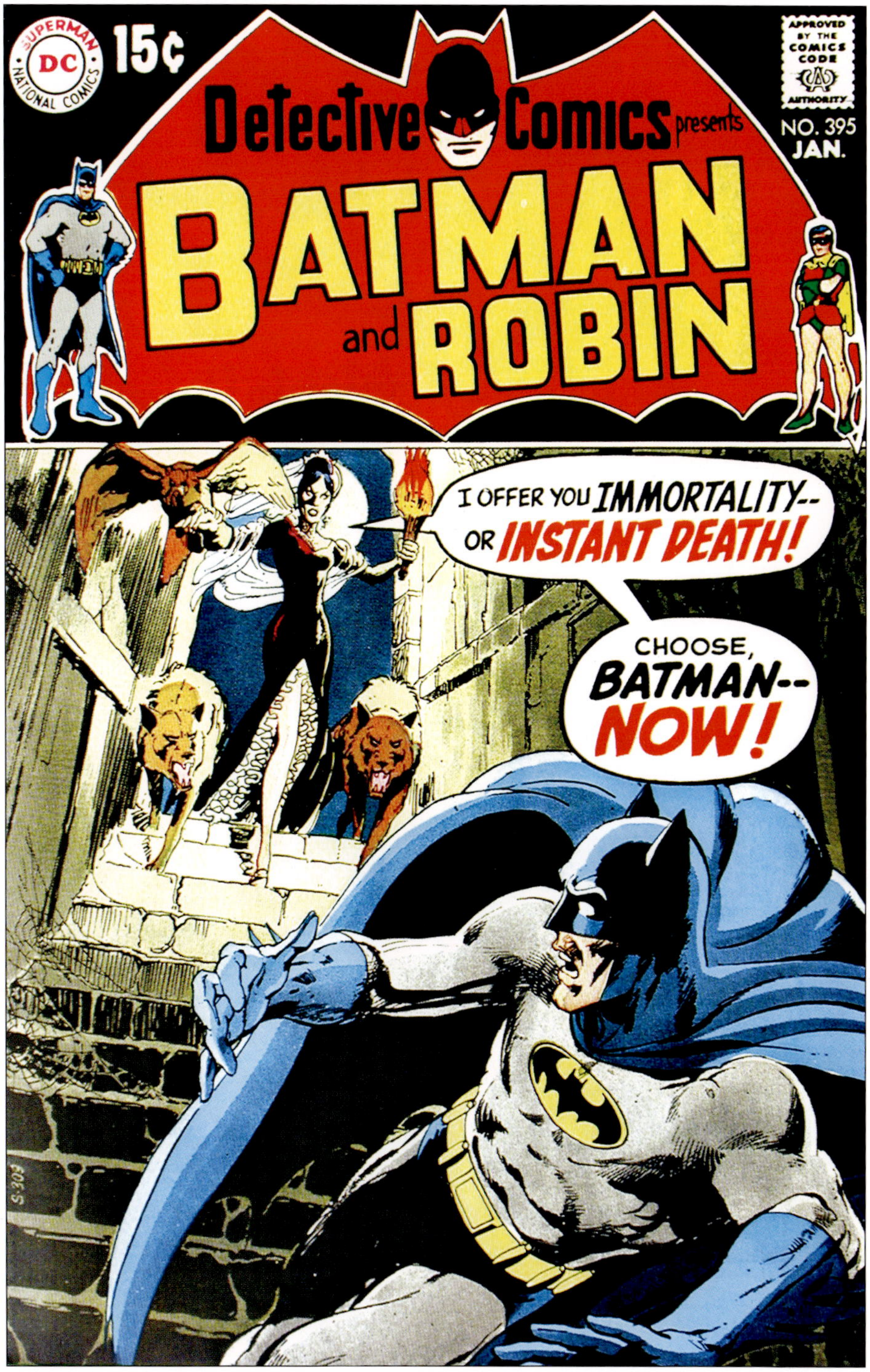

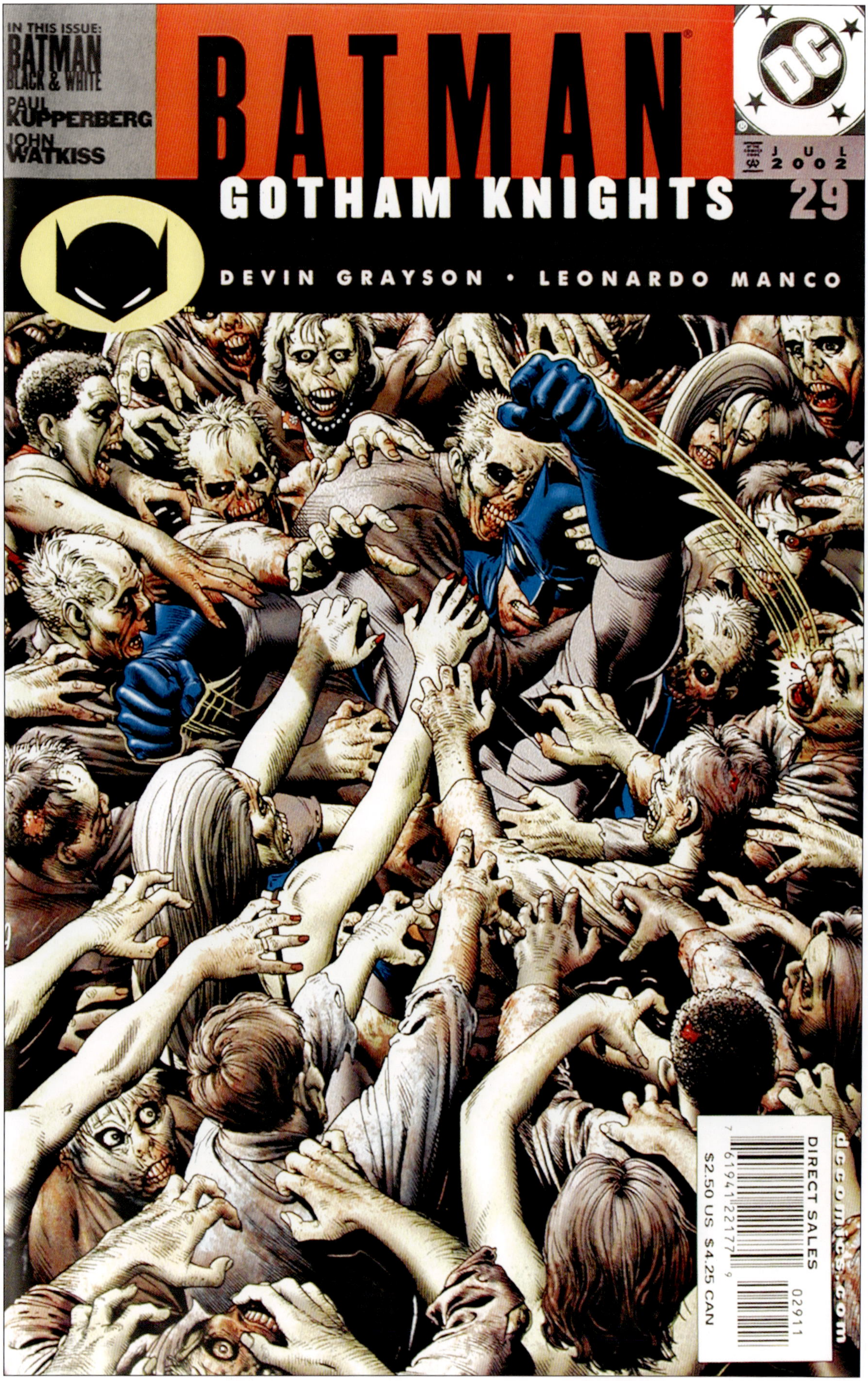

Batman: Gotham Knights #29

2002

Art by Brian Bolland

Detective Comics #443

1974

Art by Jim Aparo

Batman #202

1968

Art by Irv Novick

Detective Comics #313

1963

Art by Sheldon Moldoff

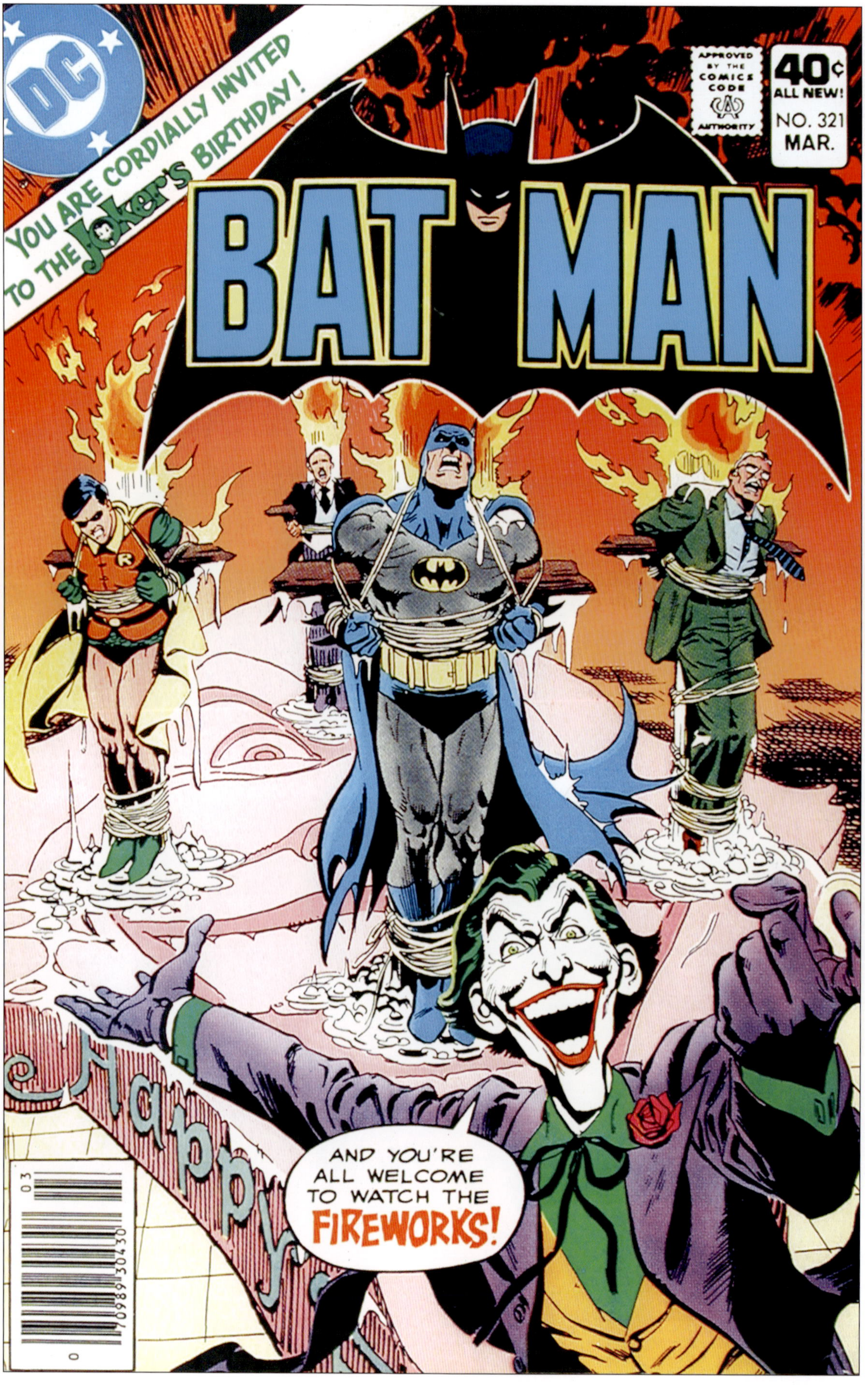

Batman #321

1980

Art by

José Luis García-López

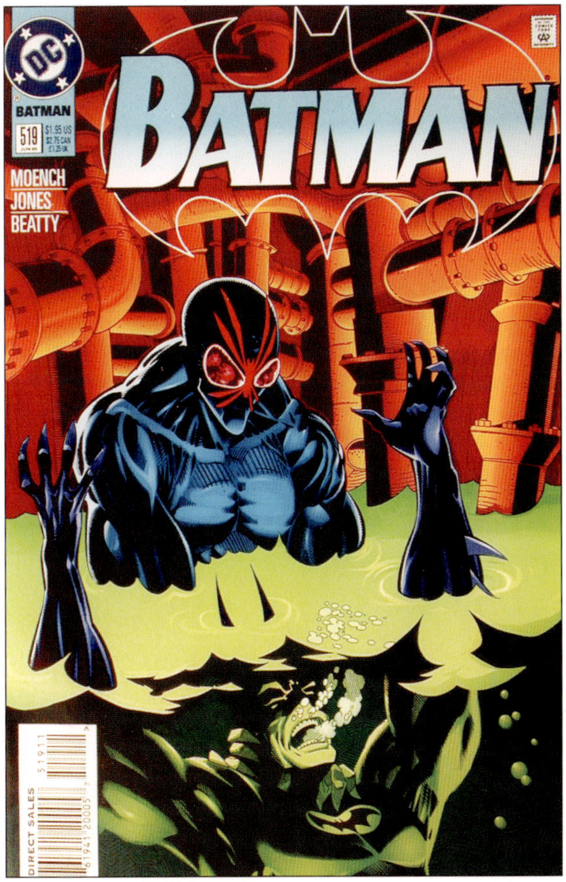

Batman #519

1995

Art by Kelley Jones & John Beatty

Batman Beyond #16

2001

Art by Brian Stelfreeze

The Batman Chronicles #8

1997

Art by Walter Simonson

Batman: Legends of the Dark Knight #104

1998

Art by Paul Johnson

It is a fine and noble thing to merely entertain people, and that's mostly what we comics guys aspire to. But once in a very long while, we can use our craft for a higher purpose. Such was the case with "Death of Innocents." We wanted to do a story that would satisfy Batman fans, but we also wanted to raise awareness about a hideous danger to the world's children — land mines. After the book's appearance, someone who should know said that we had succeeded. Nothing I've ever done professionally has made me happier. Sometimes, being a comic book writer is a splendid calling.

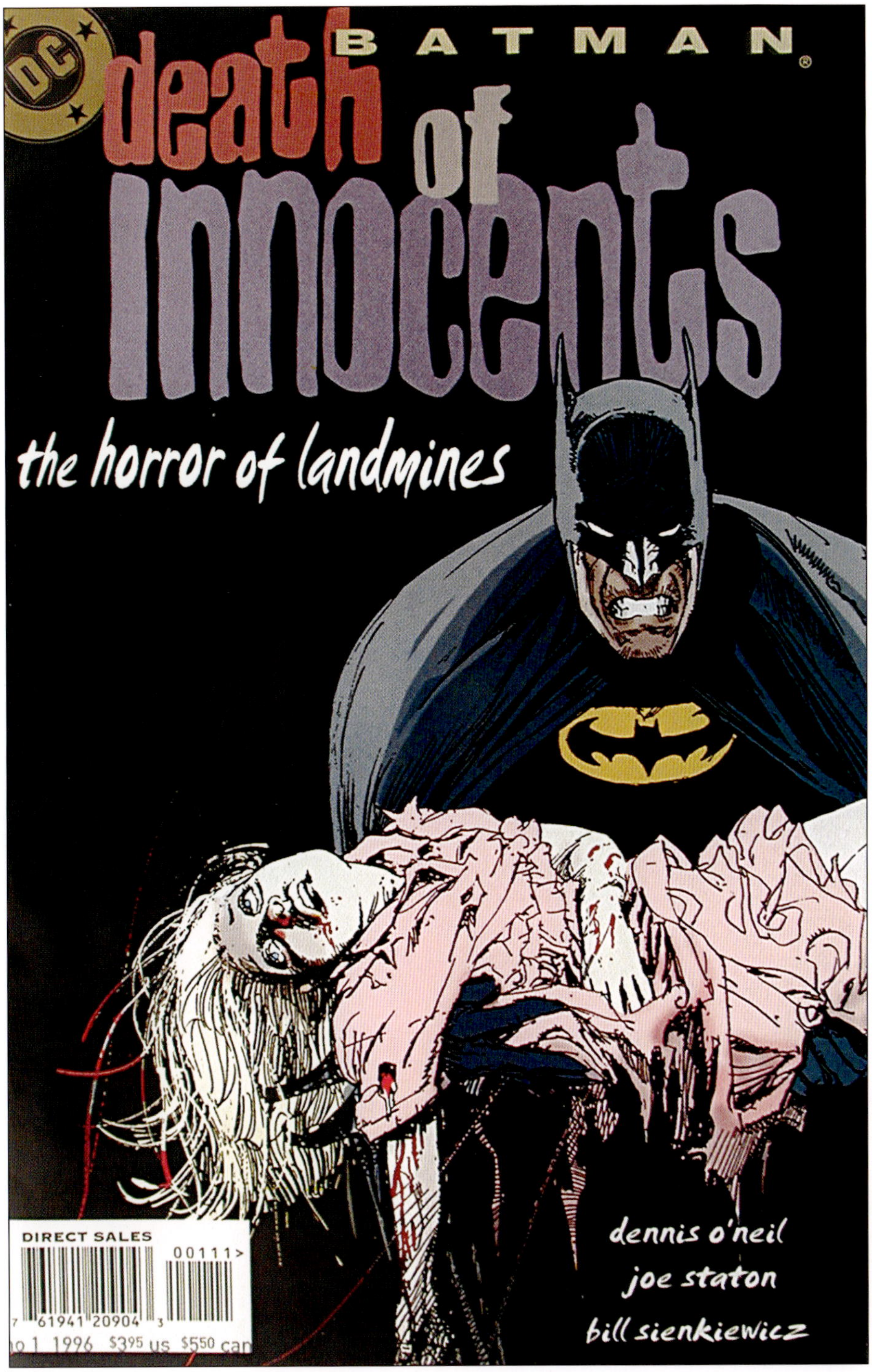

BATMAN: DEATH OF INNOCENTS 1996, Art by Bill Sienkiewicz

Page 147:

Batman #83

1954

Art by Dick Sprang & Charles Paris

Detective Comics #406

1969

Art by Neal Adams

The Brave and the Bold #100

1972

Art by Nick Cardy

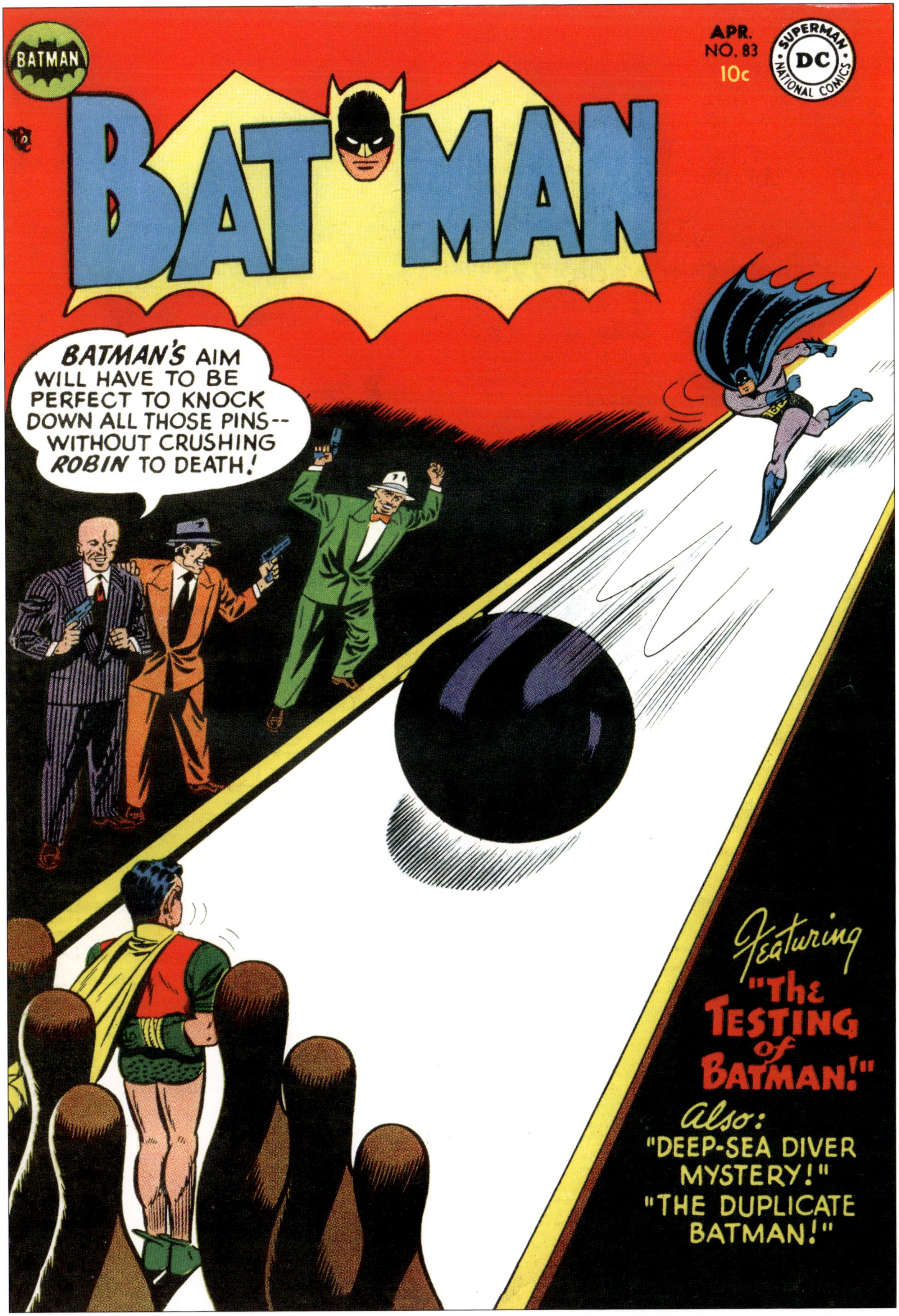
BATMAN
APR.
NO. 83
10c
SUPERMAN DC NATIONAL COMICS
BATMAN
BATMAN'S AIM WILL HAVE TO BE PERFECT TO KNOCK DOWN ALL THOSE PINS-- WITHOUT CRUSHING ROBIN TO DEATH!
Featuring
"The TESTING of BATMAN!"
also:
"DEEP-SEA DIVER MYSTERY!"
"THE DUPLICATE BATMAN!"

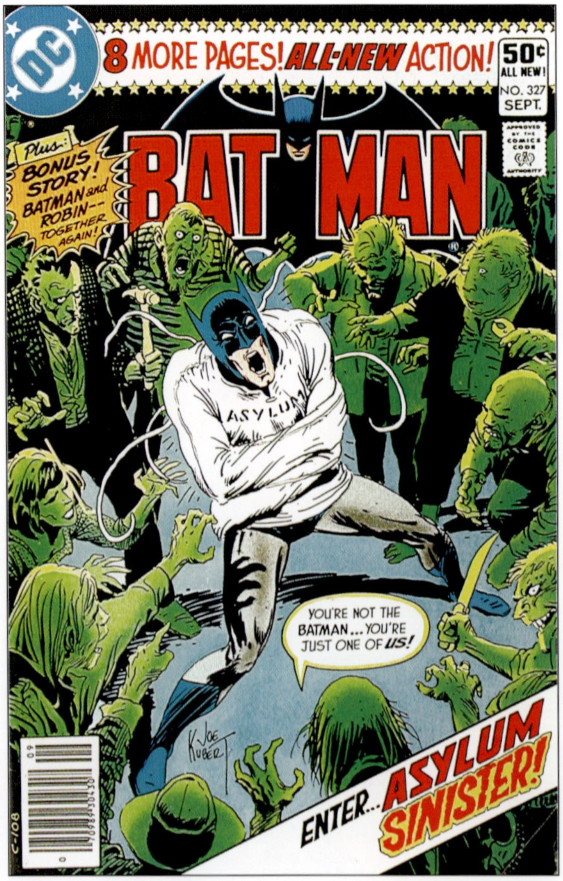

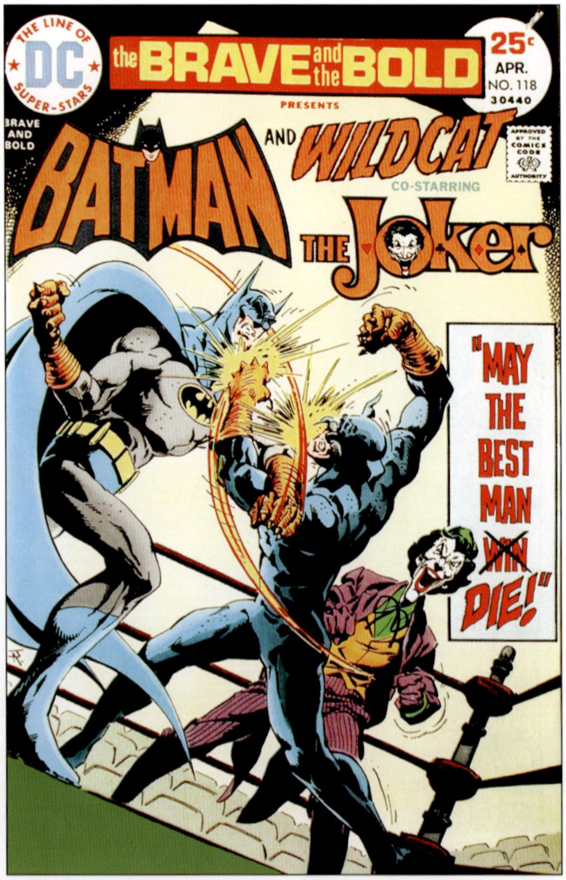

Batman #327

1980

Art by Joe Kubert

The Brave and the Bold #118

1975

Art by Jim Aparo

Detective Comics #269

1959

Art by Curt Swan & Stan Kaye

Batman #612
2003
Art by Jim Lee & Scott Williams

Even the good guys sometimes find themselves on the wrong side of the law, with dramatic consequences.

Detective Comics #377

1968

Art by Irv Novick

Detective Comics #328

1964

Art by Carmine Infantino & Joe Giella

Page: 153

Batman #128

1959

Art by Sheldon Moldoff

SUPERMAN DC NATIONAL COMICS
10¢
DEC. NO. 128
APPROVED BY THE COMICS CODE AUTHORITY
BATMAN
THE AMAZING ADVENTURE OF "THE INTERPLANETARY BATMAN!"
LET US OUT! WE'RE INNOCENT, I TELL YOU!

Batman: Gotham Adventures #27

2000

Art by Bob Smith & Terry Beatty

Detective Comics #766

2002

Art by John McCrea

Batman #329

1980

Art by Jim Aparo

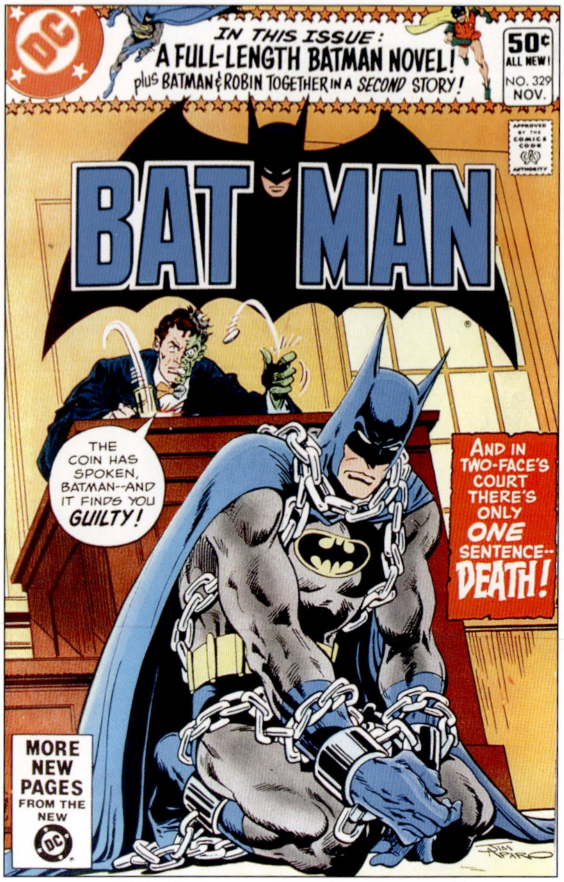

Batman: Gotham Knights #25

2002

Art by Brian Bolland

For a time, I apparently became DC's "Cover Artist," though at the time no one referred to me that way, nor did I think of myself as such.

Comic book covers had a vastly different reason for being in the '60s and early '70s.

A majority of comic book sales was to the newsstand. There was no *Diamond Previews* catalogue or grapevine. No one knew what was "coming out next month," except for the ads or mentions in this month's issue.

The cover was the only sales force. In fact, store owners looked with some small anger at a teenager who "flipped" through the books before buying. So you could buy a book with a Neal Adams cover and discover later that there was no Neal Adams art on the inside. Fans didn't like this much, but often, thank goodness, they'd buy the book just to get the cover.

Personally, I recently bought two years of *Wonder Woman* just to get the Adam Hughes covers. I'm sure you know what I mean.

Anyway, DC could count on another ten percent of sales if I did the cover, so they were happy to load me down with covers. In fact, it was a natural fit. I think of a cover artist as a problem solver. It was never the job of the cover artist, as I saw it, to simply draw a pretty picture. They surely didn't need me for that.

I'm the kind of person who likes to communicate on many levels. I like to intrigue the reader, stimulate the reader, awe the reader or even present a mystery to the reader. As far as the art is concerned, again, I'd like to mystify, ask a question, essentially make people think by using art.

In fact, good covers, I believe, are not necessarily the best drawn, but the best thought out. Anyway, that's my philosophy. That and two bucks will get you a bus ride.

When I first began working with the legendary Carmine Infantino, it was great to discover he was also idea driven.

Carmine would only ask me to use his layout if I agreed it sold the message or idea best. And I didn't make it easy for him.

His ideas were and are always simple and direct and were classically designed. It's hard to argue with those values.

Even so, 85% of the covers were my designs for many reasons. Often, Carmine was too busy to contribute, or half the time he liked what I came in with and finally, I'd talk him out of some idea or other in the course of our back and forth.

Carmine was not slow to recognize good ideas. And his true ego was always strong enough to be generous. I'd like to think his respect for my work was part of his generosity, but either way we worked well together.

For me, also, covers were a time to experiment. Most folks at old DC didn't know what the hell I was up to anyway, until some fan wrote in.

This is Neal's first Batman cover, inking over Carmine Infantino's pencils.

I remember one day when Murray Boltinoff, editor of many of the books I worked on, excitedly showed me a letter from a fan who was particularly excited about the covers I was doing on the mystery books: *House of Mystery, House of Secrets* and *Tales of the Unexpected*. Murray was literally taken by the letter. It seems this teenager, an art student, I think, would buy 10 copies of each mystery book I did the covers for. He would cut the covers off and tack them up on his bulletin board in his room and he would lie on his bed and stare at them. He wrote the letter because some of the covers, as he stared at them, became three-dimensional and he wondered if I was using some new technology.

Murray thought the kid might've been on drugs, until I explained that certain colors' wavelength is greater than others, and so those colors jump forward (red and yellow) while some colors lie back (blue and blue gray) and if you design your drawing just right, they not only seem three-dimensional, but to the eye they actually are three-dimensional.

Neal Adams *was the first of a new generation of artists to help DC evolve its look and approach to comics storytelling. At first, he was used on covers for a wide variety of titles before adding stories to his workload. His collaborations with writer Denny O'Neil helped usher in a new look for Batman as interest in the pop art television series waned.*

Through the years Batman has found himself with a host of allies. Earning the right to operate in Gotham City is not easily won.

Batman: Gotham Adventures #1

1998

Art by Ty Templeton

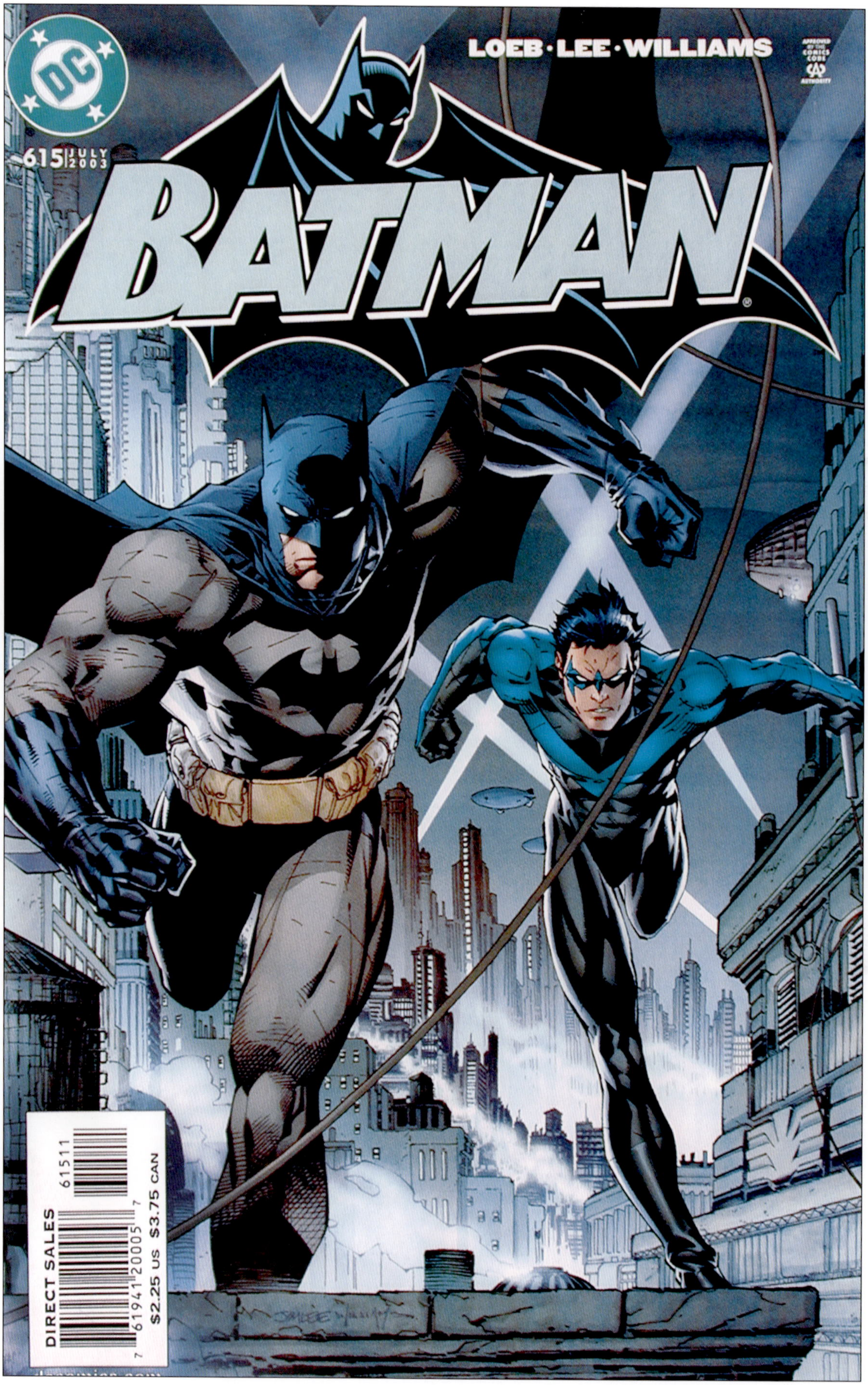

Batman #615

2003

Art by Jim Lee &

Scott Williams

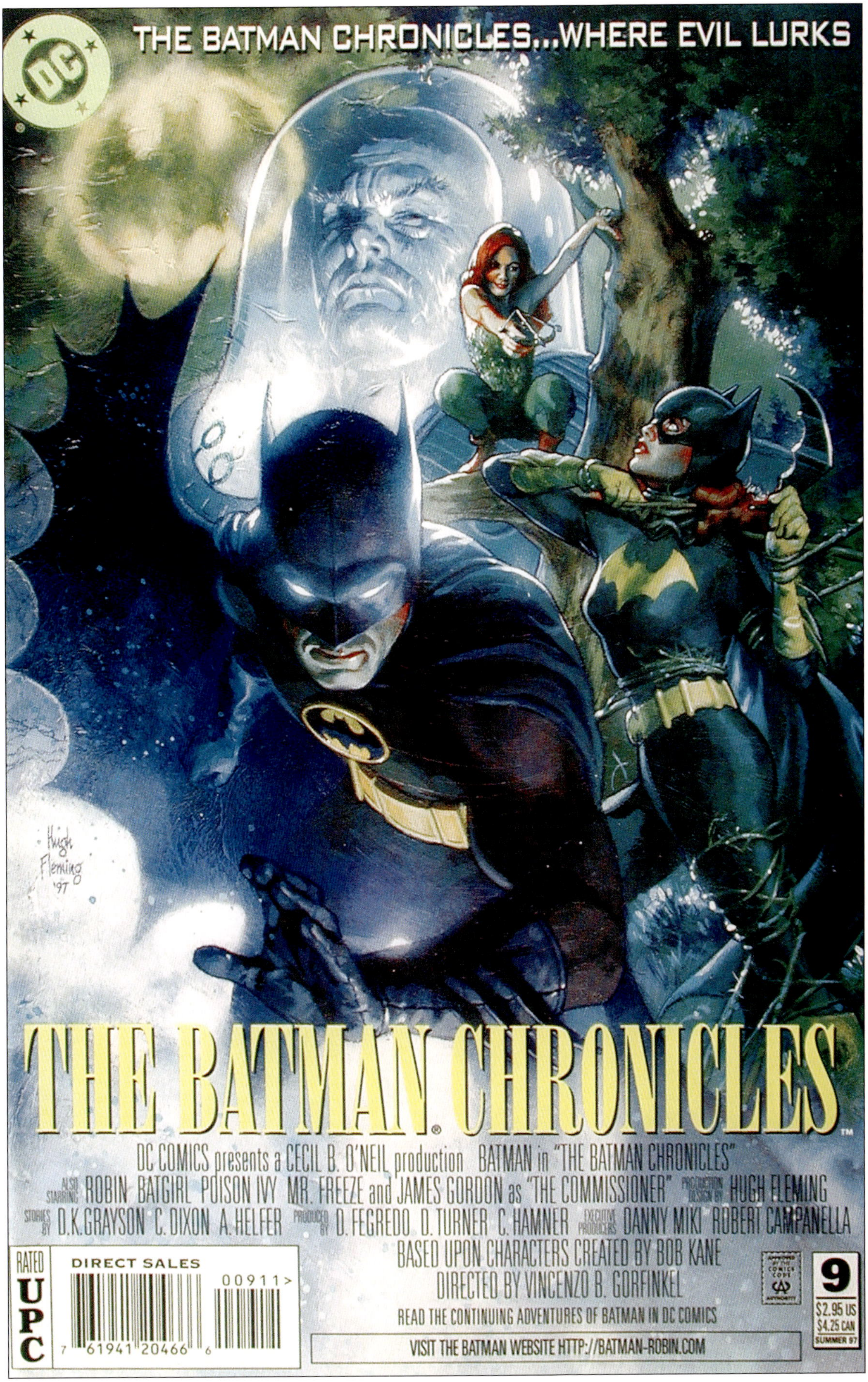

The Batman Chronicles #9

1997

Art by Hugh Fleming

Batman: Gotham Adventures #16

1999

Art by Bob Smith & Terry Beatty

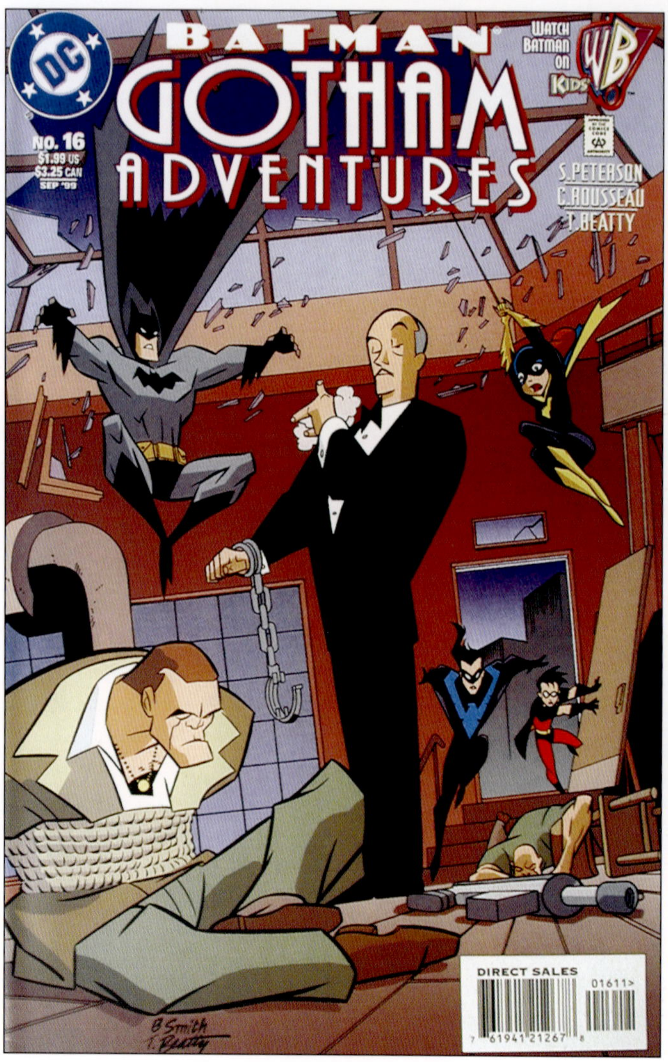

Detective Comics #484

1979

Art by Ross Andru & Dick Giordano

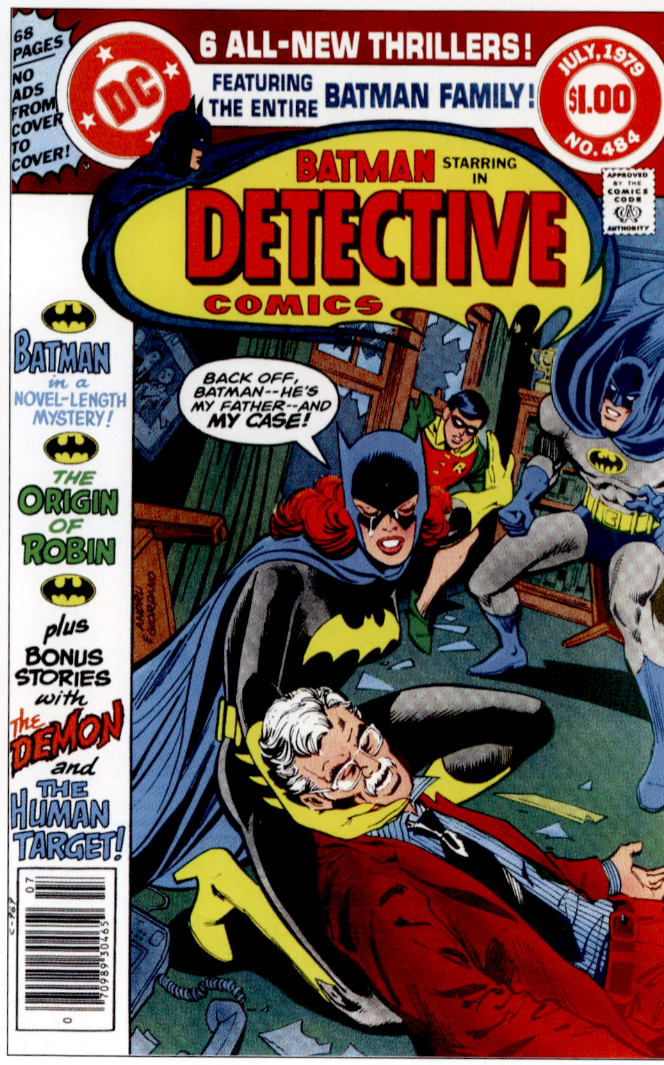

Batman and the Outsiders #32
1986
Art by Alan Davis

For a brief time, Batman formed a new team to handle problems the Justice League of America could not. A mix of new and veteran heroes, he trained them until they could fly solo.

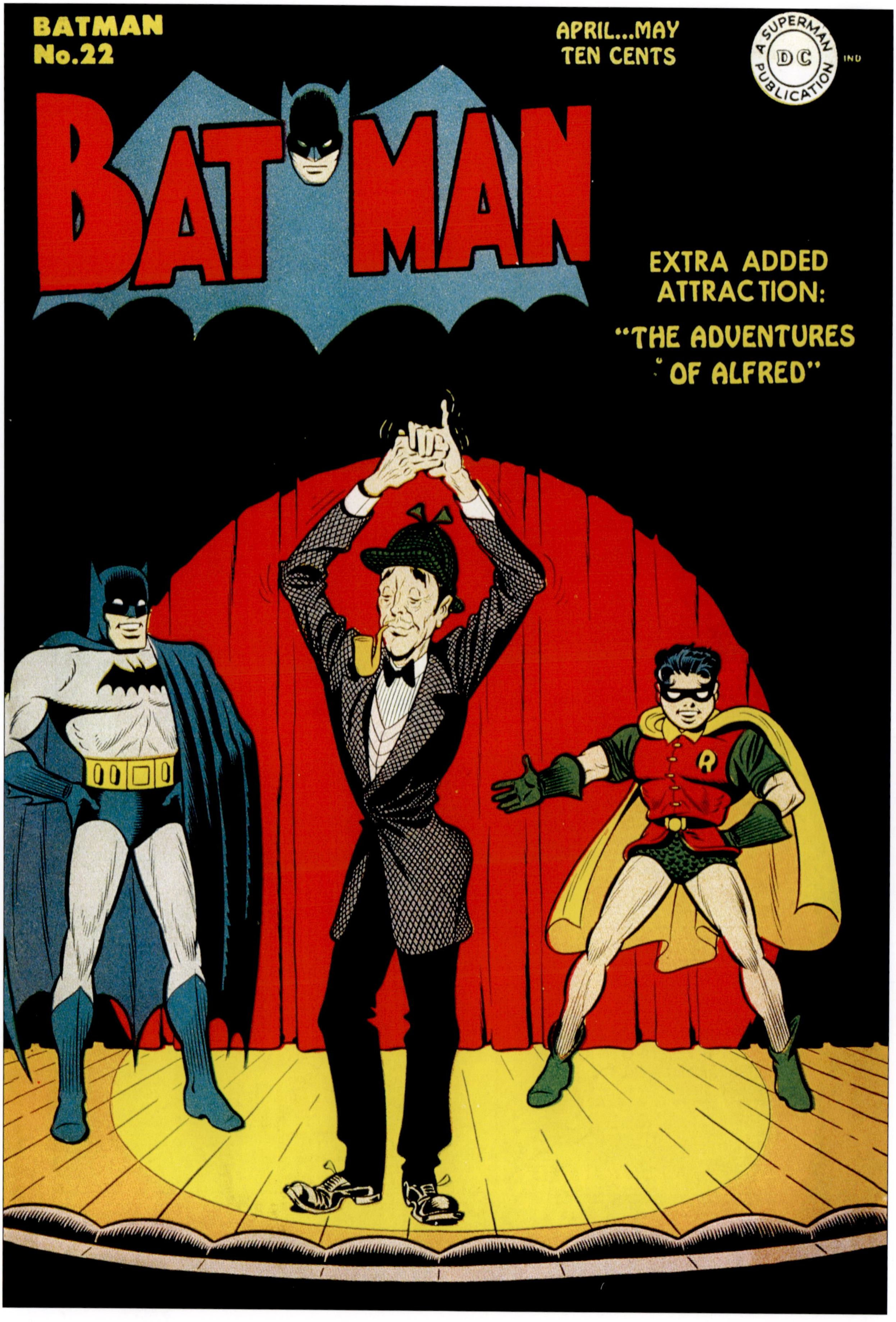

Batman #22
1944
Art by
Dick Sprang

Detective Comics #371

1968

Art by Carmine Infantino & Murphy Anderson

Detective Comics #422

1972

Art by Neal Adams

Batman #92

1955

Art by

Win Mortimer

Ace appeared regularly until 1956 but has been fondly remembered and is used on the Cartoon Network's Krypto *animated series.*

World's Best Comics #1

1941

Art by Fred Ray

After two successful oversized comics sold at the World's Fair in 1939 and 1940, DC launched this quarterly title, changing the name to World's Finest Comics *with the second issue. Superman and Batman shared the covers but didn't share the story until issue #71.*

Batgirl #7

2000

Art by Damion Scott

Detective Comics #359

1966

Art by Carmine Infantino & Murphy Anderson

When ABC asked for a female crimefighter to enhance their Batman *series, editor Julius Schwartz introduced Commissioner Gordon's daughter, Barbara, in the comics before her live action debut.*

Batman: Gotham Knights #43

2003

Art by Brian Bolland

Detective Comics #725

1998

Art by Brian Stelfreeze

Dick Grayson grew up and set out on his own as Nightwing, only occasionally partnering with his mentor.

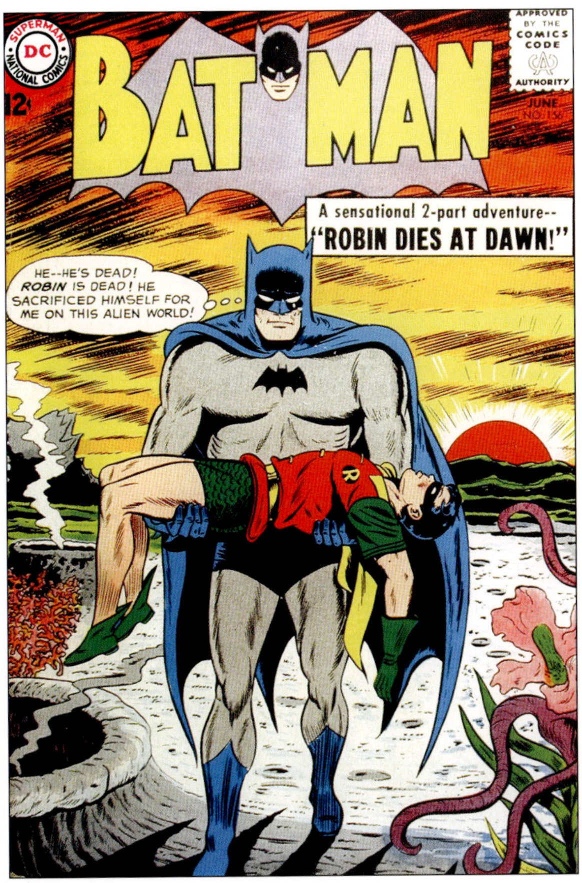

DETECTIVE COMICS #233 1956 ■ **BATMAN #156** 1963, inked by Charles Paris

From the very first cover I was asked to do by Max Gaines and Sheldon Mayer (*All-American Comics*) I have always approached the cover as a challenge. The challenge being to try and make the cover as interesting and as provocative as possible so the prospective buyer would select my magazine (because of the cover) out of the rack of dozens of magazines. And of the hundreds of covers I have done, I would say *Batman* #156, "Robin Dies at Dawn," would be my favorite. I imagine it made a terrific impact on young fans when they saw it on the rack. My other favorite would be *Detective* #233 which introduced Batwoman. I think the design and color of the cover was perfect. It had everything. Batman and Robin. The Batmobile. The Bat-signal. And the first appearance of Batwoman.

***Sheldon Moldoff** has illustrated hundreds of stories for many publishers but is best known for his work on the Golden Age Hawkman and his long tenure working alongside Batman creator Bob Kane.*

Batman: Legends of the Dark Knight #60

1994

Art by Norm Breyfogle

Batgirl #14

2001

Art by Damion Scott & Robert Campanella

Even though there have been two previous Batgirls, the current incarnation is the first to receive her own title.

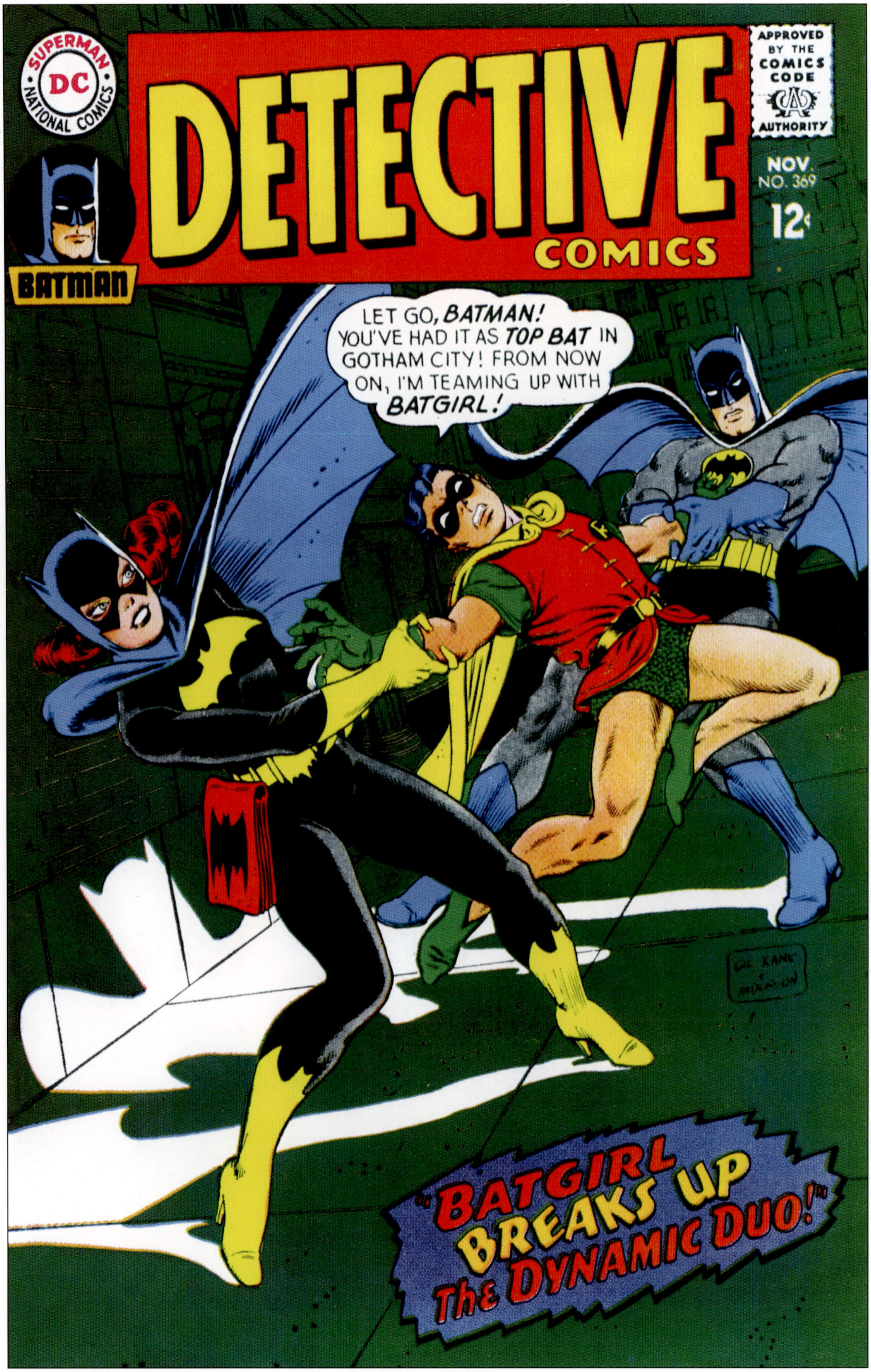

Detective Comics #369

1967

Art by Gil Kane & Murphy Anderson

Page 175:

Detective Comics #235

1956

Art by Sheldon Moldoff

SUPERMAN DC NATIONAL COMICS
10¢
In this issue: DETAILS and ENTRY BLANK for Giant 5000 PRIZE CONTEST!
SEPT. NO. 235
APPROVED BY THE COMICS CODE AUTHORITY
Detective COMICS
YES, ROBIN -- THE MAN WEARING THAT OLD-FASHIONED BATMAN COSTUME WAS MY FATHER!
FEATURING: "THE First BATMAN!"

Batman Family #17

1978

Art by Michael Kaluta

The basic elements remain the same, but every artist brings a unique approach to bringing the Caped Crusader to life.

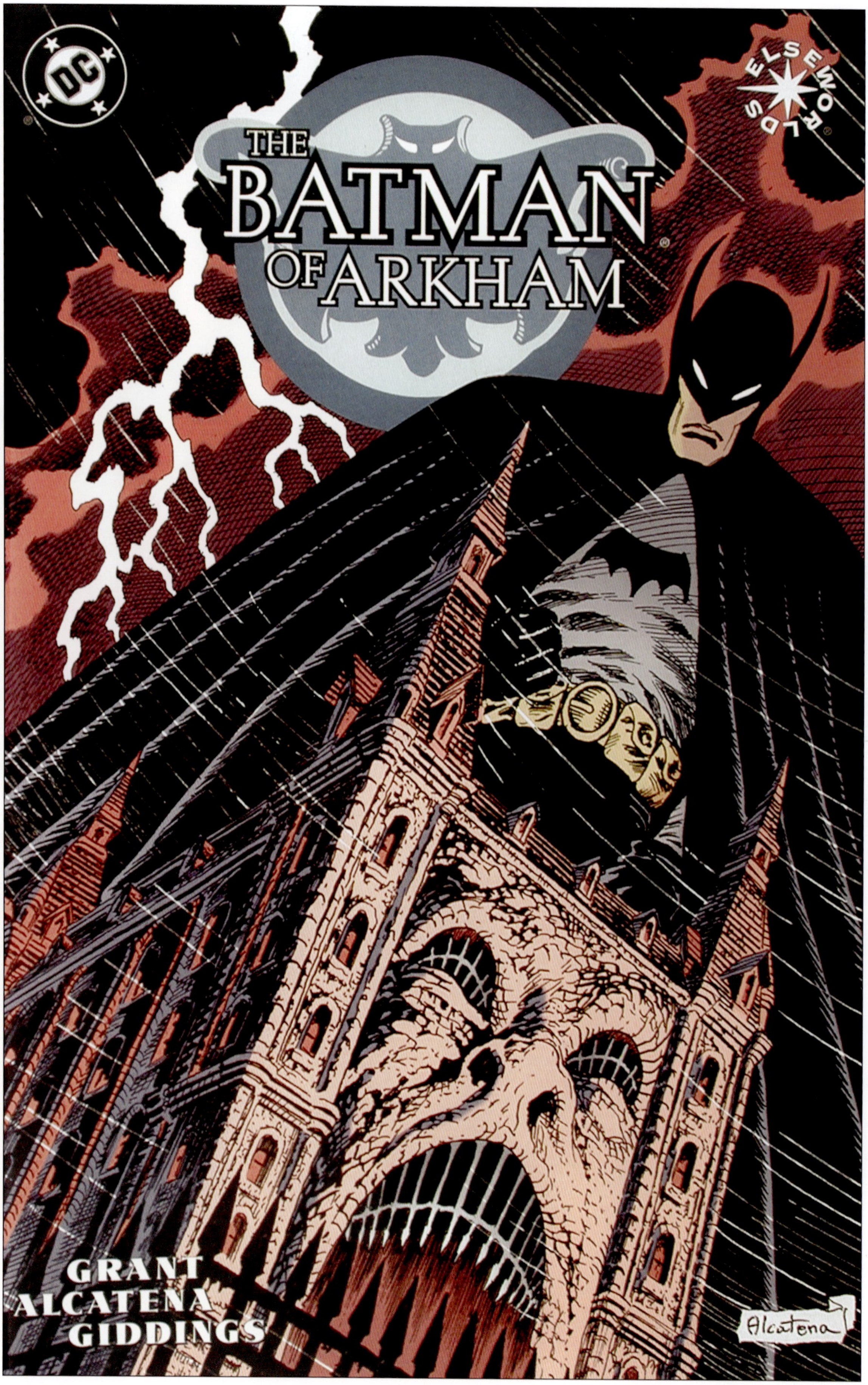

The Batman of Arkham

2000

Art by Quique Alcatena

Batman: Legends of the Dark Knight #85

1996

Art by Tony Salmons

Batman: Bane of the Demon #1
1998
Art by Graham Nolan & Bill Sienkiewicz

Batman #547

1997

Art by Kelley Jones

Batman Adventures #8

2004

Art by Kelsey Shannon

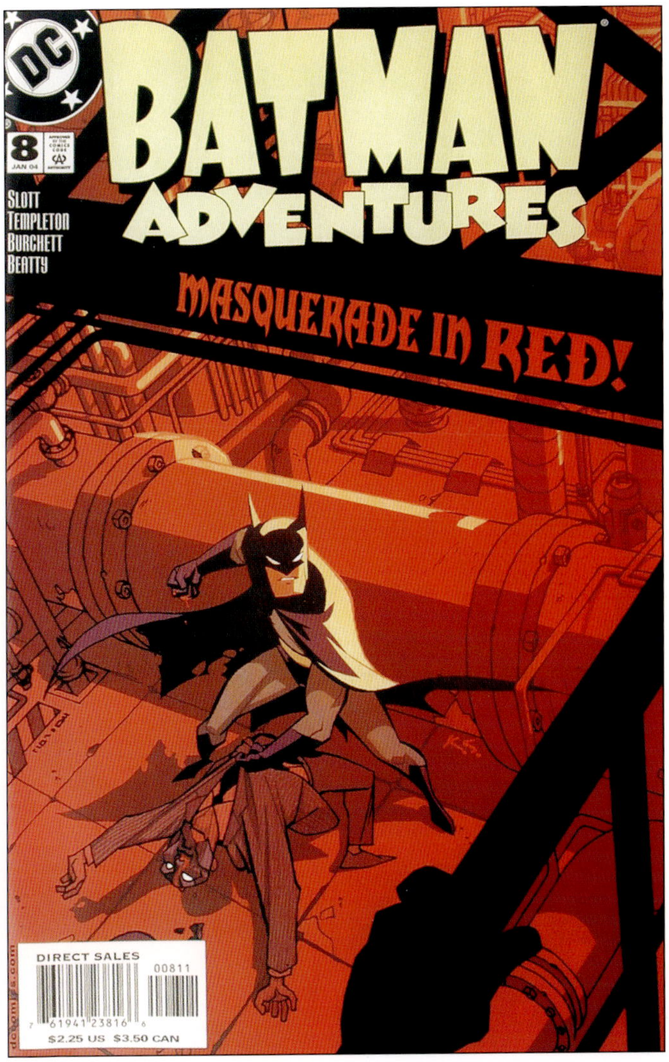

The Batman Chronicles #11

1998

Art by Paul Pope

Batman: Gotham Knights #32

2002

Art by Brian Bolland

Detective Comics #719

1998

Art by Bill Sienkiewicz

Superman: The Man of Steel #37

1994

Art by Jon Bogdanove & Dennis Janke

Note the various artists imitated to create the sense of alternate realities to confound Superman.

In today's cluttered comic shop, what elements must a cover have to get noticed?

It's tough, and getting more challenging every day. Any given cover must strive to make you stop and pay attention. By shocking you, by making you ask what it means, by making you pause due to its stark, quiet atmosphere, by making you laugh. Whatever it takes, your goal is to stop the buyer in their tracks and make them interested in your book. Every cover should have at least three elements brought together into the one image. These can include the character(s), of course, a setting, a predicament, an iconic juxtaposition (such as the Riddler's question mark), cover copy, a setting and/or the complete lack of any background setting whatsoever, and so on.

Does newsstand display play a role at all?

Yes, however we have been keeping both the newsstand and direct sales markets in mind for years now, thanks to Mark Chiarello, DC's Editorial Art Director. I believe DC has a good eye to keeping both markets satisfied.

Do you feel hampered at all by unifying elements for the Batman line, such as the cowl icon?

At times, especially when we are adding more elements to market multipart storylines like "War Games" or "No Man's Land." The covers tend to get a bit cluttered, but on a normal month-to-month basis, no. I feel that the current icons and glyphs on the line of Bat titles do a great job alerting the consumer to what it is they're about to purchase.

Should covers today be poster-shots or story specific?

There is no hard rule, and each cover must be approached on its own with your mind towards what your story is about, or how you can best represent that story without literally lifting a scene from the interior. Sometimes, lifting that scene is the perfect solution. It really depends on so many variables and ever-changing factors, like what your last few covers have looked like, the overall tone of the book and perhaps reflecting a radical shift away from that tone that the reader may be expecting every month.

What role should cover copy play? Is it necessary?

I am personally totally bored with the cover copy concept and feel it is a highly overrated holdover from our past. A well-orchestrated piece of cover art and the book's logo should be enough to pull you in. However, DC's policy is that we continue this practice, and so cover copy appears on many of the Bat titles.

Which covers during your editorial tenure worked best?

Batman #631, the concluding cover to "War Games Act 1" comes to mind. There's *Batman* #584 by Scott McDaniel and *Detective Comics* #798, the opening chapter to "Act 2." Beyond the Bat Family of covers, I'm also very proud of *Green Lantern* #154 and *Green Arrow* #18 and 19.

How do you select a cover artist? Should it be the interior artist?

I work closely with Mark Chiarello, and we look for talent that can boil down the many concepts that go into any given story (sometimes conflicting ones at that). An artist who can bring it all together and into one unified visual image that stimulates one's imagination and begs you to want to know more. It's rare that an interior artist is chosen. This has less to do with time sensitivity and more to do with the artists' mindset to do both, excellent visual storytelling from panel-to-panel and also be able to translate all those images into one iconic moment. Just as there are so few successful writer/artists in the field.

What about the increasing importance of color? What does that bring to a cover?

Color is also a major contributing factor towards bringing a cover alive. Again, from time to time the absolute stark lack of color works to have your cover stand out in an ocean of other colorful covers on the racks. It can also bring the consumer's eye to the exact moment on the cover needed to make your story's point in one single visual moment.

***Bob Schreck** is currently Group Editor for the Batman family of titles.*

Batman has found himself in some dramatic, spectacular and downright odd situations. Here's a look at some of the more unusual adventures.

Detective Comics #275
1960
Art by Sheldon Moldoff

Detective Comics #239

1957

Art by Sheldon Moldoff

(color effects by Jack Adler)

Detective Comics #256

1958

Art by Sheldon Moldoff

Batman #75

1953

Art by Win Mortimer

Detective Comics #339

1965

Art by Carmine Infantino & Joe Giella

MAD
IND
No. 289 Sept. 1989 Our Price $1.95 Cheap!
IN THIS ISSUE WE...
BATTER
BATMAN
DOWN
MURPHY BROWN
UNWIND
VIDEO RENTALS
CRASH
DRIVER'S ED
SLAP
RAP MUSIC
AND
PUT-DOWN
STAND-UP
COMICS

With all the great covers spoofing Batman that MAD Magazine has published over the years, it's difficult for me, the editor of MAD, to pick a favorite.

I could pick the cover of MAD #105, Sept. '66. It's a classic send-up of the 1960's *Batman* TV series by longtime MAD cover artist Norman Mingo. Not only is it the first time a TV series was spoofed on the cover of MAD, it also marked the first time (but certainly not the last) MAD's infamous gap-toothed mascot, Alfred E. Neuman, was substituted for a real person, in this case, actor Burt Ward's Robin. It's a great cover, but I'm not picking it.

Another great choice would be the cover of MAD #359, July '97, which featured the movie *Batman & Robin*. It would also be a clever choice because MAD #359 was actually *four* different covers by artist Mort Drucker, each featuring a different Alfred substitution of a character from the Batman movie. (I told you we tend to do too many Alfred substitution gags!) When you placed the four covers together, the words "Cheap Gimmick" appeared in the center – MAD's way of spoofing all the multiple covers being done at the time by some cheesy magazines (READ: *TV Guide*) in an effort to boost newsstand sales. (If MAD's newsstand sales happened to be boosted as well, hey, who were we to argue…?) It's another great cover, but I'm not picking this one either.

No, if I had to pick only one MAD Batman cover, it would have to be MAD #289, Sept. '89. But in order for you to understand why, you'll first need to know a little MAD history.

MAD was founded by the legendary Bill Gaines, who was the magazine's publisher from its beginning in 1952 until his death in 1992. Gaines was something of a rascal, who delighted in taunting MAD's editorial staff with bets, cons and practical jokes.

When Nick Meglin and I took over as co-editors of MAD in 1985, Gaines made us an offer. For every issue of MAD that we produced that sold over 50% of the magazine's print run, Gaines would take us out to dinner at the restaurant of our choice in New York City. If the magazine sold over 60%, Gaines would take us to the restaurant of our choice *anywhere in the world*. Now, Meglin and I enjoy a good meal as much as the next guy, particularly when Gaines was paying for it, so it was an effective carrot to dangle in front of us. Every month we worked our butts off trying to produce a great-selling issue. Try as we might, the 50% sell-through proved very difficult, and the 60% damn near impossible.

Then along came the first Batman movie. Huge buzz. Jack Nicholson as the Joker, great special effects, the highly anticipated movie quickly became a box office smash. Meglin and I managed to have a spoof of the movie out just as the film debuted. The cover featured a Richard Williams painting of an idea by Meglin. It featured – *surprise!* — yet another Alfred substitution, but with a twist. Not only was Batman replaced by Alfred, but the Batman bat symbol was replaced with the Superman "S" symbol. It was a nice, stupid MAD idea. Most readers just saw the Alfred substitution at first glance. The Superman twist snuck up on them a few seconds later. With our initial sales reports encouraging, Meglin and I quickly became convinced that we were finally going to hit the 60% sell-through. This cover would be the one that would have us eating *foie gras* in Paris on Gaines's dime. Sweet!

Of course, Gaines didn't get to be rich on his looks. Unbeknownst to Meglin and me, Gaines had quietly upped the print run on the Batman issue by several hundred thousand copies. In other words, short of just about every man, woman and child in America going out and buying that issue of MAD, there was no way it would ever crack the 60% barrier. The sly old fox had stuck it to us again.

In the end, the Batman cover sold very well and broke 50%. Gaines, true to his word, treated Meglin, Lenny Brenner (MAD's art director at the time) and me to a dinner at one of New York's finest restaurants, Gotham Bar and Grill. The meal was fabulous and expensive, though we never had Paris. To this day, whenever I look at that Batman cover, I can't help but think of my old pal Bill Gaines, MAD's curmudgeon publisher, who always seemed to be one step ahead of us.

***John Ficarra** is Senior Editor of MAD Magazine and has been poking fun at society for over 20 years. His mother still wishes he'd find respectable work.*

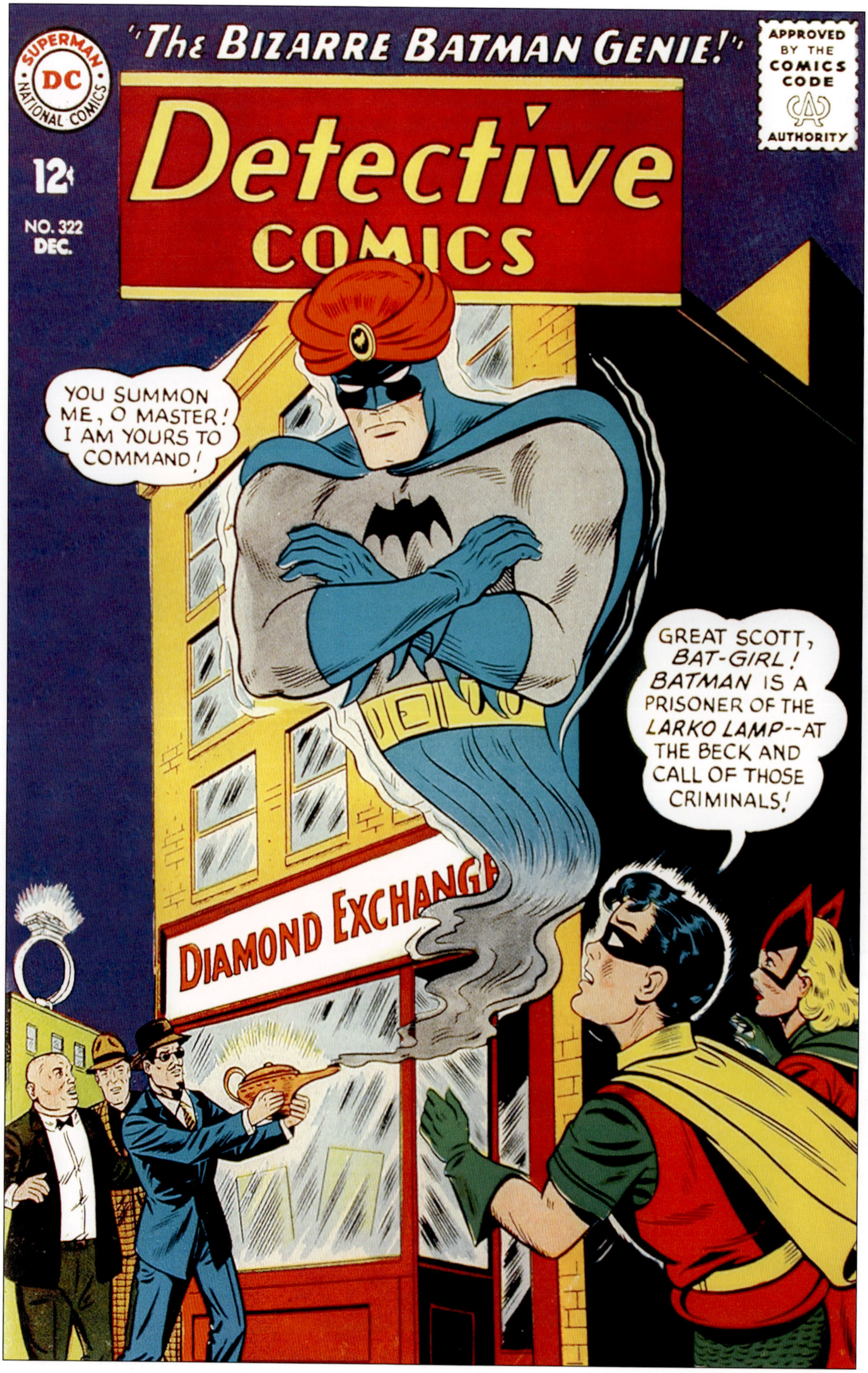

Detective Comics #322

1963

Art by Sheldon Moldoff

Batman is known for his intellect, detective skill and of course, his cool car. See where he hangs his cape, and the unique array of gadgets and vehicles that aid him.

Detective Comics #711

1997

Art by Graham Nolan & Tom Palmer

Detective Comics #561

1986

Art by Gene Colan & Dick Giordano

Page 199:
Batman #59
1950
Art by Bob Kane
(figures only)
Lew Sayre Schwartz
(pencils) &
Charles Paris
(inks)

Batman #20
1944
Art by Dick Sprang

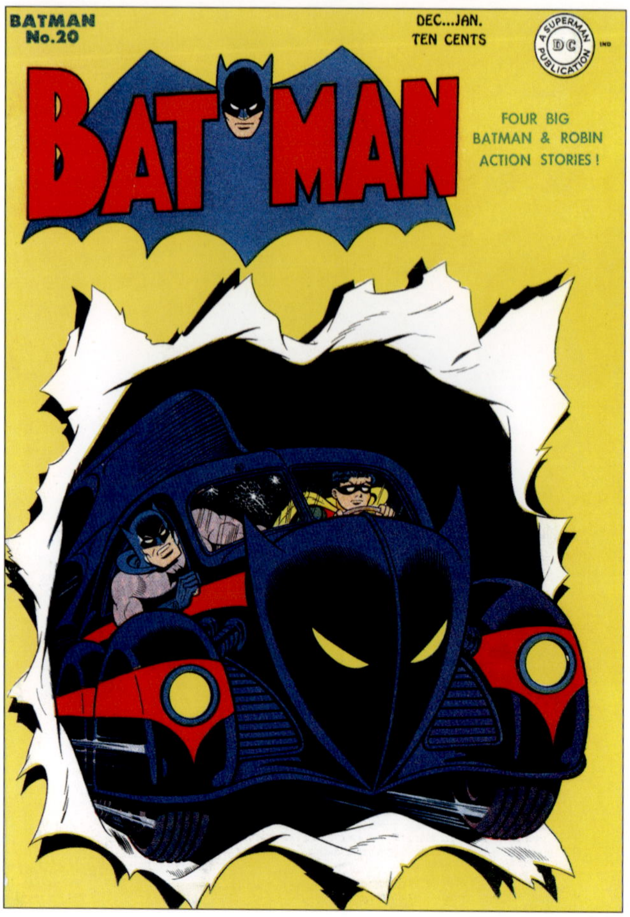

Detective Comics #156
1950
Art by Dick Sprang

52 BIG PAGES
BATMAN
SUPERMAN DC NATIONAL COMICS
10¢
BATMAN
In this issue: "BATMAN in the FUTURE!"
JUNE—JULY NO. 59
LOOK, ROBIN -- THE BAT-SIGNAL ON THE MOON! WE'RE WANTED BACK ON EARTH!

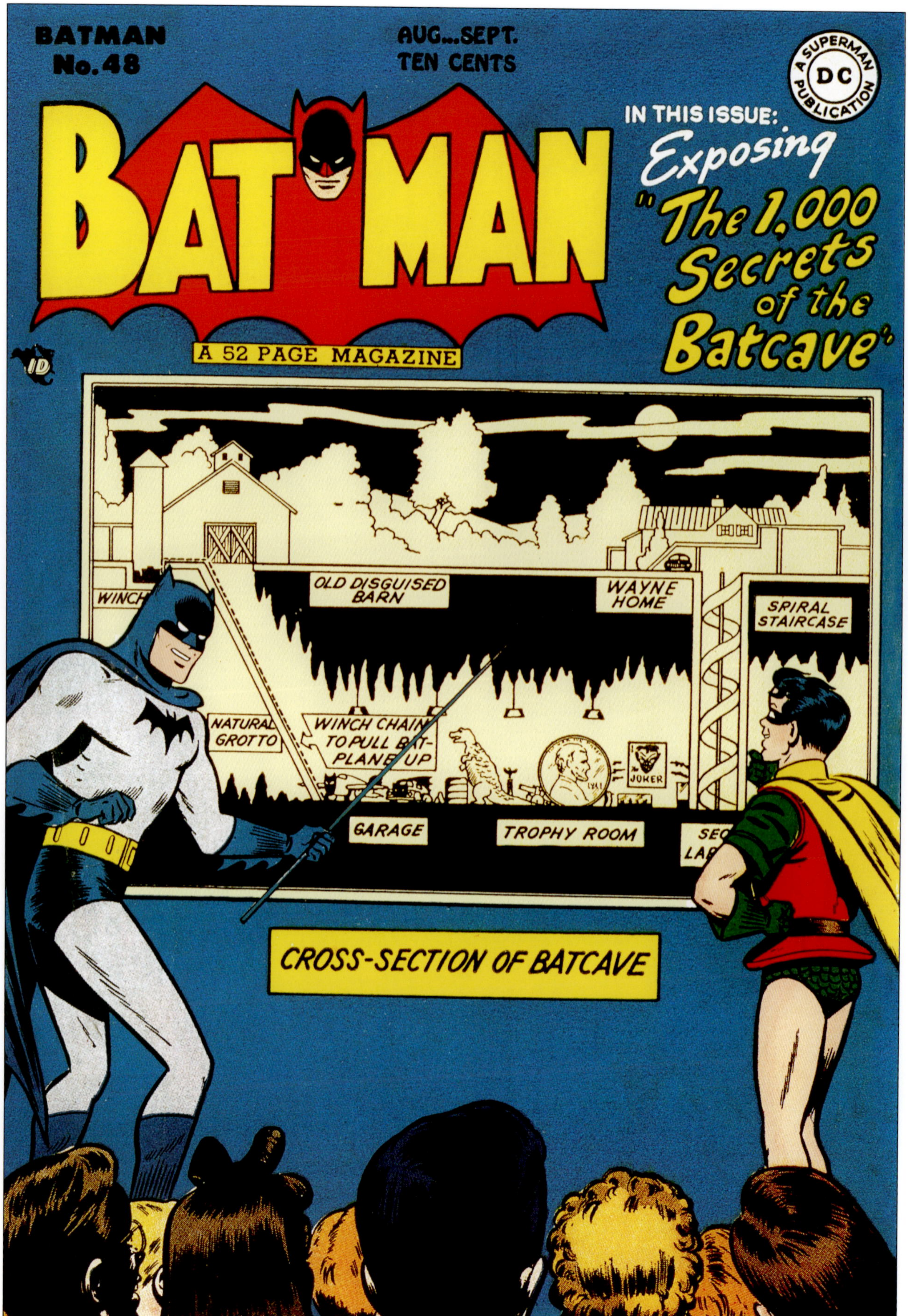
BATMAN
No. 48
AUG...SEPT.
TEN CENTS
A SUPERMAN DC PUBLICATION
BATMAN
A 52 PAGE MAGAZINE
IN THIS ISSUE:
Exposing
"The 1,000 Secrets of the Batcave"
WINCH
OLD DISGUISED BARN
WAYNE HOME
SPIRAL STAIRCASE
NATURAL GROTTO
WINCH CHAIN TO PULL BAT-PLANE UP
JOKER
GARAGE
TROPHY ROOM
CROSS-SECTION OF BATCAVE

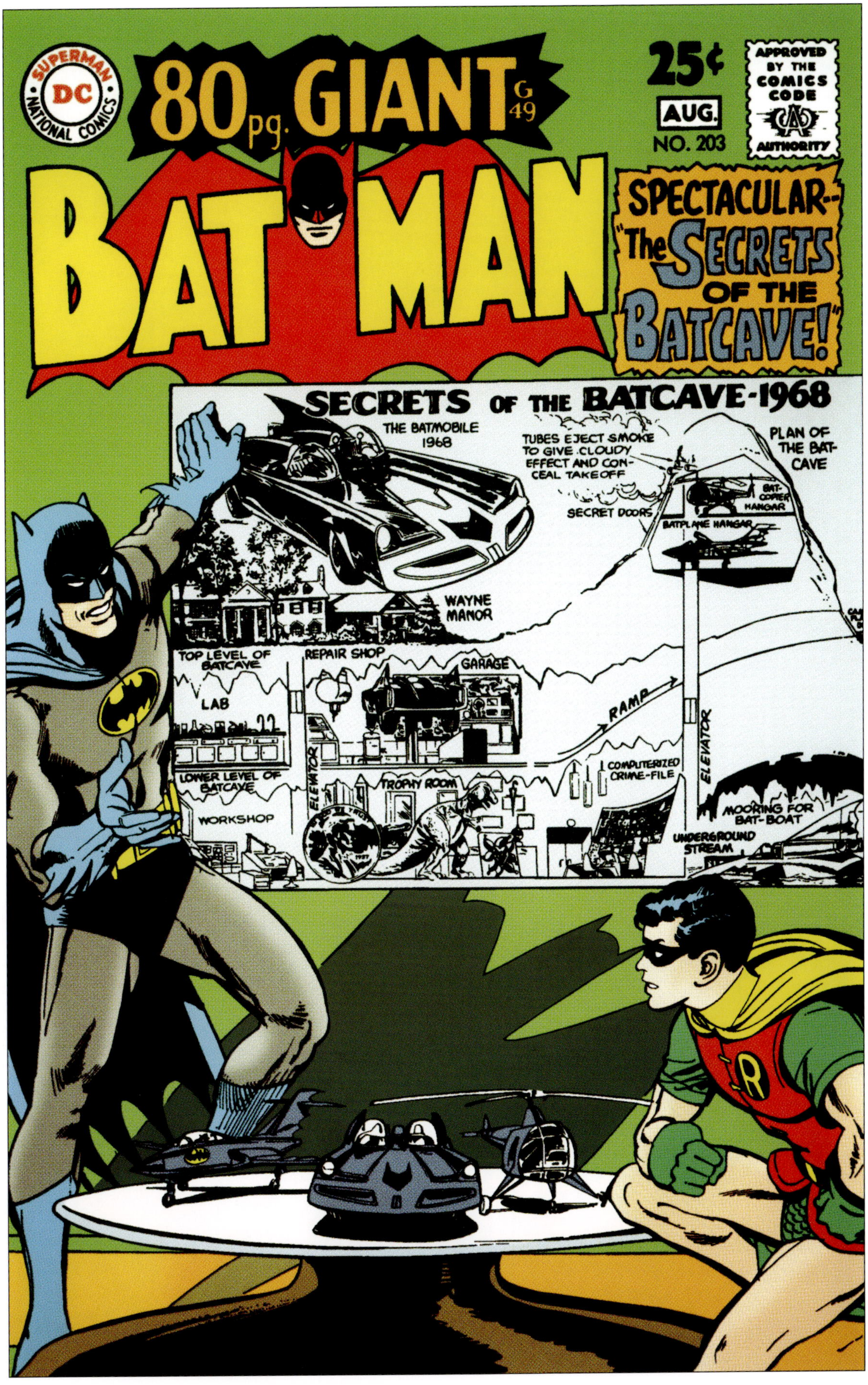

Page 200:

Batman #48

1948

Art by Win Mortimer

Batman #203

1968

Art by Neal Adams

Page 203:

Detective Comics #244

1957

Art by Sheldon Moldoff

Detective Comics #164

1950

Art by Win Mortimer

Detective Comics #619

1990

Art by Norm Breyfogle

10¢
JUNE NO. 244
APPROVED BY THE COMICS CODE AUTHORITY
SUPERMAN DC NATIONAL COMICS
Detective Comics
Featuring "The 100 BATARANGS of BATMAN!"
POLICE WHISTLE TARANG
BATMAN, YOU'RE NOT GOING TO USE BATARANG X, ARE YOU?
MAGNET BATARANG
WE'VE GOT TO, ROBIN -- EVEN THOUGH IT'S THE MOST DANGEROUS ONE IN OUR COLLECTION!
SEEING-EYE BATARANG
BOMB BATARANG
FLASH BULB BATARANG
BATARANG X

Batman #37

1946

Art by Jerry Robinson

Batman #47

1948

Art by Bob Kane &

Charles Paris

Batman #217

1969

Art by Neal Adams

A new era began for Batman as Dick Grayson went to college and the Dark Knight relocated operations to Gotham City. The move lasted approximately ten years.

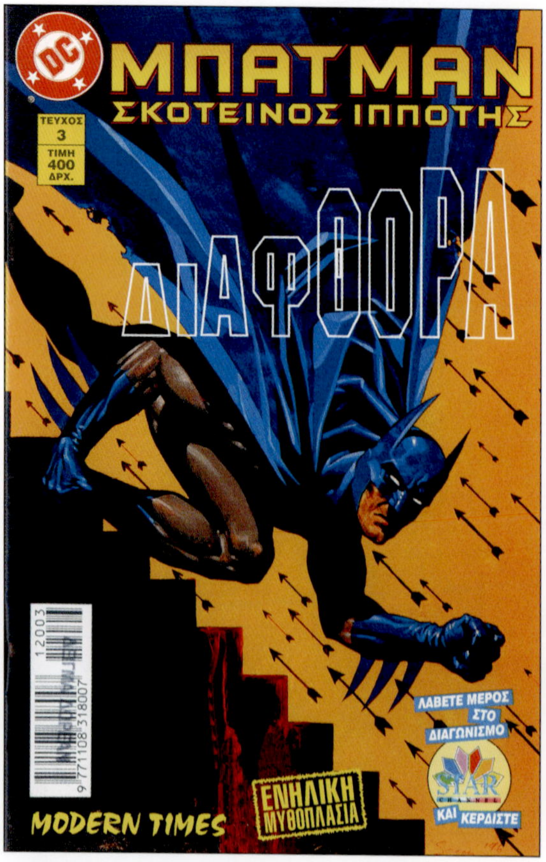

GREECE

INDIA (with stories published in five of the country's different dialects)

PORTUGAL

DC comics can be found in 70 countries around the world, with stories translated into over 30 languages. As a result, Batman has become one of the top five characters recognized globally. Each publisher chooses for themselves whether to use existing cover artwork or use other graphics for their publications.

RUSSIA

THAILAND

SWEDEN

CHINA

The seeming death of a hero definitely gets attention. The humanity of Batman and his allies makes this possibility all too real.

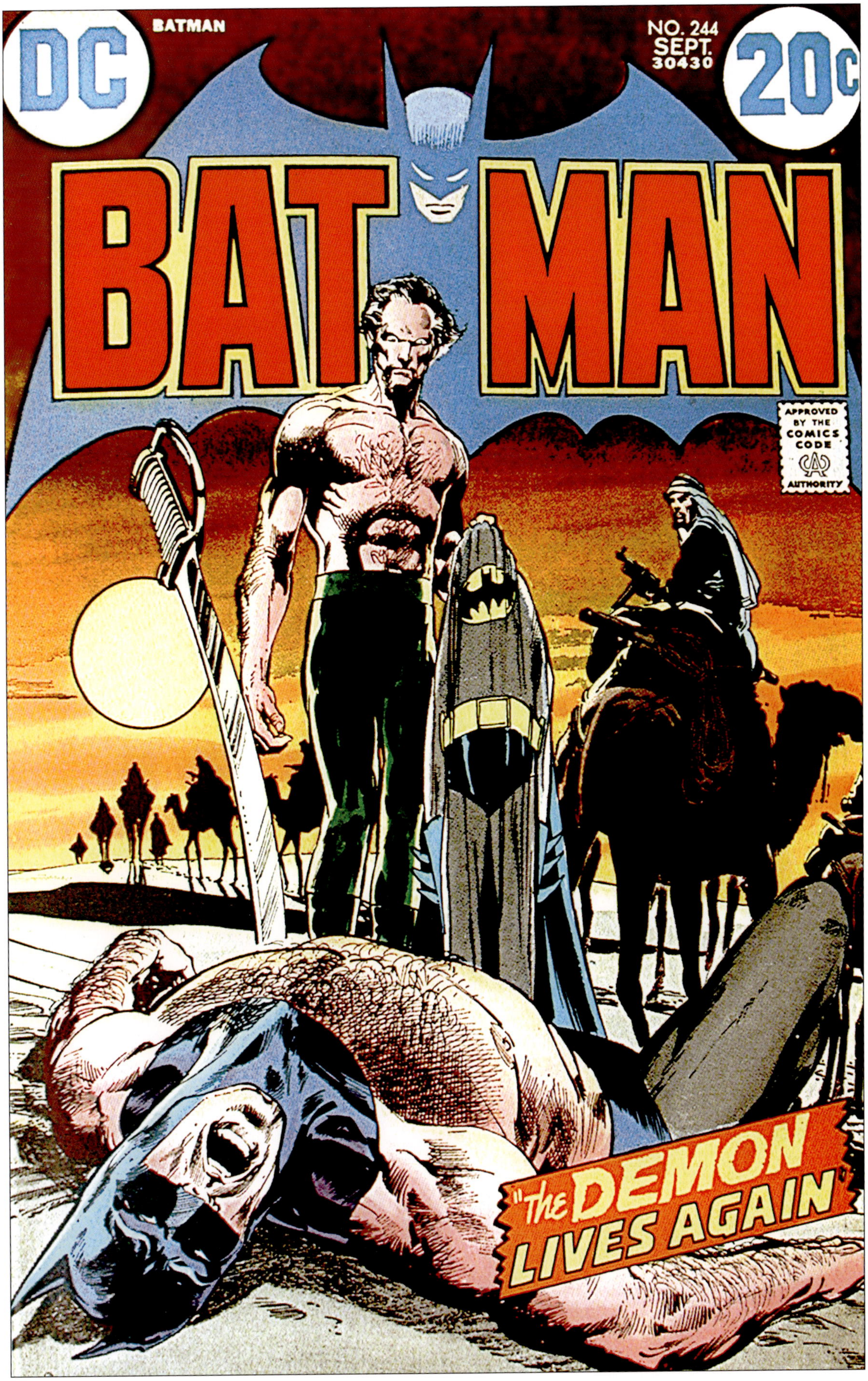

Batman #244

1972

Art by Neal Adams

Detective Comics #347

1966

Art by Carmine Infantino & Murphy Anderson

Batman: Gotham Knights #44

2003

Art by Brian Bolland

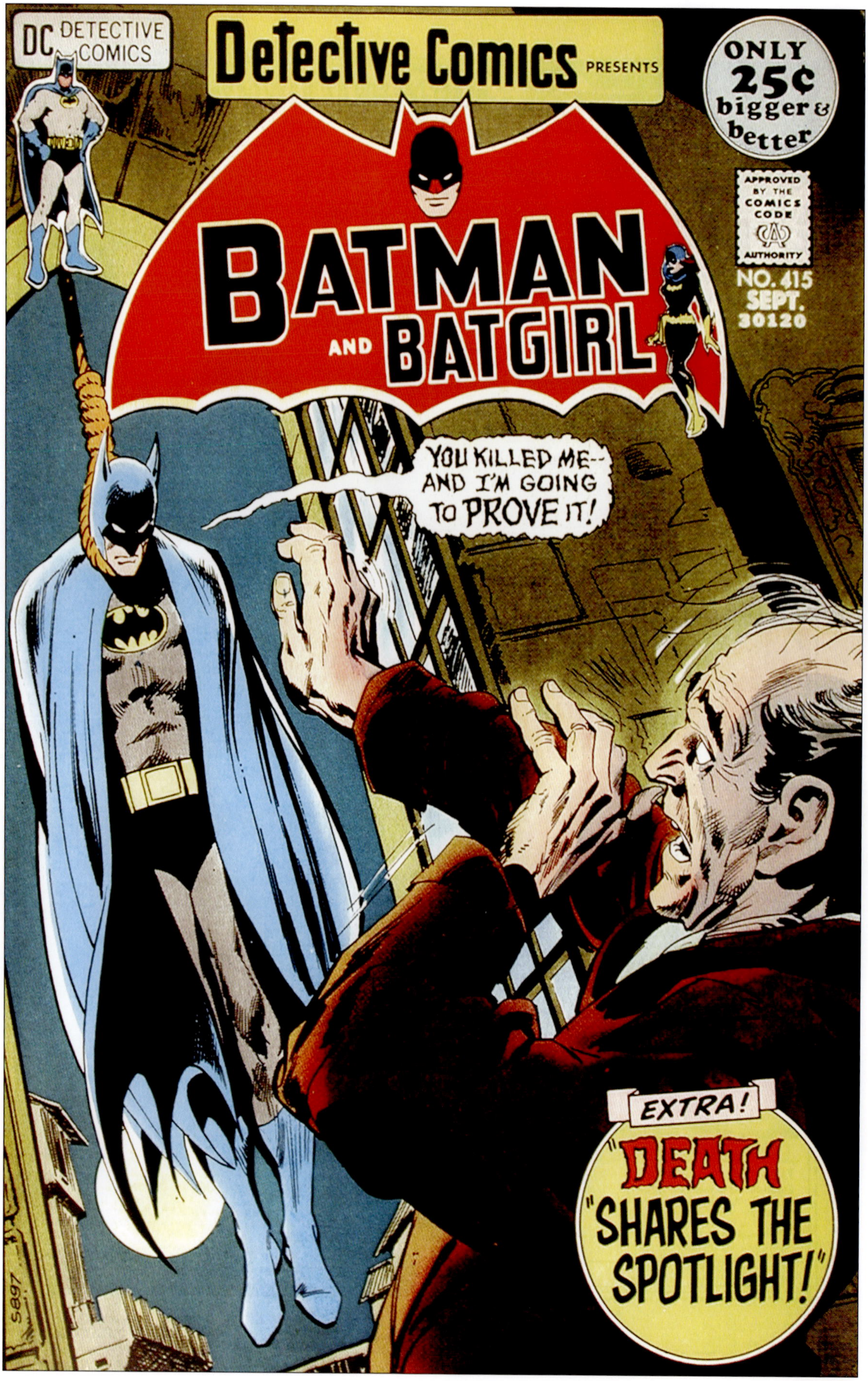

Detective Comics #415

1971

Art by Neal Adams

BATMAN #180 1966, Art by Gil Kane & Murphy Anderson

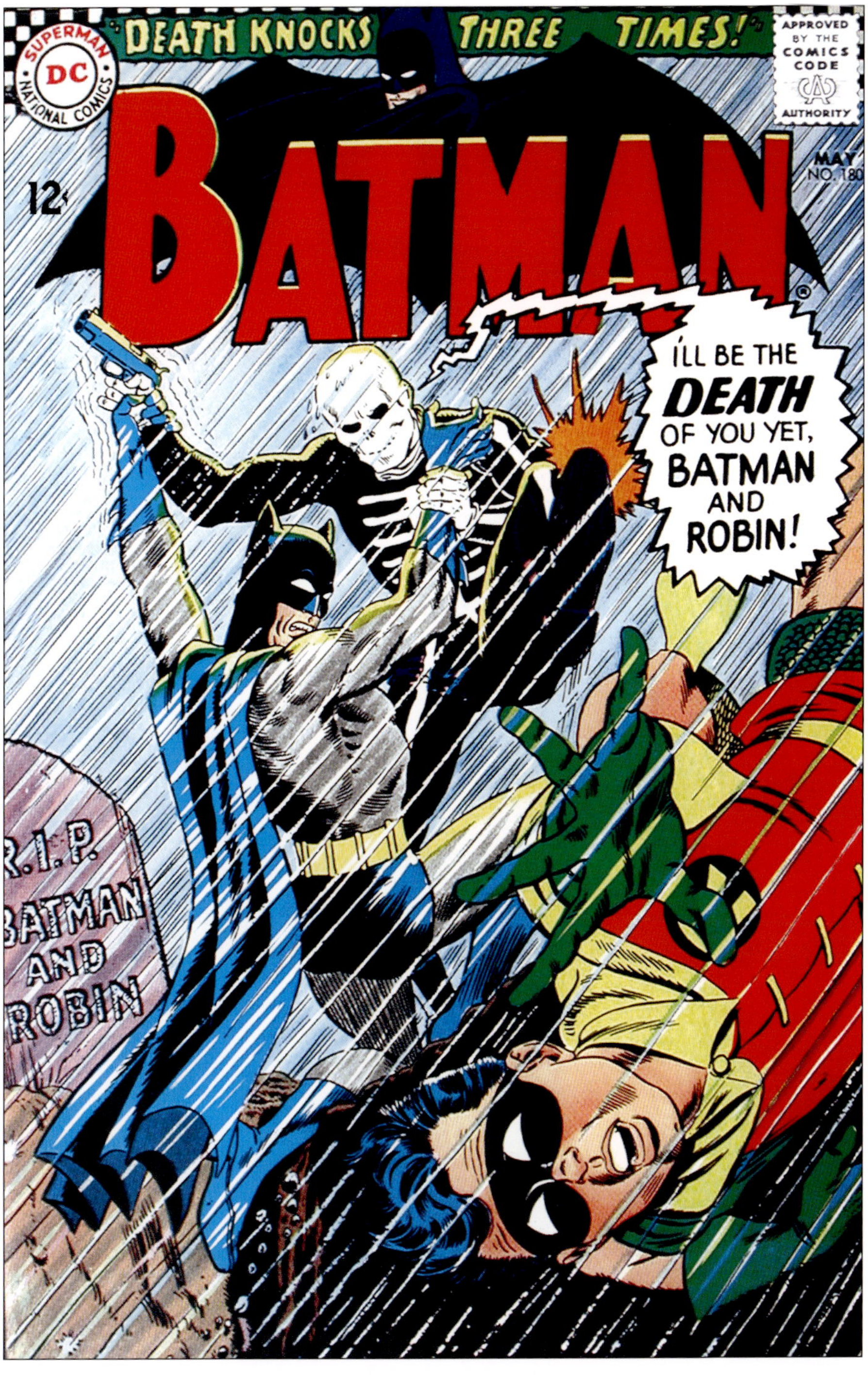

This was the first issue of *Batman* to hit the newsstands after the Adam West television series bam-powed its way onto the airwaves in January of 1966 — meaning that, as approximately 770,000 other children could also say (according to recorded sales figures), it was my first exposure to the comic book adventures of the Darknight Detective. It's a terrific composition by artists Gil Kane and Murphy Anderson, strikingly moody while still kinetic and vibrant in the best comic-book manner. Though there are other Batman covers of the period that are arguably stronger or bolder, this is the one that remains a permanent framed fixture above the desk at which I've since written hundreds of comics stories featuring Batman and his DC Comics co-stars. It's a constant reminder from the four-year-old in me that I could not possibly have chosen a more wonderful career.

Mark Waid *is a former DC editor and writer of diverse characters from* Superman *to the* Fantastic Four *to the* Legion of Super-Heroes.

Detective Comics #456

1976

Art by Ernie Chan

Batman Annual #19

1995

Art by Bret Blevins

Batman #618

2003

Art by Jim Lee & Scott Williams

THE DARKNIGHT DETECTIVE
VS.
HIS MOST
FEARSOME FOE
Ra's Al Ghul
ADV

LIMITED COLLECTORS' EDITION C-51 1977, Art by Neal Adams

One of the single greatest (and most dramatic) pieces of Batman cover art has to be Neal Adams's cover to the oversized limited collectors' edition of Batman's classic first encounter with Ra's al Ghul. The Denny O'Neil/Neal Adams epic was among the most important storylines in comics, and long before trade paperback collections would routinely put together popular issues of a comic book in one format there was…the giant comic. Often called the treasury format (because of Marvel's labeling), this larger than magazine-size periodical, measuring at 10 inches wide by 13 inches high, would be used mostly for reprint material and would eventually be a home for some of the first original graphic novel content. Sold from the mid-'70s until the early '80s, these were hands-down my favorite form of entertainment that comics ever provided. The specific Batman "issue" was of striking impact to my 7-year-old eyes, for in 1977 it was not common to see the world's most celebrated super-heroes laid out dead before you. Of course at this time Robin was not really dead (or at least wouldn't be for another decade or so, depending upon how you look at it). But he sure seemed to be gettin' dead by the first page you open up to, where he is illustrated as being shot to death by unseen assassins. Imagine my scarred young mind never fully understanding at that point, thinking, "They can't really do that to him, can they? He's on TV!" Neal's masterful rendition of the tension in Batman's screaming body, kneeling down behind the lifeless form of his teenage chum, seemed to signal a change in comics. By having such realistic draftsmanship, the world of super-heroes would have to become that much more real. The magnificent scratchboard-like effect of Ra's al Ghul's villainous visage still makes me wonder how Neal pulled off the magic that he did.

***Alex Ross** is the artist of best-selling comics, best known for his work on* Kingdom Come *and* Marvels. *No stranger to Batman, he has painted several covers as well as the adventure* Batman: War on Crime.

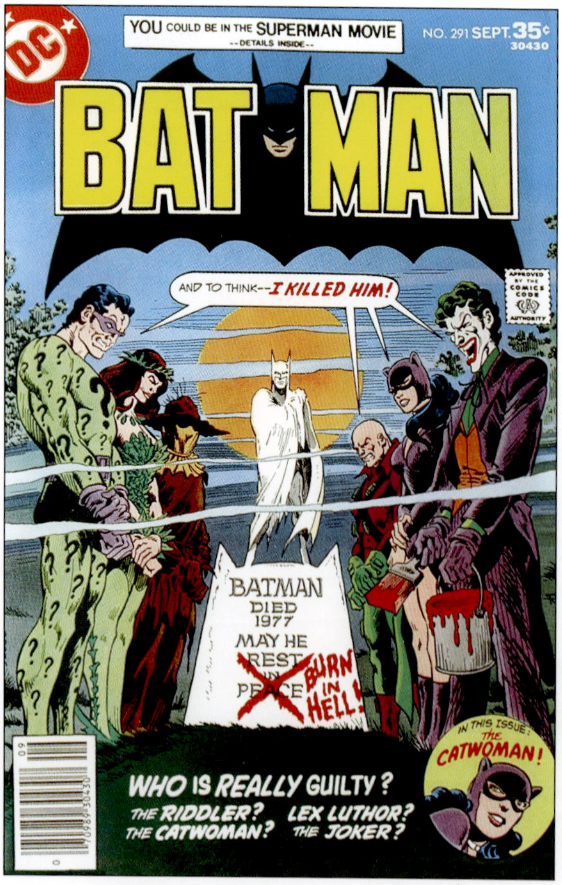

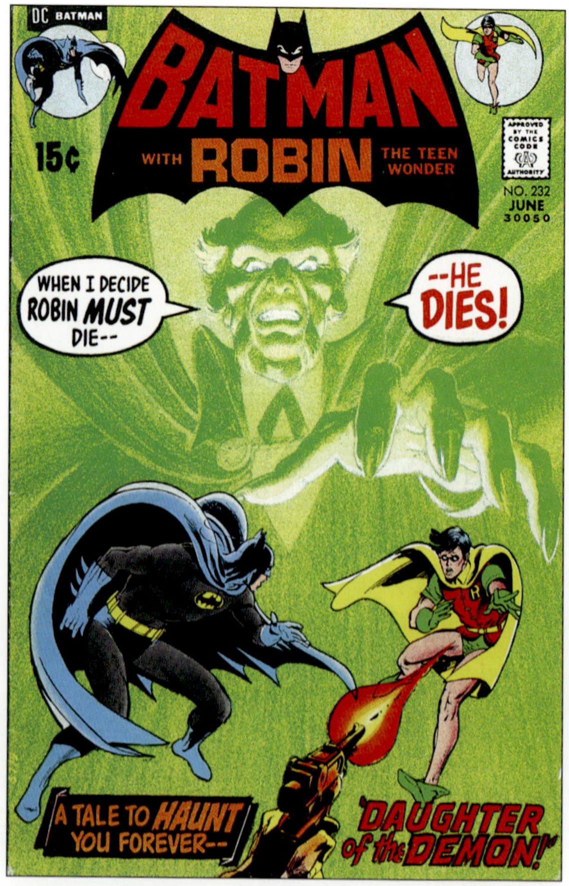

Batman #291

1977

Art by Jim Aparo

Batman #232

1971

Art by Neal Adams

This comic introduced the villainous Ra's al Ghul, the first major adversary added to the rogues gallery in years. He has remained a popular foe and will be seen, as played by Ken Watanabe, in the movie Batman Begins.

Batman #586

2001

Art by Scott McDaniel

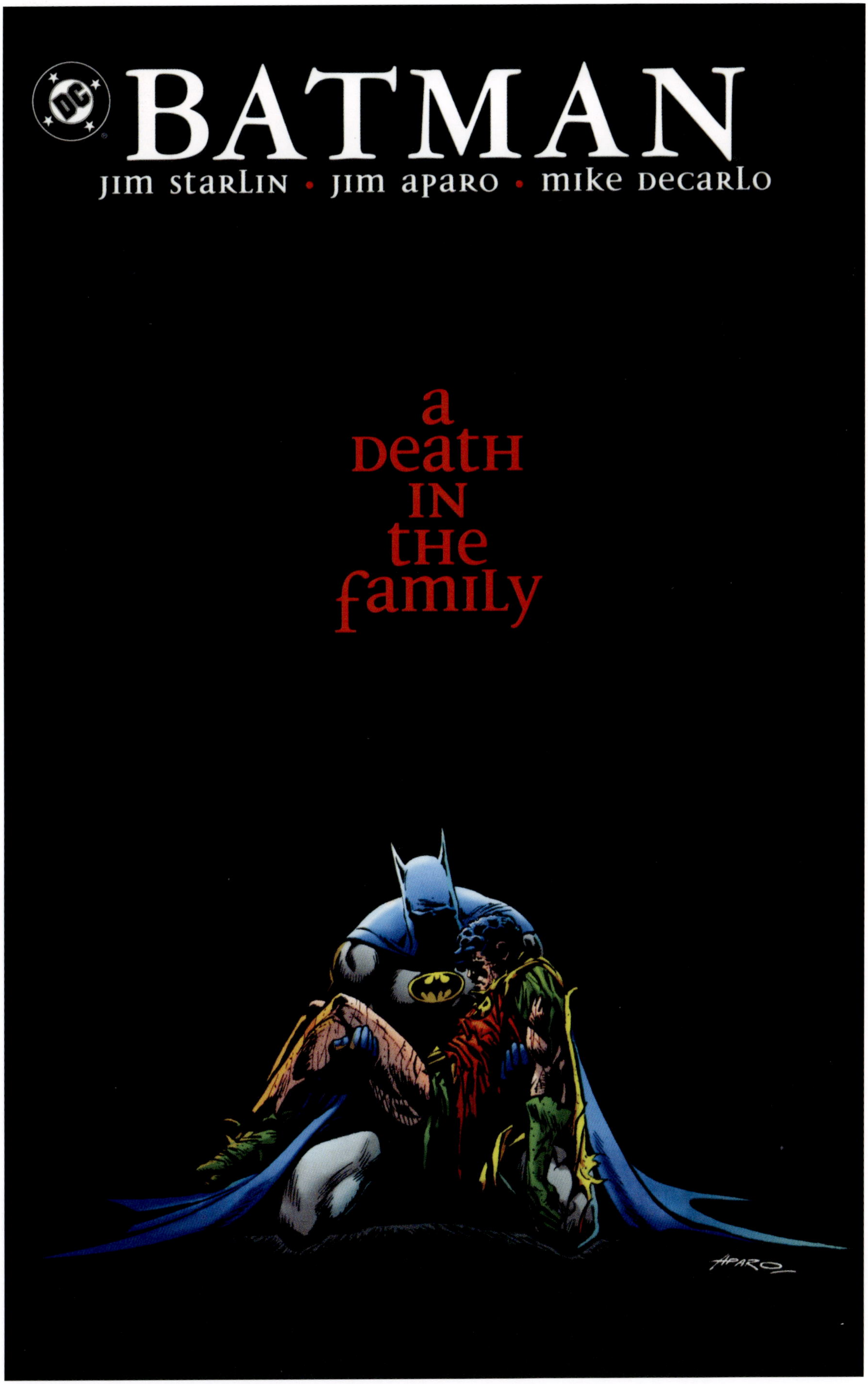

Batman:

A Death in the Family

1988

Art by Jim Aparo

This was the story in which readers had 36 hours to call one of two phone numbers to determine whether Robin would survive an attack by the Joker, or perish. The narrow totals led to his death.

For the first six decades, comic book covers were essentially assembled in the same way, using artwork, photostats, lettering and color to create an image that would encourage people to pick up and ultimately buy the comic. What follows is a look at how those covers were produced for much of Batman's lifetime and then a look at today's more streamlined methods.

Usually the editor selects a cover artist. Sometimes the story artist is better at storytelling than the single image necessary to make a cover work. Or the artist is behind schedule. When the interior artist is not used, the editor tends to select an artist whose name might help attract fans or is exceptional at the imagery required for cover art.

The editor and artist discuss the story and the artist produces several sketches, usually at comic book size, roughly indicating figures and detail, leaving room for things like the DC bullet, price information, UPC box and logo. The editor selects the best image and sets the artist to work.

The process from initial sketch to printed cover can take as long as six months since covers are used to help market the comics to retailers at the time orders are placed. The digital cover illustration, bottom right, was sketched in February, and the finished comic went on sale June, 2003.

1

2

3

1

Comic book artwork is produced one and a half times larger than the printed page, allowing for greater detail. In many cases, two artists are involved, someone to pencil the images and someone else to use indelible ink to finish the art. As in this case, though, Norm Breyfogle produced the art on his own. The editor places a sheet of tissue paper over the art and indicates where the various required elements are to be placed, including copy. Once the cover is turned over to Production, they assign a letterer to create the copy. Photostat copies of the logo, Comics Code seal and price information are made and a production artist begins adding the elements, sometimes directly onto the artwork and sometimes as a separate layer as is the case here.

2

A comic book sized photocopy of the completed cover is made and sent to a color artist who works with colored dyes, similar to watercolors. Sometimes the editor or the artists have specific color notes, which are passed on, otherwise, the color artist makes his own choices. The guide is reviewed by the editor and then approved, or marked with corrections.

3

The original art and color guide are sent to a color separation facility. Most of DC's comics were separated in either Connecticut or New Jersey. The cover was photographed and nine copies were printed on acetate. Each copy represented a color: one black, three each for magenta, cyan and yellow. The comics were actually produced using 25, 50 and 100 percent values for the three colors, plus black, to create the color. Staff artists would use opaque paint on each acetate to indicate the areas that would be required to achieve the desired color. For example, Batman's uniform would be 25% magenta, cyan and yellow. The finished acetates are photographed and combined to produce four overlays, one for each color, and that proof is reviewed by the editor.

Each of the four colors of film is reproduced on acetate. This way the editor can verify the values of each layer.

4

Each piece of color film is then used to produce a corresponding metal printing plate at the printer. Each plate is curved to fit a giant roller, which is run through a reservoir of color ink and then pressed against paper coming from a roll taller than most people. The roll of paper is at one end of the printing press and the inked image is pressed by each color plate in rapid succession. The paper then travels through a heat stage, setting the ink.

5

The corrected proof is returned to the separator who makes corrections and then produces four pieces of film, again one for each color. The film is then sent to the printer and the cover is printed on a glossy stock, usually heavier in feel than the interior paper, and is then bound on top of the comic book with pieces of metal that, when snipped, resemble staples. The edges are then trimmed and the finished comics boxed and shipped to newsstands around the country.

4

THE DIGITAL WORLD

6

For *Detective Comics*, Tim Sale provided several sketches, and this one was selected by editor Bob Schreck.

5

7

Just as before, the finished artwork was produced following the sketch.

8

Today, though, the original art is scanned and turned into a digital file. The file is then sent electronically to the color artist, in this case, Mark Chiarello. Using digital painting software (usually Adobe Photoshop), the color artist digitally paints the artwork. The file is saved in jpeg (compressed) format and dropped into a waiting folder on DC's network. The editor is then able to first check the color on screen, with a final proof printed and routed for various departmental approvals.

9

Once the final color is approved, a final high-resolution file is then used by an artist in our Pre-Press Services department. The artist will use Quark XPress to digitally add what has traditionally been done by hand. Our Lettering department provides the copy and that, along with price box, logo, DC bullet and other elements, is placed on what is effectively a digital transparent layer, leaving the artwork itself untouched. Once the final proof is approved, it is digitally transmitted to our printer in Canada. The printing, binding and shipping process remains the same.

6

7

8

9

From his first appearance Batman has proven an enduring feature, celebrating one milestone appearance after another.

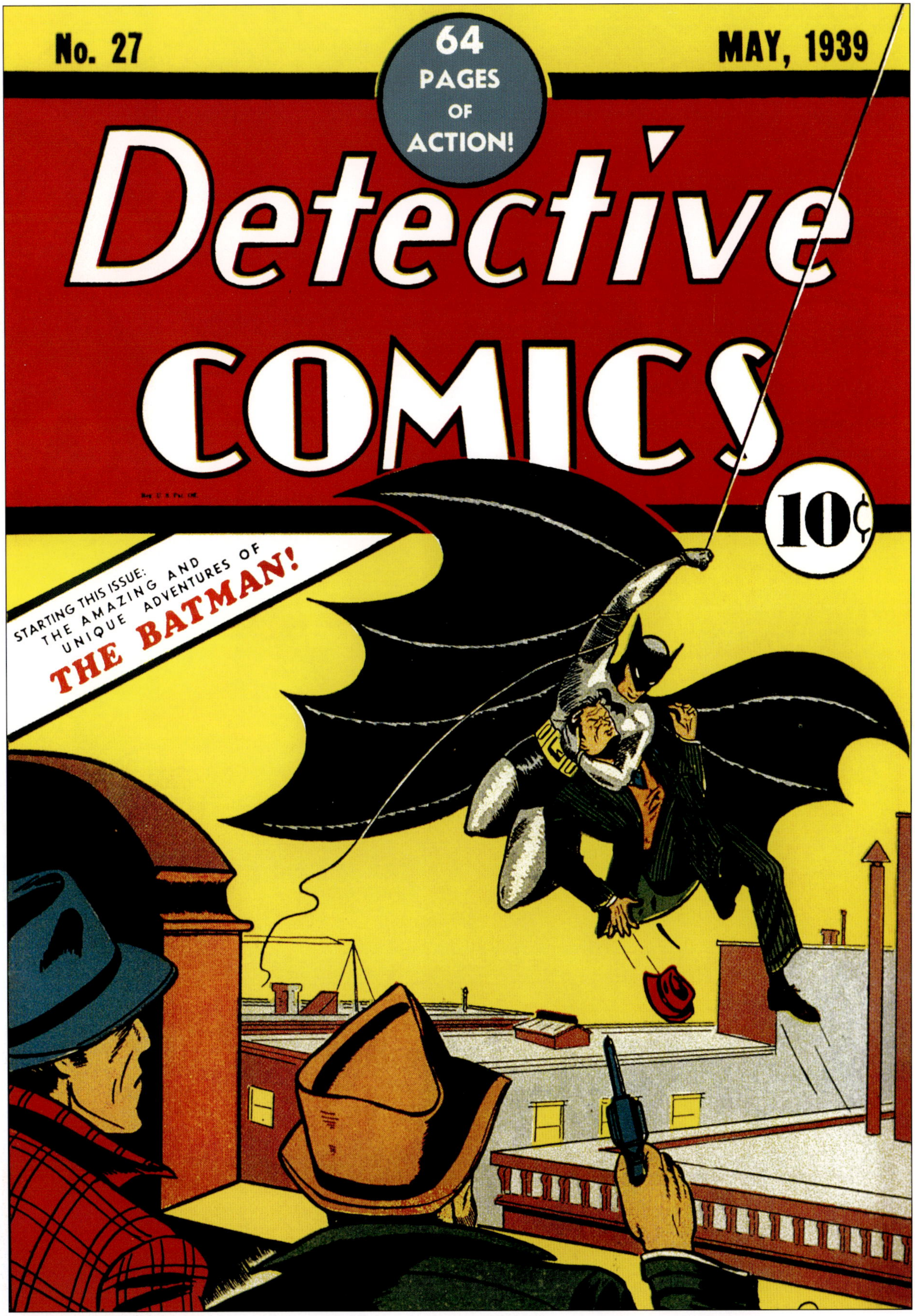

Detective Comics #27

1939

Art by Bob Kane

Batman debuted here and within seven months became the sole cover feature.

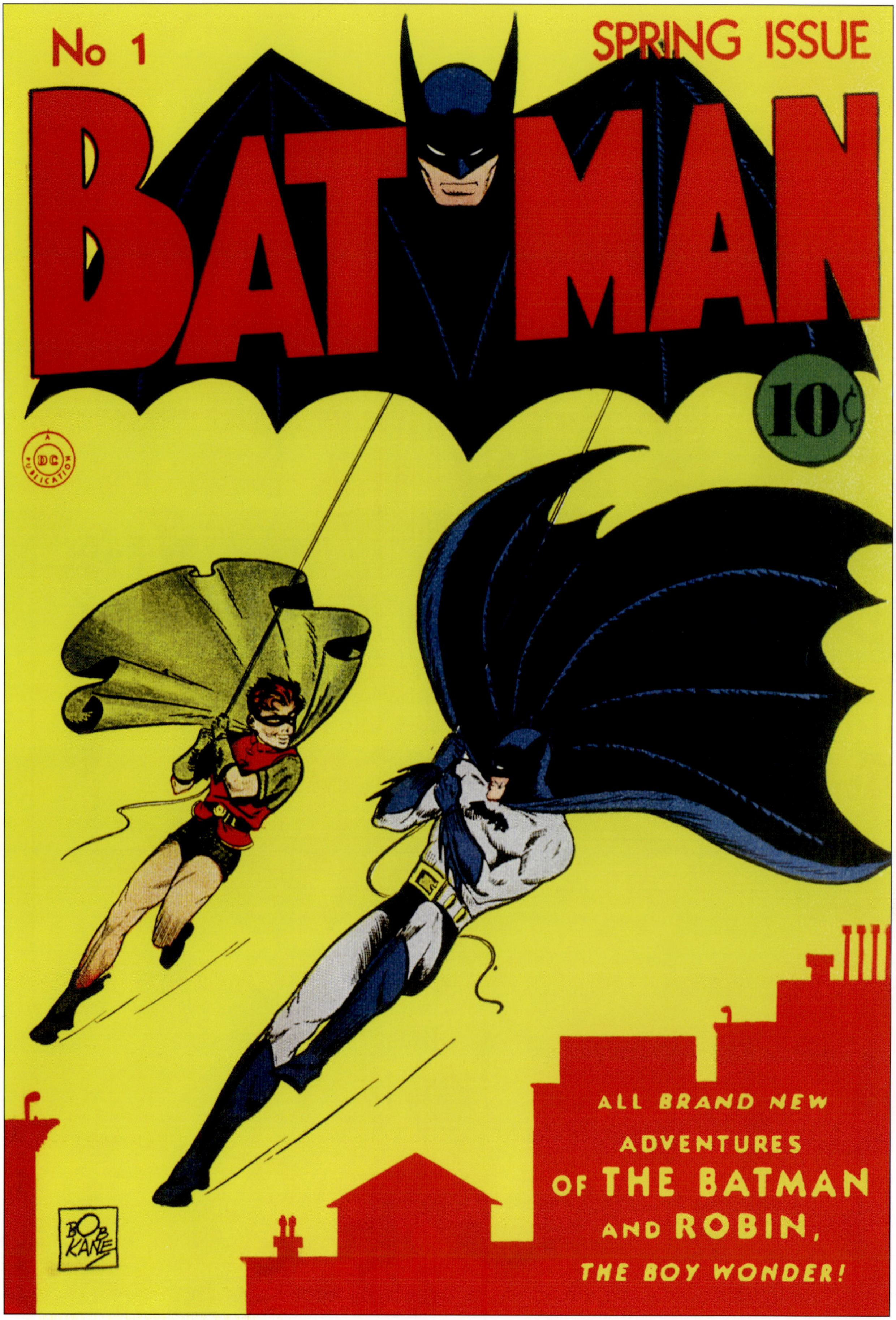
No 1
SPRING ISSUE
BATMAN
10¢
A DC PUBLICATION
BOB KANE
ALL BRAND NEW
ADVENTURES
OF THE BATMAN
AND ROBIN,
THE BOY WONDER!

Page 224:

Batman #1

1940

Art by Bob Kane & Jerry Robinson

Batman quickly earned his own quarterly title that increased in frequency over the next few years.

Batman #100

1956

Batman #200

1968

Art by Neal Adams

Batman #300

1978

Art by Dick Giordano

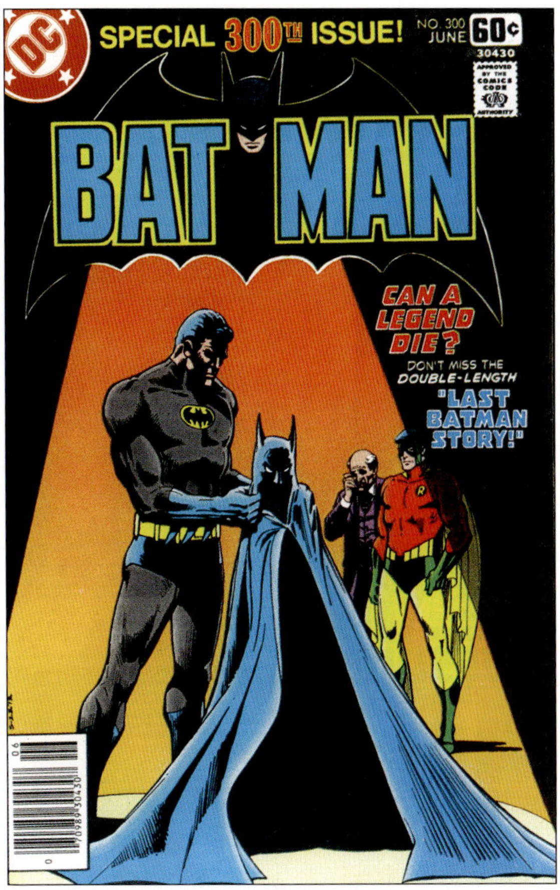

BOB LE ROSE
Detective COMICS
Detective COMICS
Detective COMICS
IS SHE HEROINE OR VILLAINESS?
WHAT IS HER STARTLING SECRET IDENTITY?
BATMAN

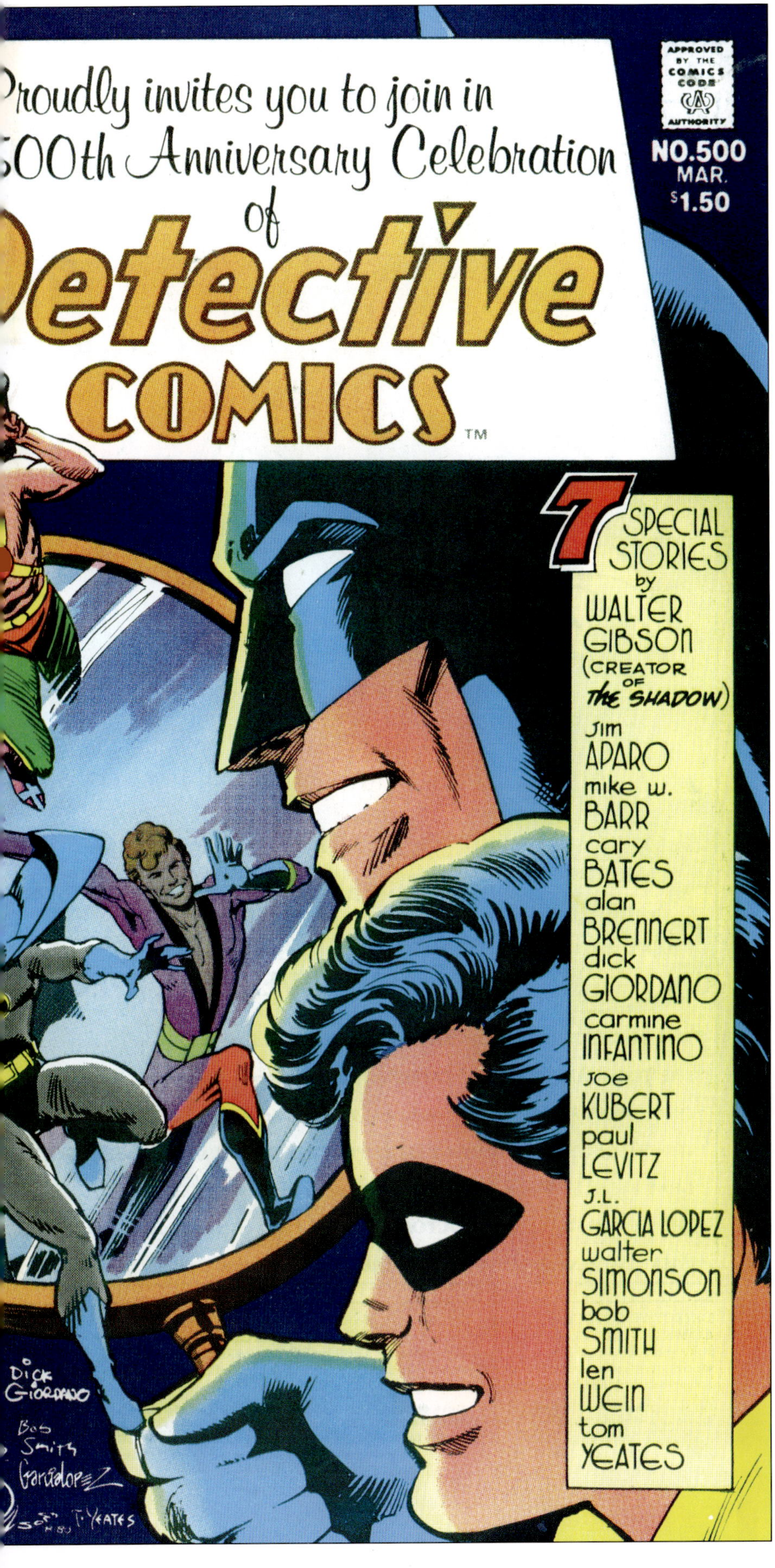

My favorite of the 80-odd Batman covers on the issues I edited, unique because it was a jam carefully orchestrated between all the extraordinary artists represented in this celebratory collection. Joe Kubert provided the layout, and he was joined by Dick Giordano, Walter Simonson, Carmine Infantino, Jim Aparo, José Luis García-López, Tom Yeates and Bob Smith illustrating it. Jam covers occasionally happened spontaneously in the studios of artists assigned to do Batman from the earliest days onward, but this was the only planned instance of its kind.

It's also special for the credit accorded Bob Le Rose, for many years the production artist who assembled DC's covers. In these pre-desktop publishing days, the only way to accurately capture and distort the old *Detective* covers used in the background was to painstakingly arrange them one by one on a camera bed in the proper twist, and then paste the photographic stats in place. This was perhaps the most difficult cover construction of the thousands Bob had done, and so he got to sign it as an artistic contributor.

It was also used as one of DC's first promotional posters for the then-small but growing group of comic shops.

***Paul Levitz** is currently DC Comics' President & Publisher, having served in a variety of roles starting as Assistant Editor and including a short stint as editor of the Batman family of titles.*

Batman #400

1986

Art by Bill Sienkiewicz

Batman #500

1993

Art by Kelley Jones

Batman #600

2003

Art by Scott McDaniel

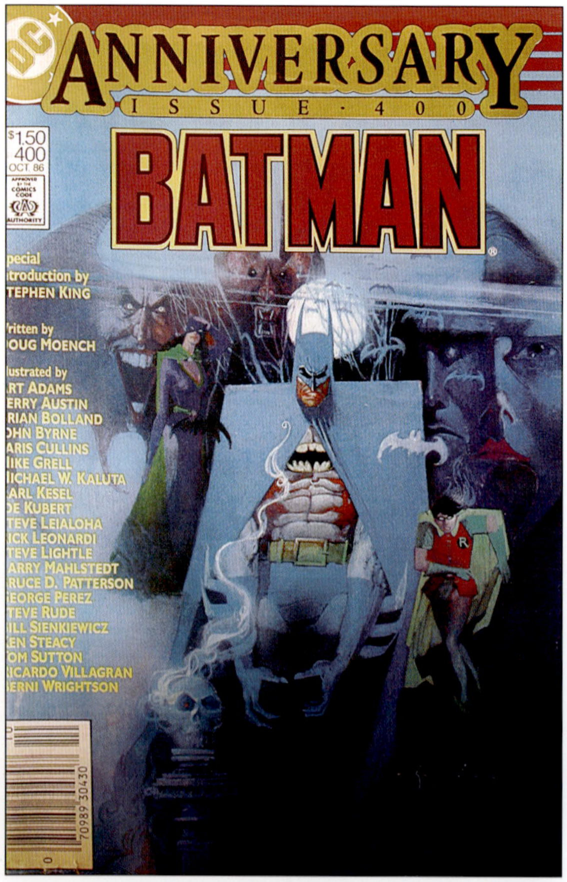

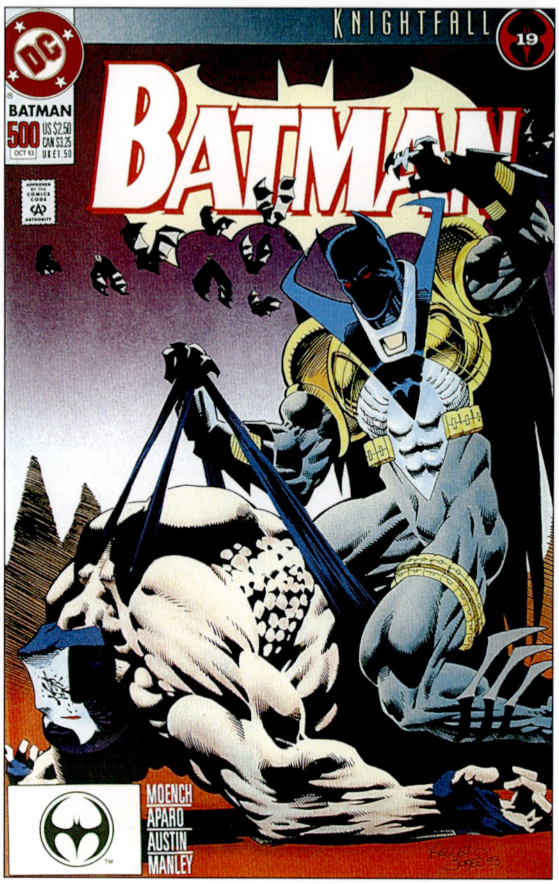

Detective Comics #327

1964

Art by Carmine Infantino & Joe Giella

With sales flagging, Julius Schwartz was asked to edit the character. He brought in new writers and artists, introducing with this issue an era dubbed the "New Look."

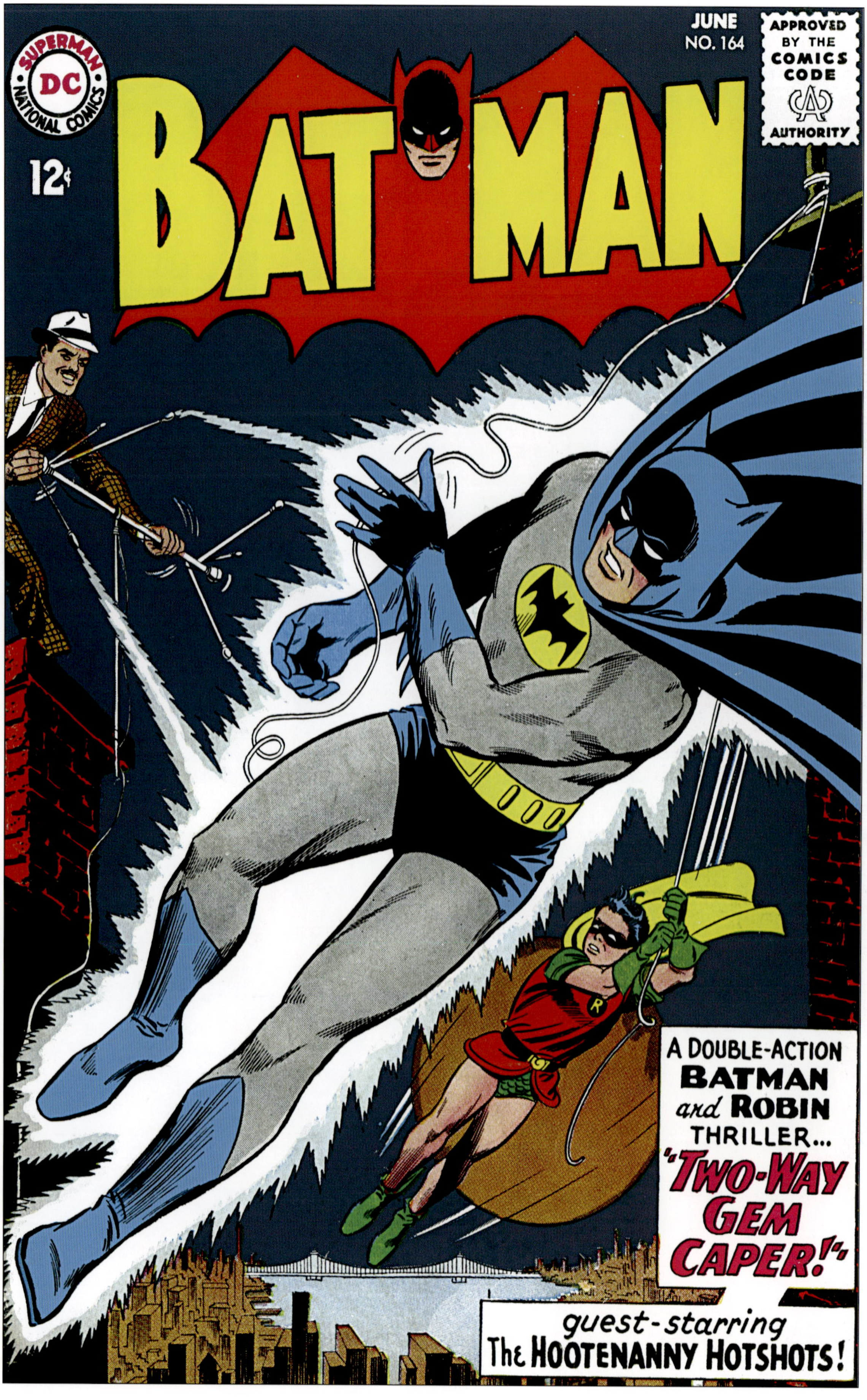

Batman #164

1964

Art by Sheldon Moldoff & Joe Giella

Joe Giella inked both Batman *and* Detective *to help unify the look while the stories took a turn from the fantastic back to crimes, familiar foes and more realistic settings.*

Batman has paired up with many other heroes in THE BRAVE AND THE BOLD comics for years. Here's a look at some of his other notable colleagues and appearances.

Superman/Batman #3

2003

Art by Ed McGuinness & Dexter Vines

Superman and Batman were paired up once again in this new best-selling series. This time, their different approaches and philosophies were explored as they faced incredible challenges.

JLA #44

2000

Art by Howard Porter & Drew Geraci

Wonder Woman: The Hiketeia

2002

Art by J.G. Jones

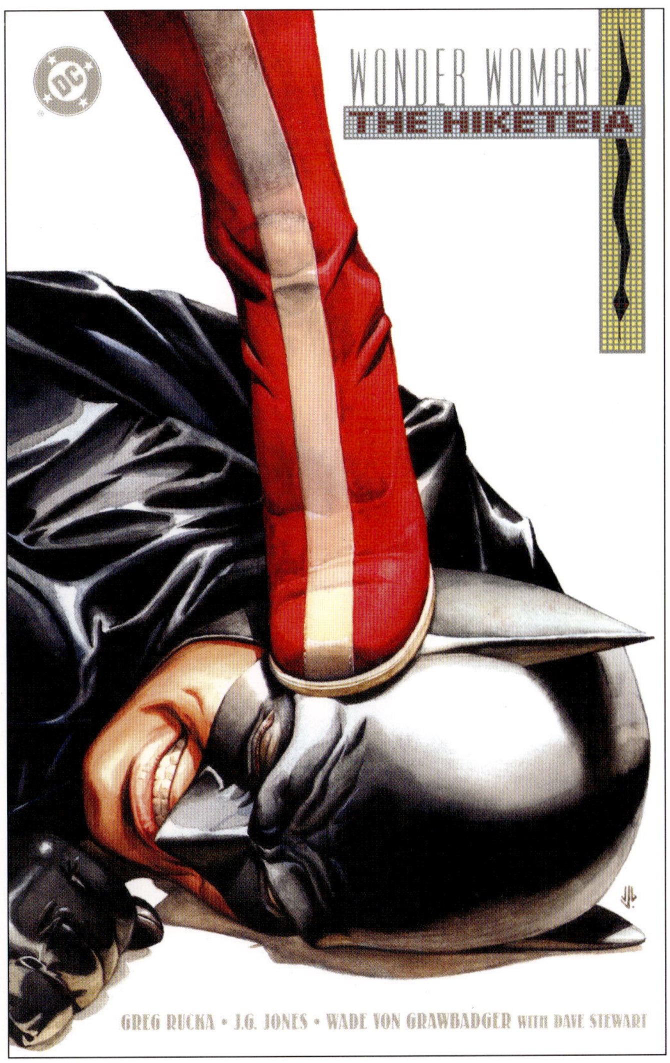

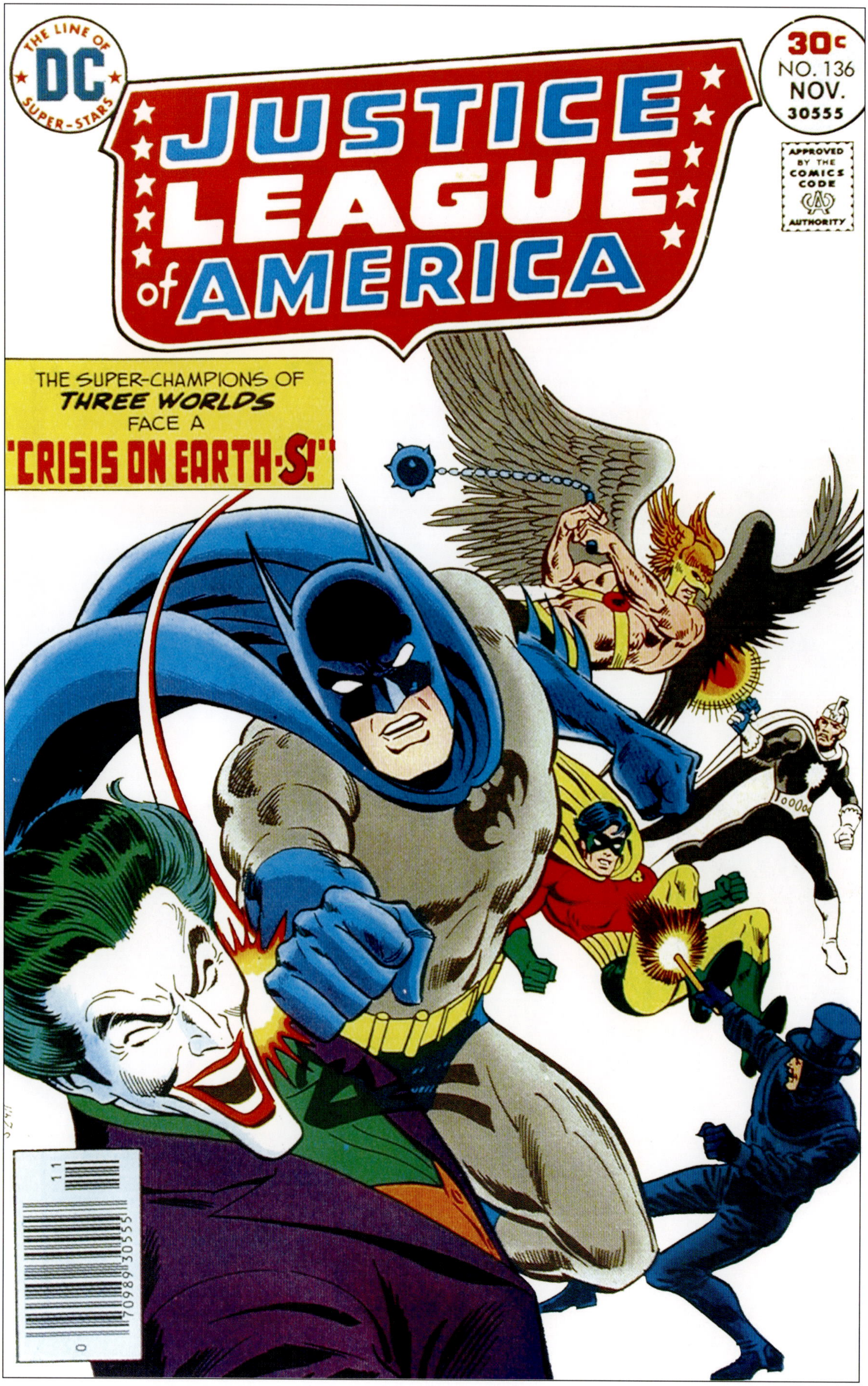

Justice League of America #136

1976

Art by Ernie Chan & Jack Abel

World's Finest Comics #168

1967

Art by Curt Swan & George Klein

Page 237:

Superman #76

1952

Art by Win Mortimer

This is the first time the heroes met in a story. Soon after, they began sharing adventures in World's Finest Comics.

JLA #90

2004

Art by Doug Mahnke & Tom Nguyen

In the heat of battle, Batman and Wonder Woman kissed, leading them to wonder if a romance was possible. Their separate responsibilities prevented them from finding a satisfying answer to the question.

World's Finest Comics #146

1964

Art by Curt Swan & George Klein

52 BIG PAGES
NO.76
MAY JUNE
SUPERMAN DC NATIONAL COMICS
SUPERMAN
10¢
SUPERMAN
DOUBLE-FEATURE!
BATMAN, THE WORLD'S GREATEST DETECTIVE, JOINS FORCES WITH THE MAN OF STEEL TO BECOME...
"The MIGHTIEST TEAM ON EARTH!"
LOIS IN DANGER! THIS IS A JOB FOR SUPERMAN!
NO, THIS IS A JOB FOR BATMAN!

DETECTIVE COMICS #31 1939, Art by Bob Kane ■ BATMAN #227 1970, Art by Neal Adams

CHIP KIDD

To diehard comic book fans I realize that this choice is hardly original — for those of us who treasure most the image of Batman as he appeared in his first year this is practically the Uncle Sam "I Want You" poster, both in familiarity and effect. But it remains my favorite because it has the elements that make this first era of the character the best: Ears that are really horns and fearsomely veering toward satanic proportions. The cape as folded wings that are just about to spring open to their full span and go in for the swoop. The surreality of Batman as backdrop. I even love that his belt buckle is ridiculously high on his chest — it gives the drawing a naïve element that both disarms and charms. This *is* "The Bat-Man."

***Chip Kidd** is an award-winning book designer and novelist. His affection for Batman is also seen in* Batman Collected.

ALEX ROSS

As a two-cover favorite of mine, the third appearance of Batman on a cover of *Detective Comics* and its re-creation by Neal Adams thirty years later stands out as one of the most dramatic compositions in the character's history. Batman had yet to become the regular cover feature for *Detective Comics* by issue 31 when Bob Kane illustrated this striking image of the then-fearsome hero looming large in the night sky, studying the scene before him.

The giant spectral vision of a heroic protagonist superimposed behind a city landscape or above their enemies was common to pulp magazine cover illustration, especially of Batman's predecessor, the Shadow. Ultimately this was among the first design-driven covers for comics, concentrating more on the graphic impact of selling this new demon-eared good guy while still putting attention on the story.

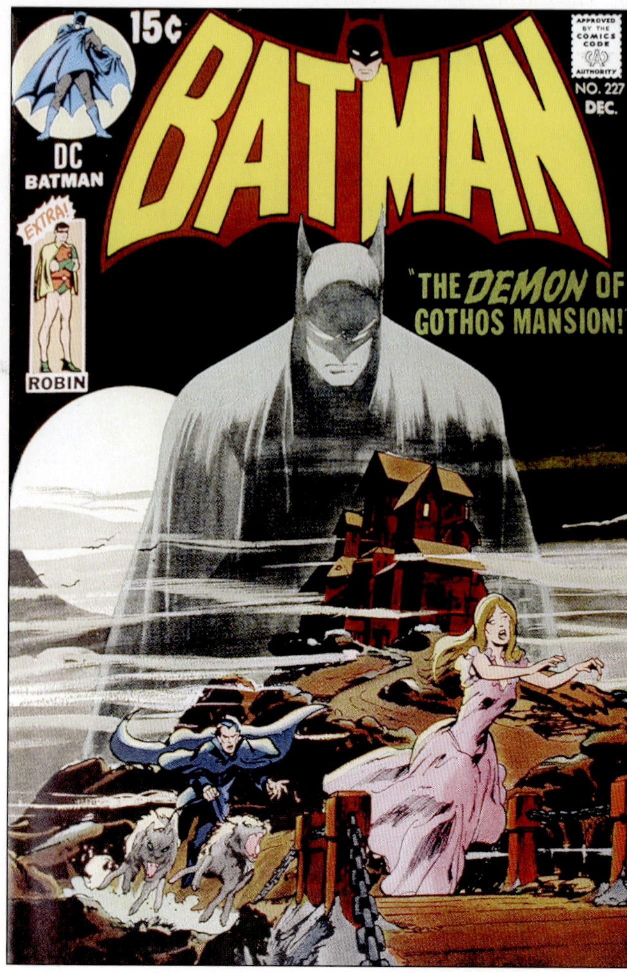

Neal Adams emerged in the late '60s as the creative force that returned the "Dark Knight"'s darkness to him. Nowhere was the link to this historic legacy made more clearly than in the cover to *Batman* issue 227, where Neal showed his dedication to the roots of the grim approach to Batman.

Since the more menacing look to the character has dominated the thirty-some years since this issue came out, it's important to note that the visual here marks the close of a different era. When Batman was given his colorful partner Robin in 1940, the grim, black-clad avenger Batman softened up considerably for the three decades that followed, topped off eventually by the campy television show interpretation of the late sixties.

Neal Adams helped lead the character and the book back to the roots of his intended design. Also, rendering this image with a radical multi-media use of watercolor and ink would speak towards the future graphic possibilities to come. Neal staked his claim on Batman like no one else, redirecting him for all artists thereafter. This one cover's lineage showed that, moreover, Neal knew what Batman needed rekindled within him, as well as giving him the respect he deserved.

MARK HAMILL

My attempt to single out one Batman cover as an all-time favorite has been, I'm sorry to admit, a complete failure.

From his initial appearance in 1939 as a sinister, almost vampire-like figure, Batman has had more incarnations than any other character in pop-culture history. Reviewing the cover art from the numerous titles over the past sixty-five years displays his uncanny ability to not only change with the times, but to reflect the deepest desires of comic book fans in any given era. The artists responsible are among the finest the industry has ever produced: Bob Kane, Jerry Robinson, Dick Sprang, Jack Burnley, Win Mortimer, Curt Swan, Carmine Infantino, Dick Giordano, Neal Adams, and Frank Miller, to name but a few.

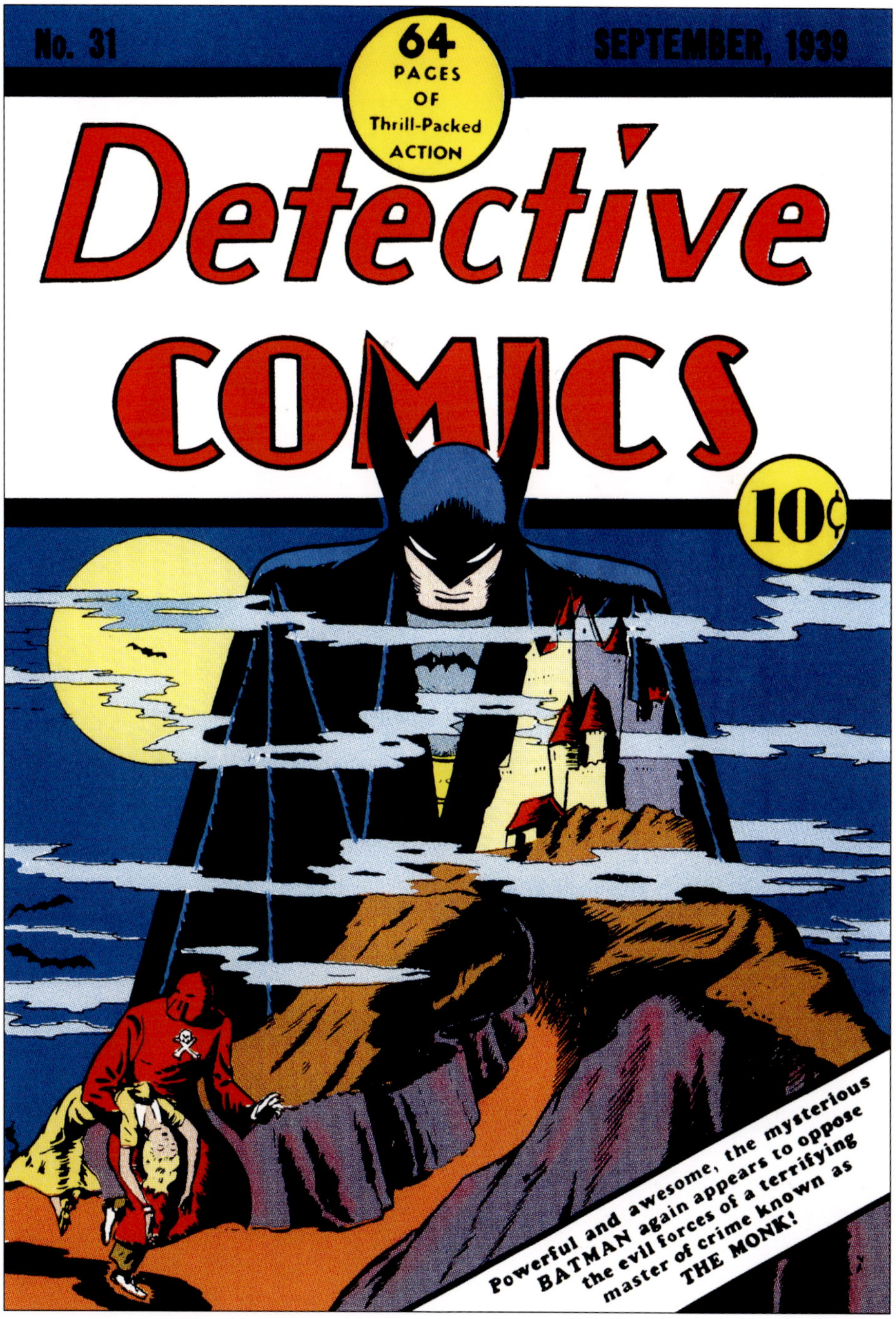

Before I began my research, I always thought *Detective* #31 was my favorite. It seemed to be the quintessential Batman imagery as an omnipotent Dark Knight towers over a gothic castle, while a bizarre costumed villain clutches his shapely feminine prey in the foreground. Now I'm not so sure. The sheer diversity of these magnificent covers had a tendency to broaden my choices rather than narrow them.

Single one out? You might as well ask the Pope to name his favorite Commandment…I love them all!

Although visually best known as Luke Skywalker, ***Mark Hamill*** *is equally recognizable as the Joker's voice on* The Batman Adventures *animated series. He's also directed* Comic Book the Movie *and written for comics.*

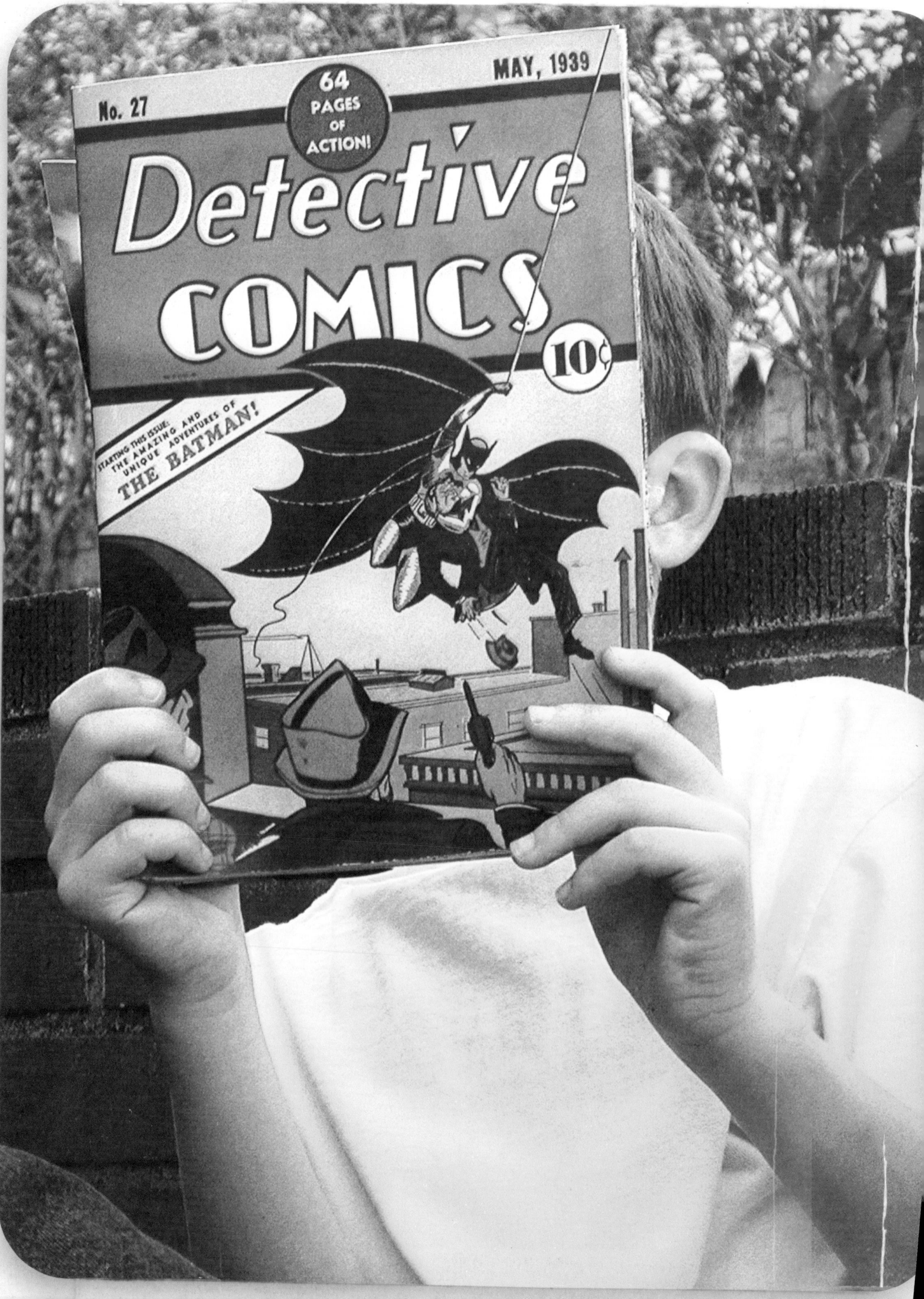
MAY, 1939
No. 27
64 PAGES OF ACTION!
Detective COMICS
10¢
STARTING THIS ISSUE: THE AMAZING AND UNIQUE ADVENTURES OF THE BATMAN!